Dr PV Dhamija was formerly professor at Central Institute of English and Foreign Languages, Hyderabad. He has doctoral degrees in both English Language and English Literature. He is deeply interested in creative writing and has published several papers on fiction and poetry. He is a creative writer of considerable standing. He has published four novels in English: *Love and Lust*, *The Encounter*, *Beyond the Tunnel*, *After Fifty Years*. He has also published two collections of poetry in English: *Cracks in the Wall*, *The Pagan*. Among his writings in Urdu are his articles on the *ghazal* as a genre and a well-known collection of *ghazals* titled *Ghazal ki Sarhaden*.

Society on a Razor Edge

A Tale of Hope in Despair

Pushya Vibhooti Dhamija

Prestige
an international publishing house

Published by
Prestige Books
3/28, East Patel Nagar
New Delhi 110 008
Ph. 9818755529

ISBN: 81-7551-188-5

This is a work of fiction. Names, characters, places and events are either the creation of the author's imagination or used fictitiously; any resemblance to actual persons, living or dead, places or events is entirely coincidental.

Printed at Chaman Offset Press, New Delhi 110 002

For all those who think and struggle
to move forward in the right direction

kahaan sab khaab jaane kho gaye haĩ

ki ham duniya meĩ tanha ho gaye haĩ

A sandstorm blew with forceful
Fury, and then another and
Then, still another and
Rudely shook and seared every tree and
Shrub and shelter, and silted
Every river and rivulet till the
Flow was choked in every channel.

The sand-age throve for countless
Years and blinded every eye
And bruised every muscle and mind.
There came messiahs of dubious provenance,
Claiming to have been timely sent
To preach, persuade and pressurize,
To stem the tide of spreading sands.

Contents

Part One

Part Two

Part Three

Part Four

PART ONE

One

I had hardly taken a bath and come out of the bathroom when I heard the telephone ringing. At the other end of the line was Robert Darwin. I asked him to hold on because I did not want to talk to him in that state of undress. I took about two minutes to dress and lifted the receiver. He was sputtering incoherently, obviously very annoyed that I had made him wait on the line so long. I soothed his irritated voice into sense by faking a receptionist's unctuousness.

'Where're you at the moment, Robert?'

'I'm just outside your door, Vigyan.'

'Then why have you phoned me? Why didn't you . . ?'

'I knocked several times. Waited for more than a minute and then knocked again. But there was no . . .'

'I'm very sorry. I was in the bathroom, and the tap was running full blast. I'm sorry again.'

'Okay, don't worry. I understand. Perhaps, I should've fixed a meeting with you.'

His wife, Elizabeth, had walked out on him close to five years before. Since my wife, Kapila, had also left me about two years later, he seemed to have a kind of sympathy with me, which had peculiarly sprung from the similarity, if not the sameness, of the 'path' which both our wives had trodden to freedom from their wed*locks*.

It was nine o'clock. My cook-cum-maid, Sheila, had prepared my breakfast and was expecting me at the dining table. I asked Darwin to join me at breakfast. He agreed without a hitch, and we were soon eating as Sheila was toasting some more slices and poaching two more eggs for the exigent demand.

A few minutes later, we were in the drawing room, engaged in small talk because we always needed hours of free time to talk over serious things. In another few minutes, we both were to leave for work and needed to fix a time for a long meeting some time in the evening.

We did meet in the evening, but at his flat this time. We were together in his sitting room not for the first time, but the place somehow presented a different look. It appeared to me a virtual museum of strange objects. I am by nature not a keen observer of things even when they are in my close proximity. And, yet, my attention was irresistibly drawn towards some of the artifacts arranged rather obtrusively in a showcase fixed on the wall in front of me. I got up to take a close look. They were all miniature figures of some extinct birds and animals. As I took my eyes off these objects and gave him a curious look, he drew my attention to a showcase on the left wall. It was full of animals starting from dinosaurs. The lowest shelf had several figurines in marble of the Homo erectus and the Homo sapiens. The Neanderthal man formed the end of the row as though it had been the last stage in biological evolution! All these figures and figurines did not excite me even half as much as the question in my mind regarding why he had at all bought and put on display those not-so-earth-shaking objects all at one go. I had never seen those objects there during any of my visits to his house in the last few months. Or had I seen them without seeing? Perhaps, they had been lying in limbo, hidden from sight. But then why were they now . . ?

He suddenly gave my thoughts a shake and broke their chain:

'Didn't I tell you that I'm a great-great-great-grandchild of Charles Darwin, the author of *The Theory of Evolution*?'

'Yes, you did, but I . . .'

'And you didn't believe?' he cut in.

'Well, . . .'

'Yes, you didn't need to,' he cut me short again. 'Nor do you need to believe even now my claim that I'm in the direct line of descent of Charles Darwin.'

We had met at a common friend's party about three years before. He was tall, well-built and yet tight-figured. He had high cheekbones and yet a nearly oval face, tapering into a narrow flattened chin. He had quite a presence in physical terms. But he had impressed me more as a well-informed intelligent young man with a keen sense of humour and a big appetite for gossip. His name, Robert Charles Darwin, created ripples of curiosity in me as well as the other guests who had not met him before. 'Charles' is a very common name. 'Darwin' is not so common, but not a rarity either. But the combination, 'Charles Darwin', sounded at that party like the spooky sound of a ghost. All of us looked at him in unison as though many eyes together could see things better than just two. With my eyes intent on him, I felt I was being transported towards the end of the nineteenth century. And then for quite some moments, I was sitting face to face with that bearded grey eminence and enjoying the seer's eloquent eyes surveying aeons of Time hurtling through space.

When my magic carpet landed back on that festive tarmac, I heard him telling the guests as well as the hosts that he was generally known as only Robert Darwin. I was not the same man now. Almost everybody had downed a few pegs of booze each and was in a state of heightened awareness. I sounded a bit too rational to a group of high-heeled men and women, who I happened to be chatting with. One or two scintillating beauties cracked a couple of boozy jokes at my 'silly' correctness of behaviour and attitude. I did not react because I found their digs too eerie. Meanwhile, Robert Darwin had joined us and was listening to those charming bimbettes. All of a sudden, he quietly passed by me and gently nudged me. Soon I was walking with him over to the hosts to express our thanks for their invitation to such a grand party.

On our way back to my flat, I did not seem to be much interested in him. I had met the old guy, the real Charles Darwin, in his real time-and-space ambience, albeit in imagination. I cannot say precisely why I felt that this new present-day Darwin could not be a descendant of the old one. I had an uncanny kind of peep into him and felt he was faking an identity. Who would not like to claim kinship with Charles Darwin? The man who had shaken everything down to its foundations. Almost all religions had lost their moorings overnight; all systems of belief had all but crashed; and most a-priori assumptions about the nature of the world had crumbled to dust.

Sheila had tidied up the sitting room and rearranged certain articles of furniture. A few little flowerpots were now on our left and a small aquarium was perched on a tabletop in front of us. The blinds had been rolled down and all the lights had been switched on. The fish aquarium was particularly highlighted. Dozens of tiny colourful fish were cavorting through their little sea. Darwin was watching their queer darting movements. Some of their capricious trajectories were not too understandable. His creased forehead reflected puzzlement. Were those strange sorties really necessary? Did they mean something in terms of the evolutionary thrust of life? Or were they just arbitrary moody tos and fros? Sheila had brought us some coffee. When she was pouring it out into our cups, a tail-deprived lizard fell down to the floor with a loud thud and, without smarting with embarrassment or pain, shot off to the wall opposite us. Darwin's eyes followed it climbing up to the point far above the aquarium. Soon she was ready to prowl for her food. Two flies and a moth were sucked into her one after the other. She was looking for a new quarry when all of a sudden her male partner, which had filled itself with the web-weaving spiders in a corner, jumped onto her and they were glued into each other for quite a while. I was curiously looking at Darwin. He was now turning his eyes over to the aquarium. I nudged him to draw his attention to the cup of coffee, which he had not sipped from even once. He was now sipping, but was too preoccupied to speak. Then he suddenly took leave and left.

After two days, I gave him a buzz. There was no response. I wanted to discuss with him a point of evolutionary biology. I do not remember now why I was in such a hurry to talk about it. I gave him a ring two or three times every day for a week. But there was no answer. I was rather disappointed because the evolutionary stuff was still rumbling in my mental stomach.

Over the next few days, the office work increased greatly and literally held my nose to the grindstone. The rumbling ended in a gentle burp, and a little later I was practically off the evolution mania hook. Back in my normal matter-of-fact frame of mind, I felt relieved that the 'zany eccentric' was off my mind.

Then, all of a sudden, he materialized from nowhere. Sheila had opened the door to him. He seemed to be fidgeting when I wished him good morning in the sitting room. He was not in a mood to talk and wanted to leave immediately. He had come to invite me to a tea party at his place, fixed for the late afternoon that day. But he had to wait for a few minutes as I was getting ready. When I came out of the dressing room, he had a little surprise waiting for me.

'I want to tell you one thing, Vigyan. In fact, I should've shared this with you right at the beginning.'

'What's that?'

'I've practically dropped 'Charles' from my name. I'm now only Robert Darwin, and not Robert Charles Darwin.'

We were among a very different crowd of people this time. Half of the guys were with their girlfriends. All of these 'girls' were of an over-painted, busty, middle-aged variety. Their husbands must have gone out with their girlfriends of more or less the same mould.

A kind of socializing was on among the individuals who had come with their wives and husbands. The women were bitching and the men were bluffing and boasting. In contrast, the twosomes were tagged together most of the time, cooing and communing. The 'nonsense' of socializing beyond this seemed to make little sense to them; and communing more closely was not quite permissible among humans in this society.

When the feast was ready, the guests were invited to the table. There was a scramble for the end where the plates lay. If the number of the guests had been a little higher, there might have been a stampede. Another remarkable thing was that all of the twosomes were behind the hungry husband-and-wife types.

The eats were all very eye-catching and delicious. I had several helpings of two Bengali preparations. My taste-buds and gastronomic desire were both more than satisfied, and yet I was going through an agonizing mental dyspepsia all the time. A very small part of the reason that might have triggered my agony lay in my inability to understand why Darwin had invited me to such a party.

I was back home at 7 o'clock. I was lolling against the sofa on the sitting room floor. But I was not exactly relaxing. The party was very much on my mind. Darwin stood at the entrance of my cerebrum. Did he want me to connect this party to the aquarium-and-lizard scene in my sitting room several days before?

Several days later, I found myself with him in a discotheque. The strobe lights were too dazzling for him, and the psychedelic music-rhythm was much too strident for me. It was clear from his angry but determined look that he would tough it out for some time. Not to betray my lack of tolerance, I too put on a bold face. Strangely, there were two separate crowds dancing to different rhythms. In one, there were mainly young men and women boogeying away to pop; in the other, there were a few young people among an older lot, who were dancing to a slightly slower rap. Darwin almost dragged me to the younger group. Most girls were glued fast to their partners and all of these two-in-ones were gyrating faster than the governing rhythm! A few of the pairs were lunging into each other in such a way that their overall body rhythm was in sync with the governing one. Their smoochings in between and slightly camouflaged orgasmic moanings were concupescing the whole atmosphere. I was getting sick, but Darwin wanted me to at least cheer up if I could not quite participate. I found a way out. I prepared myself to go to the lavatory. I passed through a hallway. A few doors were ajar on either side. Rasping, excited breathing noises punctuated by squeaky peals of ecstasy were emanating continuously. Inside the lavatory, three of the four bathrooms were closed, and I could hear mixtures of bass and shrill sounds from each.

Back in the disco, I found Darwin sitting outside the senior crowd's dancing circle and eagerly waiting for me. I told him what I had seen. He was not in the least surprised. He was keen to tell me something rather than listen to me.

What? He had seen a scene! He was dancing with a much younger partner in the senior group. A hunk who this girl had ignored came rushing in and gave Darwin a violent push. Darwin fell down upon an old guy, who fell upon a woman, who knocked against a well-glued pair. This domino-like sequence of falls rudely interrupted the gyrations of the discoing pairs. Everybody expressed outrage, but they were soon back into their grooves. When the 'jilted' hunk was telling his 'heart-breaker' a thing or two, a large dandyish dude descended there from nowhere and rained several big blows upon the jilted hunk, who now lay bleeding. The girl had taken to her heels. The dude was standing there, perhaps waiting for his bleeding rival to rise, and the gyrating crowd was dancing as before unmindful of what had happened and what more was in store at the periphery of the dancing corral.

I was in no mood to continue to boogey any more. I warned Darwin that I was not going to stay any longer. He agreed to come away. On our way back, we parted near the Qutub Enclave. I had to cross the road. The traffic was heavy and very fast on it. Even the zebra crossing did not seem to be safe for the pedestrians. But I had to go across like the dozens of other pedestrians impatiently waiting to cross. At last, the traffic light turned red and the vehicular traffic halted for a while. A large number of people were hurriedly crossing when a killer blue-line bus jumped the red signal and ploughed through a swathe of men, woman and children. Half a dozen lay dead and at least five others were bleeding. The bus had hit and run away as most killer buses usually do. All the survivors and all other people, who were waiting on either side of the road, were also gone as though nothing had happened. I found only one old man there keeping me company. Perhaps, his heart was bleeding for the dead and the wounded. When the police came, I was the only eyewitness to the 'accident'. The old man excused himself on grounds of his infirmity, but I was determined to stick my neck out. In the first two of my mandatory visits to the police station, I was frankly told by a three-star uniformed inspector that I was taking an unnecessary risk in offering to identify the killer driver. Several threatening phone-calls could not succeed in changing my mind, and thus a fake identification parade of some hired small-time criminals was held to satisfy my 'itching to do good to society'. Obviously, I could not identify the hit-and-run driver. The inspector heaved a sigh of relief. A look of derision on his face was enough to help me leave the police station at once. Not far from this place, I was paranoid about the intentions of another reckless driver when I providentially escaped a close call.

There was no sign of Darwin for a number of days after our disco meeting. There was no response to the phone calls either. At first, I was a little curious and then, after a few more days, I started worrying. But this was not the first time he had disappeared. Last time when he had re-appeared, I had tried to find out the mystery behind his unpredictability, but he had evaded my 'silly' questions. I had given up, thinking that he might feel I was too nosy. But this time I was determined to dispel the halo of mystery around his person.

After two months, I was very busy with a new assignment at the office. I was working on a new project, which my boss wanted me to work on by myself. When new worries press on you, the old ones leave you alone. I had almost forgotten Darwin. At least, I no longer missed him or puzzled over the mystery that he was becoming.

One afternoon, after I had finished working on the financial aspect of the project, I was sipping a cup of tea and smoking when the receptionist announced a visitor. It was Darwin! Where had he been? He only smiled enigmatically. I did not insist. He promised to call on me during the following weekend. On Saturday, we were at the dining table taking an aperitif. Sheila had not laid the table yet. But we were both too hungry to wait. She obliged and served everything double quick.

In the sitting room, I felt too curious not to provoke him. He appeared a little guarded initially, but I could see that he was going to tell me everything. I faked nonchalance and went on smoking and looking at the spiral of smoke rising from my cigarette. He began as though in response to a nagging question asked insistently.

'I'm going to tell you everything. Why're you so . . . ?

'Sorry.' I didn't let him complete his sentence.

'I told you I'm a descendant of Charles Darwin, didn't I?'

'Yes, you did.'

'I've been asked to work on his theory of evolution to ascertain how human beings have evolved since his time.'

'But a hundred odd years is too short a time for gauging any appreciable biological change or evolution in any species.'

'No, I'm afraid I haven't made myself too clear.'

I kept mum.

'I'm not working on biological evolution in general. I'm researching on the social and moral evolution of man.'

'But so many philosophers, psychologists and moralists have been working on this topic and have already come out with loads of findings.'

'I'm sorry to say you're off the mark again.'

I was getting irritated, but I tried to look very receptive.

'I'm not concerned with what these great philosophers, psychologists and moralists have been doing. My subject is quite different.'

'Oh,' I said.

'My hypothesis is that man has socially disevolved since the end of the nineteenth century.'

'On the contrary, he's made much greater progress in this short period of a hundred odd years . . .'

'Than in the entire period since the dawn of civilization?' he added in a questioning tone.

'Yes.'

'Well, I don't have the wonders of science and technology in mind. These things only prove that man can observe and reason, which has given them a better understanding of nature and its forces.'

'What else do you mean by evolution, or progress, for that matter?'

'*Progress* is your word, not mine.'

'What's your word, Robert?'

'My word's *evolution*.'

'It's the same thing as progress, isn't it?'

'No, it isn't. Man has made progress in the sense that they live in better houses, travel faster, talk to people at long distances, can probe space . . .'

'This is exactly what Charles Darwin meant by evolution,' I said cutting him short.

'No, not at all. His evolution meant change for the better. Better in the sense in which the modern man's better than their Neanderthal ancestor—biologically, I mean.'

'Isn't the present-day man better than their nineteenth century ancestor?'

'No, he isn't, biologically, and he's a lot worse, socially.'

My face became a big question mark.

'Isn't he much less disciplined, much more selfish?' His face was more inquisitive than mine.

Obviously, he didn't expect an answer.

So, Robert Darwin was studying this kind of evolution? But why did he have to claim a blood relation with Charles Darwin? If he was sincerely interested in this kind of research, he could have pursued it as other scientists do. So I began to suspect that there was something fishy about his genealogical claim. Maybe, he wanted to make his 'research' appear respectable? Maybe, he was not a researcher at all? Doubts such as these assailed my mind. Every day, I visualized him as more and more enigmatic. The more I thought about him, the more mysterious he appeared to be. In a few more days, my desire to know the truth about him became aggressively obsessive. One evening, I was watching a soap on TV and was intrigued by a scene in which a crackpot was being grilled over his claim to clairvoyance by a sharp-minded schoolteacher. This gave me an idea.

I made up my mind to unravel Robert's 'tangled' mind the very next time he would be accessible to me. But he was not accessible to me for quite some time. Perhaps, he had gone back into the womb of his nineteenth century great-great-great-grandfather, for all I know, from which, perhaps, there was no escape route back into our time?

TWO

For the first two years after Kapila had left me, I did entertain hopes of her coming back. But as the time passed, my hope dimmed increasingly. Now five years on, I had hardly any hope left. But I was more or less reconciled.

Darwin's occasional company had filled the void a little bit. He was not just mysterious; he was also very interesting. His queer views, seemingly weird pursuits and repeated vanishings, strangely enough, had kept up the level of my interest in life. So, his disappearance now was, in a way, a second betrayal in my life. For days, I felt very dejected and forlorn. Sheila would sometimes try to cheer me up with an unexpected cup of cream coffee and my favourite chocolate biscuits. She would also off and on tell me an interesting anecdote or two regarding certain maids and cooks in the neighbouring flats. One evening, she plied me with strange questions about my relationship with Robert Darwin. Though I knew she was pretending to chum up just to keep up my morale, I shut her up rather harshly. She blinked back her tears and disappeared into her room behind the kitchen.

A few days later, there was a little stir in my still life. It was a Sunday morning. As usual, I was busy lapping up the edit page of my favourite newspaper when I heard a knock on my door. Contrary to my normal response on such occasions, I did not feel disturbed. A young man dressed in jeans and a garish shirt was standing in front of me. He introduced himself as Rajneesh Chaudhary and told me that he had been one of my favourite students 15 years before.

I failed to place him, though he tried his best to remind me of a number of incidents on certain occasions, in which he had figured prominently. But I saw no reason why I should not have trusted him.

I have not said anything about my professional career antedating my present job of a senior planning executive in the Building Materials Research and Development for the Homeless Company Ltd. I had been a lecturer at a postgraduate college in Madhya Pradesh. I was a very popular teacher. Some students adored me, and a few even worshipped me. A very beautiful girl in her middle teens was reported to have had a crush on me. I brushed this 'stupid' report aside as nonsense. But I remember giving credence to it one day, when this girl fainted, fell off her seat and was lying on the floor face-down, mumbling some incoherent words, which included my name too. I was later on told by a very mischievous overgrown girl in her characteristic impish way that I was squarely responsible for that incident, which she called 'accident'. My lecture, she said, had so impressed that 'poor tiny teen' that she had lost her head and with it her physical balance.

It was this incident which Rajneesh tried to use as an aid to jog my memory of those days. He had, he told me, called this girl's father and then gone with them to the nearest hospital.

Two Sundays later, I was face-to-face with Rajneesh again. He breezily told me a few things about himself. He had joined as a junior manager in a Multinational Company two years before. He was now well settled. He owned a beautiful flat in a locality called Kailash Vihar and had a 'wonderful' wife and two 'very cute' children. He was very proud that his boy and girl were schooling at a highbrow English-medium institution. He did not like to call it a school because that would bring it down to the common level of middlebrow schools. I could not hide my lack of interest in his twaddle but, perhaps, he did not notice this and rabbited on. He effused over his boy's 'wonderful' English and his girl's sense of humour and use of 'big English words'. His own English was anything but passable. In fact, it was horrid, especially in respect of pronunciation. And, yet, he would have me believe that one of the strong points that had gone in favour of his selection for his present post was his 'good' English.

He hated Hindi and he hated all those educated people who spoke Hindi all the time. Though this was only his second visit to my house, he knitted his brow whenever I uttered a Hindi word or sentence to interrupt his endless yarn. Once or twice, Sheila peeped in to ask me whether we needed a cup of coffee. Rajneesh needed tea rather than coffee. When she was gone, he thought it beneath his dignity to betray any dislike for her speaking in Hindi because after all she was only an 'illiterate maid'.

Two days later, I was sitting in my study, poring over a serious article on the literacy campaign in India, when Sheila came in and stood behind me. She mumbled something and turned to go out. I guessed she had something to say but was hesitating. I encouraged her to speak.

'You mind not if I says something, Saab?'

'Don't worry. Say what you have to.'

'This man not good, saab.'

'How do you know?' I asked her rather harshly.

'He is . . .' She hesitated.

I looked at her sternly.

'You should not meet him, saab,' she said very quickly and went out at once.

On a couple of earlier occasions too, she had warned me about certain things. Whatever she had said had come true later. Therefore, the present warning set me thinking. I was beginning to believe that her sixth sense was possibly well developed.

Sheila's warning was off my mind after a few days. When Rajneesh came again, I treated him neutrally as usual. Every time, he expected some tea and snacks. This time, he wanted to stay to lunch. I saw no problem and asked Sheila to prepare some extra food. When he was eating, every morsel drew extravagant praise from him. The lunch consisted of two very ordinary dishes, *chapatis* and boiled rice. The words he was using again and again were absolutely undeserved. Their variation and repetition had a certain rhythmic pattern in that they coincided with Sheila's coming in every time to serve. I also noticed that every time he effused, he was eyeing her. When she came for the last time, I saw something like lasciviousness in his eyes.

I felt Sheila had perhaps meant this when she had warned me. But this was only a half-truth. She had meant much more than his libidinous interest in her. But at that time my mind was too tired, perhaps even too bored, to probe the matter any further.

An official tour to Bombay was in the offing, and this was the first time I did not feel like leaving home. There was a vague fear lurking in a corner of my mind. I tried to brush it aside as a mindless hangover from a bad dream, but it would not leave me. I was on the point of cancelling my tour when my boss told me in a worrisome tone that there was a new development in our Bombay office, which needed urgent attention. So, I had now no choice but to fly to Bombay immediately.

After I had sized up the urgent part of the problem in the Bombay office, I was relaxing in the Company's official guesthouse when the phone rang raucously. I lifted the receiver but was disconnected. There was a ring again. Again I was disconnected. This happened more than ten times. Once or twice, the line was cut off immediately after I had heard a blip of an urgent female voice. I was rather worried, but it did not even once occur to me that it could be an SOS or some such thing from Sheila.

On the following day, I was very busy. The afternoon was particularly hectic, what with complaints and irregularities in the official records and financial transactions. The whole office was asked to work beyond the five o'clock closing time. After a whole day's frenetic roller-coaster ride through files and falsehoods, I was able at long last to complete my work. But I was dead tired. Much too tired to leave for home the same evening.

Back at the guesthouse, I ordered a hurried supper and wanted to go to bed at once. Though very sleepy, I thought it necessary to call Sheila to find out how things were at home. There was no response. I dialled the number every two to three minutes. The phone went on ringing and its strident ring must have reverberated through the whole flat. She could not have slept so soundly as to be dead to all sound. This was an extremely worrying matter, and I was mad with fear and anxiety.

I caught the early morning flight and was at my door at 7 a.m. There was no response to the doorbell. I opened the door frantically with my own latchkey and entered the house with my heartbeats racing to an alarming level. There was no sign of Sheila anywhere! Her own room was empty. The other rooms had no trace of her either. Where had she gone? Could she have stolen a few precious things and eloped with some boy? No, that could not have happened. She was so honest, so caring, so dependable. All these thoughts crossed my heated mind in the space of just a few seconds. Then something in me propelled my steps towards the storeroom beside the kitchen, and I heard a low moan. The room was dark. When I turned on the light, I found Sheila lying on the floor, all tied up and gagged. In a minute, I untied all the knots, removed her gag and carried her to her bed in her room. She was too weak and scared to answer any questions. I rang up the police station and my doctor almost at the same time. After the police had recorded her spluttering statement, the doctor advised me to admit her into his nursing home for a check-up and treatment.

After five days, when she was normal, she told me what had happened. A man wearing a black mask had sneaked in. She was sure she had not left the entrance door open. He was quickly rummaging through the drawers in my bedroom. When she heard a low creaky sound and peeped into the bedroom, the intruder pounced upon her. He had almost stripped her and was going to rape her, when suddenly there was a knock on the door. He threatened to kill her if she dared to open the door. She was in panic. When she tried to reach for her clothes, he rained heavy blows on her. She cried in pain and shouted for help, which invited the final threat of death. She was then kicked and dragged to the storeroom, where she was gagged and her hands and feet were tied with a rough rope. He had a free hand now and, obviously, carried out his rummaging and robbing operations rapidly and escaped. Sheila had fainted and remained in that state for several hours.

The police was clueless about the burglary, though they had tried all their new computer-assisted methods of investigation. I had lost 15 thousand rupees, a gold watch, some important documents, all my academic certificates, most of my last 25 years' diaries and a register containing my personal accounts. This was the finding after the first hurried check. Another check with Sheila's help a few days later revealed that many more things were missing. I could not be sure about several articles because I did not know till that day about what articles—jewellery, cosmetics, other valuables—Kapila had taken away with her.

Greater than the loss of some very valuable articles was the loss of my vital documents and certificates. The apprehension that cost me my sleep for several days was that this criminal, whoever it was, might misuse some of those papers and blackmail me for years. To balance out this apprehension was a feeling of relief that Sheila was alive and had resiled to her earlier self.

Rajneesh did not come for over a month. Since I was not much interested in him, I did not bother to find out what had happened to him. Then, one day, there was a phone call from his flat; his wife, Raveena, was on the line. I was surprised when she asked me about his whereabouts. When I expressed surprised ignorance, she told me that he had not been home for over a month, and that she had had no news of him from any of the probable places he could have gone to.

A few days later, Sheila surprised me by reporting that she had seen Darwin in the vegetable market. I had a suspicion that she had not yet fully recovered from her trauma and had possibly occasional hallucinations. Without telling her that I suspected she had a psychic problem, I called in my doctor to give her a check-up. The report was normal, but he advised her to take more fruit and milk as part of her daily diet.

I received another jolt when she told me on her return from the same vegetable market several days later that she had seen Darwin again. When I asked her in a sceptical tone whether she had wished him or spoken to him, she complained that he had not answered her 'good morning, sir'.

THREE

Weeks later on a Sunday morning, as I opened the door to go out for a walk, I saw Rajneesh standing there with his left hand reaching for the doorbell. We were back in the sitting room in a few seconds. Sheila was in a state of blue funk. I did not understand the cause of her perturbation and thought that it was perhaps due to her recent trauma.

Rajneesh was at pains to explain why he had not met me for such a long time. When I asked him why he had upset his family by keeping them in the dark, he said he had been in touch with them all the time. Obviously, either Raveena or he was telling a lie. My feeling was that he was a liar, and not she. This also showed that either there was a serious discord between husband and wife or they were colluding to slip a fast one over on me. When I searched my mind later, I saw no reason why they should have been trying to dupe me at all.

These thoughts exercised my mind for a few minutes. Rajneesh was still sirring me overpolitely, apologizing for any 'inconvenience he might have caused to me' and at the same time emphatically justifying his disappearance. He needed some money very badly, he said, and had gone out to settle some old accounts with one of his uncles and his sons. He expressed great disappointment over the failure of his mission. His face was now a perfect reflection of misery and disgust, and my face was betraying sympathy for his plight. When he saw me melting, he hummed and hawed a little and gabbled something that could be called words.

'Sir, I ne—t twenty thousand rupees.'

'I beg you pardon.'

'I need some money, sir,' he said in a measured tone. The words were now clear.

'How much?'

'Twenty thousand . . . or any amount you can spare, sir.'

'But I can't spare more than five, and that too for a month or so.'

'Even this amount will be a great help, if you can't spare more, sir.'

'Okay.'

'I'm sorry, sir, to bother you. I'll return your money next month. This month I'm paying up the last instalment of my home loan.'

'Good.'

'From next month, I'll have money enough and to spare. My pay packet is big enough to take care of everything. I shouldn't have any problem from now on. Thank you very much, sir.'

Immediately after he left, Sheila stood before me, struggling to find words to say something.

'Yes, Sheila?' I said, to help her say her say.

'You given him money, saab?'

'Yes. Any problem?'

Perhaps, my tone rather than words discouraged her, and she left mumbling something abashedly. If I had helped her open up, she might have told me something about this man. Was there some connection between the recent assault on Sheila by that burglar and her hostile attitude to Rajneesh? I asked myself this question several times in the next few days.

A few days later, when Rajneesh visited me, Sheila blanched again. Though she was as obedient as ever, she could not quite hide her sulk. I was this time very serious about probing this 'connection'. But Sheila's last visit to the vegetable market dispelled my suspicion. She had seen Darwin again, which confirmed to me my doctor's diagnosis or guess that she most probably hallucinated in reaction to certain kinds of stimuli.

Rajneesh did not come for many days. Because of his frequent visits in the last few weeks, I had started expecting him almost every week. When my expectation was frustrated for about four weeks in a row, I rang up his house. There was no response. I contacted his office and was told that he had been fired. I was a bit worried. Because there was no response to repeated telephone calls, I went to his flat and pressed the doorbell button. The man who opened the door was anybody but Rajneesh. He was a new tenant! Obviously, Rajneesh did not own this flat or for that matter any flat. To pay his 'last instalment' for the flat, he had borrowed money not only from me but also from several of his company colleagues and 'friends'.

Sheila's sulk had changed into respectful sympathy. I did not look straight into her eyes for several days. When finally I did, her eyes had anything but a questioning or accusing air about them; they oozed only solicitous care for me. I felt guilty and even slightly offended that she cared so much. Guilty perhaps because I had not made use of her sixth sense; offended perhaps because her excessive care reminded me that I should have taken it seriously.

My doctor was wrong. Sheila had never hallucinated. The vegetable market Darwin was Norman Darwin, a lookalike of our Robert Darwin. He was the latter's twin brother, who had come to Delhi looking for his brother.

Norman Darwin had drawn a blank after days' vigorous search for his brother. He had met a number of people, who had anything to do with Robert in the last few years. He had lost all hope and was packing up to leave when an insurance agent, who knew both Robert and me, directed him to me.

He met me in my office. If I had not known that he was Norman, I would have hugged him.

'You're my last hope, Mr Verma. I'd almost wrapped up my search when . . .'

'Thank you for coming to me,' I said, interrupting him, 'but I know as little about him as you.'

'I'm told you were great friends.'

'Yes, we met quite often. But when he suddenly left here, he left no trace behind. In fact, I realized he'd gone when I didn't see him for two months and found to my dismay that he'd quit his flat and left bag and baggage.'

'Have you tried to look for him? I mean, do you have any clues as to where he could've gone?'

'No, none at all, though I've tried all my means to unravel the mystery of his sudden disappearance.'

'Are you still trying to . . . ?'

'Well, I've not closed the file yet. I'm sure I'll find him one day. But do you know something about this weird subject, he claimed, he'd been working on?'

'Oh, evolution! That's been his craze since his school days.'

'Did he take any formal course or training in biology or evolutionary biology or biotechnology or this new-fangled thing, called bioinformatics?'

'None at all. In fact, all these sound Greek to me, and he wasn't better educated than me.'

'His "pet project" was man's social degeneration since the time of Charles Darwin. In fact, he was obsessed with it, so much so that he hardly talked about anything else.'

'Yes, he'd had this obsession from his late adolescence to the time he suddenly left home.'

'Why did he leave home?' I asked.

'I don't know for sure. But he's said to have told an old school mate on the eve of his disappearance that he was "leaving his kingdom like the Buddha in search of Truth".'

'Was there anything that suddenly worked as a stimulus to his decision?'

'Not to my knowledge. He did see beggars and lepers in the streets as all of us saw them there and as all of us see them here. And a few murders and rapes and heists so common everywhere.'

'Thank you. I understand things a shade better now. What, however, beats me is why he's disappeared from here without leaving any clue.'

'Oh, that's his old habit. He learnt it in his hide-and-seek days and uses it now unhampered by "any roadblocks across his progress towards Truth".'

This meeting certainly enlightened me quite a bit on Robert Darwin's own evolution in the past rather than on his obsessive interest in man's evolution before or since the end of the nineteenth century. Norman left without any success other than securing a promise that I would inform him if ever I found any clues to Robert's possible whereabouts.

FOUR

Sheila had now recovered from the hangover of her horrible experience. Strangely, she was on the whole more cheerful these days than she used to be in her pre-trauma days. And, to my pleasant surprise, she appeared to be a little more clairvoyant as well. She was not aware of this psychic power herself. Whatever she said in her simple, innocent way often came true. One morning, she visualized a lorry running over a boy, and that afternoon we saw a big crowd of people in front of our house, raising hell. A five-year old had been knocked down by a lorry and reduced to gory pulp. A few days later, I found her kneading twice the normal quantity of dough. She said she was expecting guests. I had invited two office colleagues for that evening to dinner and forgotten all about that.

This clairvoyance thing was an asset, which I should have been happy over. But I was anything but happy. It put me in mind of certain mistakes I had committed, which, I thought, could have been avoided had I bothered to listen to her spontaneous, innocent remarks off and on.

There was a dark day ahead for our area in the city. And, this time, I was determined to make use of her foresight. A Hindu girl working as a maid in a Muslim household had been reportedly raped and killed brutally in our apartment building. The grapevine led to rampant rumours, resulting in people gathering into big crowds. As usual in such cases in this part of the city, there was a big communal flare-up. I came to know of the riot before anybody else, because Sheila had forewarned me, and decided not to go to the office. The following day, when I came to know that two of my junior colleagues had been killed on their way to the office, the pain of the tragedy was much too much, but it could not hide my sense of relief.

Exactly three months later, there was another riot in another part of the city. This time, a Muslim maid was raped and then done to death by a 25-year old brute of the Hindu household in which she was working. The print media found their favourite pastime after months of peaceful dullness and published it in such lurid detail that the inflammable passions on both sides of the fence caught fire and a most dreadful communal riot followed. No amount of police vigilance and damage control effort by a politically engineered Hindu-Muslim peace committee was able to stop it. For two days and three nights, it was a widespread free-for-all, resulting in dozens of deaths and a loss of property worth billions of rupees.

For days after this bloodshed and destruction, the religious politicians of the two communities first vented their spleen against each other and then rent the air with their raucous loud-speaker-amplified tributes to their great religions.

Sitting in my office a few days after this gory drama, I found myself busy with something other than the files, which helplessly stared at me for immediate attention. The wall in front of me had become one vast file page. I could not exactly decode the mysterious writing on it, for the magnification had distorted it beyond recognition. The words were still expanding and assuming a human profile and then gradually taking on the lineaments of our Darwin's face. Just at this moment, my secretary, Firoz, came in, and the hazy lineaments that could have hardened into a definite shape dissolved. When a project draft landed before me for my approval and signature, my heated imagination had cooled into solid reason and cold calculation.

For a number of days after this, my mind was continually haunted by Darwin's cartooned face. I wish he had come back and spelt out to me once again what he had been trying to say. But the next moment, I remembered what Norman had said about his being a 'fraud'.

Was it a mere coincidence that almost every day after the apparition of Darwin's looming face showed up, a new beggar knocked at my door and begged food? One day, it was a Muslim *faqeer* with his geometrical beard; another day, it was a Hindu *baba* in tatters and with three vertical white bands on his forehead; still another day, it was a Sikh offering Guru Nanak's postcard-size picture as a blessing. And one day, even a Buddhist *bhikshu*, the like of whom I had never seen in this city, was at the door extending his jug-shaped bowl towards me. And they were all fawning and begging. How were they different from one another? In the style of their apparels, or their language of abject flattery? In the cloying clichés they mouthed to coax the alms-giver?

The pre-Norman and post-Norman Darwin revealed now two different personae to me. Several days after the last riot, I was in my office, very pensive and angst-ridden. The immediate cause was the surfacing, in my mind, of a few dreadful images from the riot, the most revolting of which was the brutal killing of a hapless lanky old man. Two young macho men with scorpion moustaches had first bludgeoned him with heavy clubs and then stabbed him a dozen times with their bloodthirsty daggers. The sight of the blood shooting out of a writhing body was still alive before me. From behind this image emerged a stern, distorted visage of Darwin. I focused on the eyes, which seemed to be winking to remind me of one of the remarks that he had made more than once. Religion, he had said in his tongue-in-cheek tone, was not only not necessary, but was the 'main' cause of man's degeneration since Charles Darwin's time. I had dismissed the remark out of hand as many times as he had made it. And I did not like the look of it now even after the two recent horrible bloodsheds. After all, Robert Darwin was a 'fraud' as Norman had said. As I recalled Norman, the post-Norman persona of Darwin, fobbing off charlatanism as wisdom or prophecy, welled up from Norman's creased forehead and dispelled his pre-Norman persona. I was at peace with myself, was I?

An afternoon two Sundays later was bright and hot. It was much hotter than on the preceding few days. I had some important work on hand, but I was feeling too lazy to do it. I felt like relaxing a little bit and soon dozed off in the chair. When I woke up, it was well past five o'clock. A couple of visitors had been waiting for me for over an hour. A clerk in my office, Jaggu, had brought with him a cousin of his, Ram Niwas, who was badly in need of a job.

Ram Niwas was introduced as a multi-skilled young man, well-suited for the Public Relations section of our Marketing Department. I looked at him keenly from head to foot and felt there could be some truth in what Jaggu had said about him.

'Can you tell me something about one or two more important of your skills?' I asked him, with my eyes still scanning his face and gestures.

'I can make good posters and banners of all kinds, sir. I can sing folk songs, sir. I can act in comic scenes, street cameos, sir.'

'Good, very good,' I said in a tepid tone.

'He also knows a few juggler's tricks, sir,' chipped in Jaggu a little enthusiastically.

'Where do you come from, Ram Niwas?' I asked, my eyes still fixed on his face.

'I come from Gumanpura, sir. It's a village in the Sikar district, sir.'

'You mean in Rajasthan?'

'Yes, sir.'

My eyes narrowed and my forehead creased to search my memory. 'Isn't it the village which Rajneesh belongs to?' I asked myself. My eyes then turned to Ram Niwas.

'Do you know somebody by the name of Rajneesh?'

'Yes, sir. He's my cousin, sir.'

'Where's he nowadays?'

'I don't know, sir.'

'But he's your first cousin, isn't he?' I asked rather quizzically.

'He is, but he left home about three years ago and hasn't come back, sir.'

'You mean you've all lost touch with him?'

'Maybe, some of my people know about him. I don't, sir.'

Sheila came in to ask if I needed some coffee. Seeing these two people, her body language changed, reflecting uneasiness. Later on, when I asked her what had happened to her, she was not too clear about the change herself. I wanted to tap the promptings of her sixth sense in the matter because Ram Niwas was a cousin of Rajneesh. Her confusion over this point was in a way useful to me in that I now knew her somewhat better than before. I was now quite clear about the working of her sixth sense or clairvoyance: it had not only embedded in it an off-and-on toggle switch but also a scale switch that adjusted its power or intensity.

Monday was a lazy day. But I could not avoid the office. Lots of work was pending. My car had been at a garage since Saturday afternoon. Since I did not find any taxi at the Kailashpur stand, I decided to foot it to the office. It was quite an adventure because I had never undertaken such a long walk even in my younger days. Half way through my rather brisk walk, I wanted to relax a little. On my left, there was a park known for its rose varieties, orchids and strange-looking exotic plants of all forms and shapes. There was a culvert very near the entrance. I preferred to sit on it, though there were quite a few stylishly sculpted stone benches discreetly placed everywhere.

I had hardly lowered myself on to the culvert when I lost all sense of time and place! The garden had dissolved. I was in a new world, which had nothing to do with our world of gardens and garbages. I saw hundreds of hairy midgets, some tailless and some tailed, but most of them horrible-looking and emitting unbearably foul smell. When they saw me seeing them, they growled loudly and rushed towards me. I panicked and ran for my life towards the gate. But there was no escape. I almost fainted and felt my life-breath oozing out of me. But they perhaps wanted to keep me awake to their great brave drama. I suddenly saw one of the tailless midgets growing into a huge, tall monster and striding towards me to make a morsel of me? That was all I saw. I was no longer 'awake' in spite of these monsters and midgets.

In the afternoon, I was present in my office only physically. I tried all I could to rationalize what had happened in the park. But I could not visualize that dreadful scene clearly. My repeated attempts to coax my mind to recede in time met with stiff resistance. I succeeded in snatches only to espy a few small hazy parts of that *night*mare in the *morning*.

That evening at home was a very difficult one. The midgets and monsters kept coming back every few minutes. A little later, they came accompanied by another phenomenon. Now, every time they broke into my mind, Darwin also bobbed up with his old visage, sometimes in his original form and sometimes rather monsterised!

When Sheila appeared with a cup of coffee, I suddenly returned from my hallucinatory ramblings. The clock had come full circle. She perhaps spotted the same kind of look in my eyes that I had found in hers for a number of days after the burglary in the house. That was, perhaps, the reason why she was so concerned.

'May I called the doctor, sir?'

'Why, Sheila?'

'You does not seem very good, sir.'

'I'm quite well. Don't worry. You may go.' But she lingered for a while, trying to muster courage to say something. Finding no encouraging response from me, she left very dejected.

The next day was much less gloomy for me. My mind had broken free from its illusionary visions. I was now on a clear, hard plane of solid reality. The files on my table were staring at me rather rudely. When my secretary, Firoz, asked to come in, the files looked more menacing. It was a relief that he had not come in to remind me about the pending work. He was in just to announce two visitors.

They had come to invite me to a grand Convention of World Religions, commencing on the following Sunday. To be honest, I found the invitors more interesting than the invitation. They were husband and wife. The husband, Javed Khan, was a bearded Muslim dressed in a white *churidar* and a black *sherwani*; the wife, Anita, was a very beautiful, ideally-figured, bindi-wearing Hindu, clad in a red-bordered purple *saree*. And they had come to invite me on behalf of their respective religions.

Firoz had some tea sent in. When Anita was pouring tea, I was scanning alternately the invitation cards and their faces. After I had read the invitation between the lines, Javed drew my attention to a little brochure accompanying the invitation. I saw in the margin of the first page the figure of a hand with its index finger pointing towards the three-line matter printed in red ink. The highlighted matter was excited, as it were, about the addition of a new religion to the Convention. The new religion was Atheism. The excited red lines were followed by a cool-headed explanation for its inclusion in the list of the world's religions.

When the visitors were gone, I read a new meaning into the style of the invitation card and the brochure. It was an attempt to shock the invitees into taking interest in the Convention. That was why two oddly matched man and woman were sent to invite people on behalf of their respective religions.

I was still preoccupied with these thoughts when Firoz popped in again, this time to remind me indirectly that I had to attend to the pending work without any more delay. The MD wanted the project-in-hand blueprint completed within two days.

The deadlined two days could not have been more frenetic. Even my long yoga practice had never given me an experience of such a single-minded focus. The night was hardly different from the day until the project was almost ready. A few hours before the deadline, I took ill and my office's focus shifted from the project to my person. Firoz took over the work, and I was forced to relax in the anteroom behind my office. A yoga-type thoughtlessness, which I had often failed to achieve even after hours of practice, was my mindscape for good 30 minutes. Then, gradually, the thoughts started to sneak in. The first bunch of them related to Sheila and my house. I had not gone home for 48 hours. Then came in the thoughts pertaining to the Convention, which had been dispelled unceremoniously by the MD's deadline 'ultimatum'.

I had three days off after the completion of the blueprint. I badly needed this time to recoup. Sheila's almost 'motherly' ministrations helped me to recover within 24 hours. Thanks to my brief illness, which entailed this forced rest, I had the luxury of pondering over that intriguing invitation to the Convention. A number of thoughts crossed my mind. First, I tried to figure out why I was being invited at all. The only reason that occurred to me was that I was considered a well-informed public speaker in this region? Second, I was going over my own earlier reading of the drama inherent in the very nature of the inviting couple. Third, I found myself enthusing over the fascinating novelty of Atheism being given the status of a religion and its being put on a pedestal along with Christianity, Hinduism, Islam, Buddhism, Shintoism.

It never occurred to me till I joined office that my five-year old book, *The Futility of Religion*, must have impelled the organizers to invite me to participate in the Convention. My publisher had not given the book any publicity and thus had nearly killed it. I earned neither royalty nor name. Nobody except my shrewish and cynical wife, a few colleagues and friends knew that I had published a book. And none of these people ever bothered to read it because it had not been hyped. One very sound but lightweight academic had appreciated its merit and published an honest review, which was not noticed. So, I lost interest in the book and soon forgot all about it.

The invitation to the Convention now assumed a new significance in my mind. Some of those guys must have read the book and concluded that I was an atheist without even considering the possibility that atheism could have a far broader and far more meaningful meaning than that stereotyped nonsense usually attached to it.

I had a sneaking suspicion that the organizers must have drawn up a plan to have 'atheists' like me pilloried. The red lines in the brochure with an index finger pointing towards them gave credence to this suspicion. I knew I was not an atheist in the popular sense of the word and had no doubt in my mind that I was more than capable of presenting my point of view very forcefully and convincingly from any platform. Nevertheless, I found it difficult to convince myself that it was not futile to engage in any rational dialogue with priests, *pundits* and *mullahs* on their exclusive turf.

Anyway, the Convention was still a few days away and I had quite a few mundane things to attend to. So, I decided that I would cross the bridge only when . . .

Three days before the Convention, I had an unexpected letter waiting for me at home. Sheila had perhaps gauged the letter without opening the envelope. She brought it on a platter, which conveyed to me a bit of irony because she had never 'served' a letter like this before. When I was opening the envelope, I had a feeling that I was opening a mysterious door. The mystery did not lessen when I read it. It was a brief note from Robert Darwin from *nowhere*:

> Dear Vigyan,
> I don't need to be sorry that I left you abruptly, leaving no trace behind. This was exactly how I'd come into your life—abruptly and without telling you where I'd materialized from. Anyway, let's not waste our time over these trivial things. The important thing is that I want you to attend the Convention to which you've been duly invited.
> Kind regards,
> (Signature)
> Robert Darwin

The mystery deepened. For the next few hours, I was nothing but a speculation-producing machine: Why did the fellow want me to take part in the Convention? How did he know I had been invited to it? Was he one of its behind-the-scenes organizers? Why was he not attending it himself? All these questions and caveats were propelling the motor of my mind.

The next day also was a Darwin-shadowed day. My speculation overflowed the confines of the letter and inundated the whole Darwin question: Was he by any chance a real 21st century avatar of Charles Darwin? Or was he a fake, an impostor, tricking 'gullible intellectuals' like me into the belief that he was another earth-shaker, or prophet in the making, who people would ignore at a heavy price? Two days later, these speculations narrowed and spiralled into a decision. I made up my mind finally to attend the Convention—at least, for fun.

FIVE

The venue for the Convention was Shanti Van. An unprecedentedly vast area had been canopied with a snow-white marquee. The stage was a splendour that even a wildest wedding of a heavy-dowry-fetching son of the richest *Marwari* could not have equalled. Was it, as they say, a paradise on earth? A huge round table, with a flat side facing the audience and alcove-like spaces carved into it to accommodate high-backed velvet-upholstered chairs, could have been the envy of any Indian Maharaja's royal conference room. The background of the stage was a plush red-silk tapestry covering the entire length.

Behind the scenes, an eclectic ceremony seemed to be going on. I was able to hear a buzz of voices becoming louder and louder. In a few minutes, the buzz tapered into a silence, and the curtain rose. A galaxy of personalities led by a high-ranking Christian priest, called Father Anthony, filed in and occupied the alcoved chairs, fixed for them at the table. The Father was supposed to 'anchor' this session. He was seated at the extreme left end. A globe-headed baton was placed before him, giving him the authority to begin the proceedings. The microphone before him was much too sensitive, it appeared. I could clearly hear even his heart throbs, not to speak of his heavy rasping breathing. When he cleared his throat to start, it emitted something akin to a grunt. The microphone was adjusted to ensure that his voice quality might remain somewhat audience-friendly. The Father's face now turned from the stage to the audience.

"Ladies and Gentlemen
It gives me great pleasure to address an august audience like this. I feel so honoured to have been asked to give an inaugural address. Any of the personages seated on my left could have performed this function much better, I suppose. Therefore, I do not think I will have words ever to adequately thank your Holinesses at the table and you all, ladies and gentlemen, in front of me. But I think I can use this privilege to alter the schedule a little. Rather than giving an inaugural address, I would inaugurate the Convention by first underlining its objectives very briefly and then calling upon my friends at the table to represent the points of view of their respective religions.

"The objectives are outlined in the brochure, copies of which should be with some of you, if not with everybody. The aim of religion, in a nutshell, is to enable individuals to realize themselves and unitc with the Heavenly Father. This is the summum bonum of all religions, to my mind. But different religions have carved different paths to the same goal and set them down elaborately in their scriptures. So far, so good. But we have come far afield and all of us are facing problems of all kinds. Over the last three centuries or so, these paths, instead of taking their travellers towards their goal, have been coming in the way of other paths. The cumulative result today is, to say the least, most frightening. The fidelity to your own path seems to have become much less important than hostility to others' paths. And we have had discordance of a highly raucous kind, leading to bloody battles, holocausts, genocides. We have now an atmosphere of utter confusion and disorder. Everybody is befuddled—the clergy and the laity alike. Alas, the path is lost, the goal is forgotten!

"The chief objective of this Convention is to deliberate on our fiercely fighting 'goalless paths' and ascertain whether there can be some viable alternative to this horrendous mayhem and anarchy that could lead to Harmony and Peace. If we could all agree that the goal is more or less the same, it should be possible to sort out the problem of paths.

"I do not want to stand any longer between you, ladies and gentlemen, and our learned friends on the dais. By your permission, I would first of all call upon his Holiness Mahaacharya Brahmananda to give his discourse."

There was a big stir on the dais. As the Mahaacharya was preparing to rise with his files and papers, I could hear some bickering voices to his left. I was in the third row of chairs meant for the invited guests. And yet I was too far from the stage to make sense of the few words that reached me. But my cynical mind was keen to put words into these words' mouth. Were they not grumbling that the Father was clever enough to put the cart before the horse so that he might have the last word? At least two voices were grouching that the fellow would like to have the 'last laugh'.

I was too busy enjoying my snide snooping on the holy men's unholy voices to realize that the Mahaacharya had already started his address. The ovation had not yet fully died down. I report from the point at which I was able to catch up with him:

"Hinduism is an extremely broad-based religion. It is a fascinating conglomerate of seemingly diverse but essentially similar beliefs and practices. Its core part is the fundamental unity traceable through its bewildering diversity.

"Hinduism believes in one Supreme Being, Brahma, Who permeates every atom in the universe. To those who know, He is manifest in everything in the cosmos; to those who do not know, He is unmanifest.

"Hinduism was not founded by any one individual. It is an accretion from the spiritual experiences and insights of seers, sages and saints, extending over several centuries. It is, therefore, free from regimentation, and individuals are free to seek Brahma in their own way.

"Hinduism is anything but paganism. It is a *positive* way of seeking the Supreme Being—sometimes, even via the worship of natural objects and icons of gods and goddesses; paganism, on the other hand, is a *negative* way of peopling the objects of nature with supernatural powers and worshipping them to appease them lest they should cause harm.

"Father Anthony's word, 'paths', comes in very handy here. Hinduism is a path towards the Ultimate that does not cross or come in the way of other paths. Its cardinal structural ingredients being its broad-basedness and its unity in diversity, it is a byword for tireless tolerance and assimilative accommodation. That is the reason why India is a land where so many religions and creeds flourish side by side.

"We firmly believe in *vasudhaiva kutumbakam*, meaning, the entire world is one family. Therefore, I would conclude by saying that we have to look for reasons for the present-day religious intolerance and strife elsewhere."

As the Mahaacharya was going back to take his seat, I could hear some loud voices from somewhere in the back. Soon, they waxed into a noisy brawl. A Police Inspector with his posse of 20 constables rushed to the point and threatened to arrest the mischief-makers. But the potential for trouble was still there as the young people from different religions, chiefly the Hindus and the Muslims, were left there as they were.

The cynic in me was perhaps overactive again. Did I actually see or just visualize some Muslim hoods making dirty comments on the Mahaacharya's address and the Hindu goons reacting violently?

Peace having returned, Father Anthony now called upon Maulana Saifuddin to give his address. The Maulana's grey beard gently touching his *sherwani* below conferred a graceful eminence upon him. He walked with measured steps to the lectern and stood there for half a minute or so surveying his audience. Then he looked at his great colleagues at the table and began:

"Khwateen-o-Hazaraat:
The word *Islam* means submission to the will of God. It comes from the same root as *salam,* which in Arabic denotes 'peace'. Thus, Islam teaches that, to achieve true peace of mind, one must totally submit to God and strive to live in accordance with His divinely revealed law.

"The paramount truth that God revealed to mankind through Prophet Muhammad and His earlier messengers is that nothing is divine or worthy of being worshipped except the Almighty. A Muslim is one who totally submits to the will of God and strives to live in accordance with His message as set down in the Qu'ran. He should take the Qu'ran as the literal word of God, which was revealed to Prophet Muhammad over a period of 23 years.

"According to Islam, God is one and his oneness or unity should never be compromised by associating partners with Him. All Muslims are required to maintain a direct relationship with Him, and therefore all intermediaries are strictly forbidden. They are obliged to observe all the tenets of Islam in word and spirit, and individuals are not free to indulge in any experiments or practices to explore or intuit truth on their own.

"Some religions and philosophies portray God as an impersonal higher power, Who is unconcerned about His creation; others invest Him with human attributes and hold that he is present in His creation. Islam, however, teaches that God is loving, compassionate and merciful, but He is very much above His creation, transcendent.

"The Holy Qu'ran also teaches us a great deal about the life hereafter and the day of judgment. God is merciful and just, and all human beings will be justly judged by Him for their beliefs and actions in their earthly lives. Sincere belief in the life after death induces human beings to live a balanced and righteous life."

There were several interruptions during the Maulana's speech, especially when he was talking about the 'folly' of individual freedom or experimentation and appeared to refer in a veiled way to the concept of *kufr* and *kafir*. But towards the end, there was continual hooting, which subsided only when the Maulana was on his way back to his seat.

Father Anthony was now on his feet, appealing to the audience to listen to every speaker patiently and respectfully. 'Respectfully, my foot!' a slew of voices from the left-back end of the pavilion shouted. At this, the Father lost his cool and threatened to close the proceedings if the troublemakers did not stop misbehaving. This time, there was a loud yell from the right-back end: 'You'd better close shop. We haven't come here to take the brunt of the stupid homilies you all have been hurling upon us.' The Father had no option but to swallow his threat. Trying hard to look calm and composed, he this time made a threatless appeal for cooperation from the audience and called upon Ananda Tiratha, a renowned high-ranking Buddhist monk, to address the audience. When his Holiness was walking towards the lectern, his personality exuded vibes, which wafted over the whole *pandal*. A closely cropped big head stuck out of a saffron-robed torso, giving the impression that it was a Buddhist stupa in motion. When he reached the lectern, the audience gave a new kind of sitting 'ovation'—a big buzzing silence in lieu of a big hand.

"Your Holinesses on the dais and my dear friends," he began. "I am here to talk about the basic tenets of Buddhism. Lord Buddha founded it over 2500 years ago and laid down its cardinal principles and practices in a simple and straight language. The aim was to liberate the individual from their sorrows and miseries and lead them to happiness. All sorrows stem from the tyranny of desires. Therefore, the key to happiness lies in our triumph over desires.

"The Buddha's Eightfold Path expounds the essential principles that should guide and govern our lives. If we follow these principles, we not only achieve happiness in our life on earth but also attain total liberation from the cycle of life and death and move towards *nirvana*. Since these principles are available in print at affordable prices at the market, I should not presume on your time by expounding them here.

"Bhagwan Buddha never enjoined his followers to worship him. They are free to worship him or just look upon him as the fount of wisdom and truth, and follow and mould their lives according to the principles enunciated in the Eightfold Path."

The monk finished his speech before the hooligans had their chance to hoot him down or even show their appreciation by a few catcalls. They must have felt seriously cheated because when the Mahaacharya rose to announce the name of Father Anthony, there was a sudden burst of jeering noises and dirty slogans. The Mahaacharya ignored the boos and jeers stoically and motioned Father Anthony to take the stand.

Father Anthony had a written speech. He opened his file and began his address very loudly so as to rise above the din emanating from the back half of the pavilion and engulfing the entire space.

"Christianity is named after Jesus Christ, the Son of God. He was born to redeem mankind from their sins and establish the kingdom of God on earth. His crucifixion was his ultimate sacrifice. He took upon himself the punishment for man's sins. The Bible is . . ."

The words after *is* were drowned in the loud uproar of yells and shouts between groups of people in the back-half of the audience. As Father Anthony looked up to see what was happening, he had red and white missiles landing upon him. Quite a few eggs and tomatoes hit him and fell off the lectern. He was not the only victim. All the holy men had their share. The guests in the chairs near the stage were also pelted generously. When the missiles were exhausted, hoots and boos and obscenities followed . The audience panicked and were all up on their feet to escape. A number of them stampeded to flee the scene of mayhem. I was very scared like all other guests and was looking for an escape route. All of a sudden, a heavy stone landed on the crown of my head. I was 'seriously' hurt and taken to hospital. The injury was not as serious as some people thought it was. I was discharged late in the evening.

I was ready to attend the Convention the next day. In the morning, I received a phone call from one of the organizers, saying that the holy men would like to take a day off and, therefore, the Convention programme had been modified accordingly. The real reason was that no lectures or talks or deliberations were possible unless there was some guarantee from the authorities that at least a semblance of order would be maintained. The gossip mills had gone into overdrive. One strong view was that the local politicians would not like the Convention to be successful? Another slightly more reliable opinion was that some fanatical elements from the three 'main' religions wanted the whole thing disturbed in order to keep their pots boiling.

Anyway, the Convention resumed its work on the third day. From now on, it was a subdued affair. Formalities and speeches were curtailed so that more time was available for a discussion and a summation.

'Foolproof' arrangements had reportedly been made to maintain order. There were police all over the place. The speakers and the audience felt quite secure on their seats, it seemed.

The representatives of the 'minor' religions were calmly waiting for their turn. But it appeared that there had been successful lobbying for the 'atheists'. That is why the person who was asked to speak was a flamboyant young man, with his face oozing loads of attitude and reflecting belligerence.

"Friends," he began, "I must make it clear at the outset that I'm not an atheist in *your* sense of the word. I firmly believe in a Supreme Power, Who runs the whole universe. I don't believe in any of the silly gods and prophets and avatars that your silly religions have created for silly reasons, one of them being the exploitation of the gullible . . ."

The speech was interrupted by a deafening hullabaloo, which arose somewhere in the middle of the audience mass and spread outwards like ripples in a pond. The policemen scurried from the periphery towards the middle and were able to restore some order. But some articulate 'labels' in the audience would not have any more of that 'wicked speaker's nonsense'. As this peace-restoring effort was going on, the speaker, who had steadfastly stayed the course, would not have his 'right to freedom of speech' curtailed at any cost. So, when tomatoes and potatoes flew towards him, his words and tone became more and more vituperative and bellicose. A few sentences that I could hear above the horrible din were: "Religion is dead. I'm here to read out its final obituary. What you are doing now is what *your religions* have taught you; and what I am doing in response is what *my religion* has instilled in me. Your religions are tomatoes and potatoes, instruments of torture and tyranny that are more perishable than the objects and objectives they hit; my religion is rationality, humanism . . ."

At this point, a hard stone, certainly a much less perishable instrument, landed on the speaker's lectern. As I looked behind, I saw a number of young men yelling at him and charging towards the stage.

The speaker was not deterred at all. To my, as to my neighbours', great amazement, he went on speaking at a volume automatically adjusted to the ever-increasing pitch of the angry uproar. I had never seen such a committed, courageous, foolhardy young man before. Something suddenly happened inside me. I got up and darted towards the lectern, forcibly wrenched the mike from his steely grip and shouted at the charging brigade. The pitch of my voice was perhaps the loudest and angriest that they had ever heard before, and they stopped in their tracks. But they did not understand why they had suddenly stopped where they were. Seconds later, when my pitch climbed down a few notches and they heard clearly-audibly articulated words, their fury had abated and they were listening attentively as if to a useful announcement. I needed some more time to ensure that they would not resort to violence and, therefore, I thought it prudent to utilize this buffer time to say my own say:

"Ladies and Gentlemen and Young Men:
At least some of your religions teach respect for some individual rights, including the right to the freedom of speech. I myself don't quite agree with what the honourable speaker,

standing to my right, has said. But I would defend to my last breath his right to say it. My atheism is certainly very different from his atheism, but I have no right to pelt stones at him in the same way as you can't pelt me with your beautiful red tomatoes and your ugly earth-coloured potatoes."

The angry brigade was still standing. Confusion had overlaid their anger, and they did not know how to react to this kind of absolutely unexpected situation. The relatively less bemused audience around them were acting as a kind of gravitational pull on them, as it were. Sure that I could go on for some time, I resumed my speech:

"Atheism's not an anti-religion; it's a religion on the same footing as your religions. But the difference makes it the most important of all religions. It's an individual's religion in that the individual can observe and think and reason on their own and chart their independent course of action, unhampered by the baggage of mythology and blind belief. Your religions, one and all, are mass religions, which curb the individual's freedom of thought and action and impose upon them heaps of ritual, dogma and myth and kill the vital force in them. Borrowing the word of the speaker on my right, I condemn all these 'silly' religions and urge you all, my dear friends, to jettison them and continue progressing on your great journey of life unencumbered . . ."

I was not allowed to continue with my 'balderdash'. There were yells of 'shame, shame' from every direction. The charging brigade had rallied round them lots of more fiery young men and even women and rushed towards the stage. Our holy men were also on their feet now, seething with anger and emitting strident and abusive noises.

I got very scared and wanted to flee for my life, but my fellow 'atheist' would not relax his grip on my right wrist. There was no time to persuade him to see reason and leave the stage with me at once. The holy men took a 'conscionably neutral' stand, and we were both engulfed in a wave of violence. I do not know how many blows must have rained upon us. We were seriously injured and when we regained consciousness on the hospital beds, we were told that if those 'kind' policemen had not rescued us, we would have been killed. I for one had received a much greater injury on my mind, and lying supine there, I could not quite decide whether I should praise or curse the cops for saving me.

My co-patient did not seem to be too much of a thinking type. I did not have any idea of what he was going over in his mind. He looked very sombre. Was he going to bare his chest to the hoods' bamboo sticks or bullets again, or was he quietly pondering his next strategy to counter the 'collective stupidity' of the profession of 'mumbo-jumbo'.

His name was Subodh, on the hospital ticket. I called out to him softly, but I found him asleep. For the next few minutes, my eyes were automatically fixed on his face. Without my knowing about it, my mind was scrutinizing every line and lineament of his face. But I got no clue to why he was such a madcap. My mind now spontaneously zoomed in on the face behind the face, and I suddenly saw recognizable features. Robert Darwin was peeking at me from behind the mask of Subodh's face?

In hospital, I did not get to know much of what had finally come out of the Convention. I was not allowed to read any newspaper till I was about to be discharged. Later on, when I tried to catch up on things, I only came to know that at least three people, including a woman, had been killed and about a dozen wounded as a result of the Convention. Because of the generally bad and biased reporting, I could not quite know what exactly had led to the riot towards the end of the final day. A few days after I joined duty, I lighted upon a leftist paper in our office reading and archives room. Its editor had put an intriguing spin on the Convention and the 'bloody riot' that followed it: "The atheists were *pulverized* (he perhaps meant attacked and seriously wounded) for their *insanity,* and the theists' *sane* discourses led to *insane* blood-letting." The irony behind these lines was too obvious to need any intelligent reading. And the play on words, so typical of the style of reporting of the writers's tribe, smacked of sadism rather than of concern for the people being reported about.

The Convention did not leave me alone for a number of days after I had left hospital. I looked sick to everybody. At office, I was able to silence solicitous enquiries because of my position. At home, I could not evade Sheila's persistent questions. I had to tell her everything, though I still did not appreciate the wisdom of sharing such general concerns with her.

But she did not say anything in response, though the eloquent concern in her eyes was a personification of deep sympathy, which was a source of solace to me. Once I was in a receptive frame of mind, she quietly told me about the phone calls she had received during the period of my hospitalization. The most important calls, from her point of view, were from Rajneesh, whom she called 'Natwar Lal'. He must have called more than a dozen times, more often at very odd times. He wanted to come 'home'. At least twice, he sounded lewd and lecherous in his tone as well as words. Sheila warded him off with great tact. But she confided to me what she had felt during these nasty calls. She had a kind of feeling that this fellow had something to do with that burglary and the accompanying assault on her. This confirmed the suspicions I had entertained in my mind for some time without ever sharing them with her.

The second set of calls was from Norman Darwin, who had asked after me very solicitously. He had also told her about Robert Darwin's whereabouts! Robert, according to him, was now living somewhere in Lakshadweep and propagating his 'stupid' philosophy there. Sheila, without in any way being critical of Norman, discounted this canard of Darwin's whereabouts, and I was inclined to agree with her.

SIX

After the Convention, I was willy-nilly scripting a new chapter of my life. I was gradually finding myself a much sought-after person and at the same time a much dreaded and hated man. The 'mavericks' in the city and around were very keen to meet me, and the 'conformists' were opposing me at every place and from every platform. It gave me little comfort that I was becoming a sort of celebrity. I traced all this morphing to the moment I had rushed to the stage at that most crucial juncture during the Convention when the rioters were surging forward to kill that rebel, Subodh.

Since I was being talked about in the print media, my friends, relations and acquaintances must have been passively keeping track of how I was being transformed from an unknown opinionated officer to a high-profile controversial figure. I received quite a few letters, which I could neither call my junk mail nor my fan mail. I cannot quite describe the feeling I felt when I went through this kind of unwanted mail day after day. But I am sure I did not feel flattered, and ignored it all as a meaningless, if not malicious, interference in my life.

But, one day, I just could not ignore one of these letters. The cursory reason was that the whole letter was in capitals. When I went through it to the end, I discovered the real reason: the writer was Robert Darwin:

DEAR VIGYAN,

I CAN'T ASK YOU QUESTIONS, NOR DO I NEED ANY ANSWERS FROM YOU. YOUR CONVENTION MUST'VE PROVED TO YOU AS TO ANY SENSIBLE OR BLIND MAN THAT MAN IS

RATHER DISEVOLVING THAN EVOLVING. YOU MAY GRAB THIS OPPORTUNITY TO STRAIGHTAWAY BEGIN TO SWIM AGAINST THE CURRENT, OR GET SWEPT AWAY INTO THE SLIMES OF PRIMORDIAL TIME."

This letter could not have made much sense to anybody but me. But even I was not too sure of the exact sense of words like *disevolving* or *slimes of Primordial Time*. As I had not received any letter from him before, the style of this letter could not help me much in identifying the writer. The theme of the letter, however, did point to the possibility that the writer was Robert himself, and not any trickster or impostor.

This letter tended to put the clock of my life back. Even at the best of times, I was not an optimist in any sense of the word. But now with this Capital Letter looming over the vistas of my mind, I tended to look back to things rather than looking forward to life's immense possibilities. Robert Darwin was giving me a kind of an either-or ultimatum. It was extremely silly of him. Even if I had instantly started to swim against the current of Time, would the current have stopped or even slowed down by a whisker? And what on earth was he himself doing towards stemming or reversing the tide of Time? Just preaching or issuing warnings to me, or gallivanting around there in the 'primordial' waters of Lakshadweep!

Have you ever seen a caterpillar wiggle out of a can of treacle? The more I tried to squirm out of the trap laid by the letter, the deeper I slipped into it. Until one day I was almost neck-deep and about to drown. Catching at a straw, I pulled myself out. Sheila was on the bank, reviving my spirits with her answered questions. She had understood everything. Had she instilled something in me? Could she have done such a thing? Anyway, my stupid imagination was on the wing again, and I understood everything, it seemed. From now on, I had to do things according to my own lights. I was not required by any power on earth to mount on my head anybody's torchlight or headlight. So, I was quits with Darwin and at peace with myself. Sheila's answered questions were now simple answers without questions.

Just at this time, Sheila whipped out a long envelope from somewhere inside her person! It was another letter from Darwin. It sounded more apocalyptic than its predecessor. It deserves a good read, if only for its prophet-like directness of style.

MY DEAR VIGYAN,
I'M SURE YOU'VE RECEIVED MY FIRST LETTER. UNFORTUNATELY, YOU HAVEN'T PAID HEED TO IT. BUT PLEASE DON'T IGNORE THIS ONE.

" THE WORLD IS HURTLING DOWN INTO A BOTTOMLESS ABYSS. I WANT YOU TO STOP IT LIKE OUR GREAT ATLAS. BECAUSE ONE ATLAS IS NOT ENOUGH, I AM PREPARING MANY OTHER ATLASES TO PUT THEIR SHOULDERS TO THE HURTLING EARTH TO STEM ITS DOWNWARD MOTION.

BEST WISHES.
ROBERT DARWIN

Unlike the first letter, this one did contain the writer's name, though not his signature.

The first letter had made some sense to me. But this one, despite its very urgent tone, or perhaps because of it, did not. It sounded more like an alarmist warning from a false prophet of doom. The best thing was to ignore it, and I did ignore it with a flourish. I tore it up and asked Sheila to throw the pieces into the kitchen bin.

I knew as any sensible person did that the world was in a bad shape and India was in a worse shape, and yet I was sure that the world was not hurtling to its doom.

I was soon back to my routine self. I had put Darwin behind. The Convention was already far behind.

My 'spam', however, continued to pour in unabated. When I could not cope with its volume, I stopped reading it. Sheila suggested that Ram Niwas could perhaps spend an hour or so outside his office time to deal with the spam. There was enough sense in the suggestion, but I did not quite like the idea of Ram Niwas coming home every day and reading my fan or hate mail. Sheila understood my objection because she remembered all of a sudden that Ram Niwas was a first cousin of Rajneesh. As a result, we did not mind the unread letters piling up into tall columns.

As the print media had had enough of me and turned to greener pastures to fatten themselves on, I receded into my normal less-known persona, and my mail dwindled into a trickle. But my office work increased twofold. The MD had taken on two new ambitious projects without engaging any new hands. I was very busy day and night. Every evening, I came home with heavy office files and pored over them till late in the night. Needless to say that Sheila had now become my 'guardian angel'. She would not approve of my working till so late since she was worried more about my health than about anything else. She would often compel me to go to sleep as soon as the clock struck 11:30. She would not go to sleep before she had packed me off into bed. Though I liked her ministrations, I could not hide my irritation, sometimes, over her unbroken persistence.

The next few days saw my health improving steadily in spite of a heavy spill-over of office work. Perhaps, Sheila's care veiled as surveillance worked its way to my mind, and I was a total convert to the concept of physical morality: physical health, which is as much a cause as a result of mental health, began to take precedence over everything in my reckoning. I kept regular hours and divided my time rationally between 'work and play', as they say. I had now sound sleep every night, and woke up totally fresh and satisfied. Sheila could not have been happier.

One morning, when I opened my eyes, she was gently massaging my forehead and temples. My sleep-shedding eyes automatically looked to her face. She did not feel in the least conscious, not to mention awkward. Lost in her holistic approach to things, she was doing the massaging act as though she were doing any of her routine duties. When I wanted to get out of bed, she routinely but affectionately took her hands off me and asked me if I needed my cup of coffee immediately.

In the bathroom, my educated mind started to read meanings into Sheila's latest 'attentions'. At breakfast, I was unusually preoccupied. She must have noticed this but did not react. As a matter of principle, she normally kept her sixth-sense insight switched off. When I was leaving for the office, she did give me the impression that she was surveying me. On my way, I felt unusual tremors in my mind. I felt myself reacting to the morning scene in my bed, but I immediately pulled myself back from overreading the gesture. Even the files and meetings in the office did not quite set me free from Sheila's seeing-me-to-the-door face scrutinizing me. It was the same face which I had seen for years. But, that day, it seemed to be the most bewitching of all the feminine faces I had seen till then: a perfectly chiselled face, ensconced in a normal-sized head, bedecked with lustrous black tresses and mounted on an extremely well-formed tight figure. In my charmed mind, I was comparing her with that Plain Jain she had been at her first entry in my house nearly 14 years before.

I do not remember ever telling her to do this or that. Her idea of her household duties revolved round my needs. Every time she realized I needed something in addition to what she had been doing, she added it to her duties. Massaging must have come in like this only. She must have felt I was too tired and needed a soothing touch as a palliative. For her, it was like making me a cup of cream coffee when she felt I needed it. Nothing more, nothing less. She would not soothe me with her caressing touch unless my temples were tingling with real tension.

One afternoon when I returned home from office, I was much too tired and tense. The moment I lay down on my bed, I dozed off. Sheila knew she had a job to do. She was soon pressing my forehead with a feather touch of her soft fingers. I woke up with a blissful sensation coursing though my nervous system. Suddenly, without any premeditated plan or calculation, I pulled her onto myself. She feather-kissed me on the forehead and very gently disengaged herself. When I looked into her eyes, I did not see any blush of shame or embarrassment creeping up on her face. Before I could decide how precisely I should react, she knew I needed her help to get over my painful feeling of guilt.

'Saab, you doesn't need this thing.'

I gave her a bemused look.

'You would feeling bad, saab, if you did . . .'

'I'm sorry,' I said, still lost in a welter of confusing thoughts.

'No sorry, saab.'

I went on looking at her face speechlessly.

'Rather I should felt sorry for not . . .'

I did not quite gauge her meaning and firmly focussed my eyes on her face to understand her.

'But I did not wanted you to do anything which might caused you the pain of regret later.'

My eyes did not blink for a while. I could see that her face was undergoing a slight feeling of unease to see that I was disturbed. She was, perhaps, searching for words to set me at ease.

'I respects you all the more, saab, for the gesture you made. You are a very honest person, saab. You letted me know your affection for me. You did not hided it, saab. Thank you . . .'

She wanted to say more, but she was interrupted by the tinkle of the doorbell. In a few minutes, she ushered in Ram Niwas. I did not remember asking him to come over. He called it a 'courtesied' call and asked me over-respectfully if he could do something for me. I looked towards Sheila, whose look assured me that she had never told him to come and help me with those tall columns of spam. His 'courtesied' call was in actual fact a discourtesy call. He wanted to curry favour with me by spying on his colleagues. On a few earlier occasions too, he had tried to cosy up to me by hinting at some people's 'undesirable' activities. I had not encouraged him. This time, he was trying that trick in my house, thinking that I would be more receptive here. But I wanted to put an end to his growing mischief forever. So I told him in as many words that he should give up his evil habit, the sooner, the better. When he had left, Sheila realized that I was right about him and gave me an understanding smile.

The spam had practically stopped now. Stray letters did come in on certain days. Most of them went straight up to the top of the columns. Sheila had an uncanny knack of separating the grain from the chaff. If, occasionally, she felt that a particular letter would be exciting or even interesting, she placed it on my desk. Her 'hunch' was invariably right. One such letter a few days before had wanted to know about my sex life, especially because my wife had left me. Another letter a little later gave me a 'sound piece of advice': the writer felt that a person of my 'sterling' qualities should be a 'hero' in some high-profile field rather than a 'zero' in a dull invisible field.

When I read out the hero-zero part of the letter, Sheila was not quite amused as though she had already known its contents. Actually, she did not like the flippant tone of the letter because she was sure I was much too respectable to deserve it.

At office that day, Sheila was too much with me. That brief episode of my romantic gesture towards her welled up from my mind in all its detail. When I was poring over a most important file relating to that deadlined project, her face zoomed in and zoomed out several times. When I was through with this file, I asked Firoz to get me a cup of coffee and keep even the most important visitors off me for the next two hours. For Firoz, I was reading an important project-related book. For myself, I was busy reading Sheila's simple face as a gateway to her rather enigmatic inner self. The recall made me live over the dialogue we had had following my gesture. To my mind, no normal girl in her situation could have reacted so calmly and empathetically and said such wise and selfless things. But there still sat a stray suspicious thought in a corner of my mind, which was searching for some possible dark cave behind the backmost wall of her mind. I did not find any such arcane place, and yet I could not dispel the lingering suspicion that, perhaps, her response was a measured stratagem to entice me into a permanent relationship. The more I thought about this, the more confused I became.

In the evening, after I had had my coffee, I wanted Sheila to get me an aspirin tablet. She brought one along with a glass of water. Her simple, innocent face disabused me of the suspicion. I made bold to try proposing to her, and I was not doing this just to fathom her. I was serious, very serious, though I had a sneaking feeling that she was too wise a person, despite her apparent illiteracy, to be on the leash of a wedlock.

'Sheila, would you like to marry me?'

In response, she scrutinized my face and gave a smile that expressed a degree of respect I had never seen before. I waited as her lips moved to form words. I was sure she did not need my help, but the silence was too long for me not to fill the vacuum.

'Can I marry you, Sheila?'

'No,' she replied reverentially. 'I respects you too much, saab, and I loves you too much, saab. I wants this relation to continue as it is, for ever and for ever.'

I could not hide my sense of shock, though what she said was not totally unexpected of her. Silence lasted too long for an uninterrupted normal dialogue. My face was changing colour in spite of me, and she got the impression that she had hurt me.

'Great saab, you are my god, saab. I cannot hurt you. I am yours for ever, and you can ordered me to do anything, saab. You does not need my permission, but . . .'

'But your "but" shows your're not willing?'

'Yes, I am not willing, if you asks me.'

'Why're you not willing?'

'I have given you my reason, saab.'

'Don't you know that the marriage will raise your social status.'

'I knows that, saab.'

'Don't you know that you'll become a mem-saab from a mere housemaid overnight?'

'I knows that, saab.'

'Then, what's the problem?'

'I have already telled you the reason, saab. A marriage binds two souls too tightly and demeans them.'

My eyes were wide open, more in amazement than shock.

'I loves you too much to be willing to marry you, my saab.'

I was not exactly thinking of marrying her for my sex needs, and so I did not feel guilty on that score. Her response was so healthy and ennobling that even a hardened sex maniac would be at peace with himself after such an exchange. Despite my share of evil as a normal human, I was on balance a good man. My reaction to her, therefore, was very positive. Every single moment, she was rising in my estimation. And I too felt uplifted that I was so gracefully appreciative of her view.

Later on, in my calm thinking moments, the full significance of this wonderful 'master-maid' relationship began to dawn upon me. It was going to be a permanent alliance, founded on totally selfless and dedicated love on her part and supported by my unflinching subscription to it: Wow! What a 'family' we would be together! And what potential it had for my happiness, for her happiness!

SEVEN

Rajneesh's telephone calls started trickling in again. Every time he called, Sheila was the victim. In fact, he timed his calls to suit his urge to speak to her only. When the trickle became a big flow, I laid a kind of trap. One day, I put myself off duty to be at home for his call time. There was a ring within his usual span of calls. Sheila lifted the receiver, heard his voice and gave the phone over to me. He at once recognized my voice and modulated his voice and tenor to suit his unexpected interlocutor. He tried his usual lies in order to gloss over his lewdness in his several recent attempts to seduce Sheila on the phone. He wilted under the force of my no-nonsense words and apologized in his usual obsequious tone. I did not respond because I was busy conjuring up his real face behind his sycophantic speech mask. He went on begging for forgiveness, and I kept silent. When I could not stand his shenanigans, I blasted him again and asked him to get lost. Exactly at this moment, Sheila looked at my contorted face, and I changed tack. When he found that I was relenting, he immediately begged one last meeting with me. I told him he had no business to come 'home.' He said he would meet me at any place any time.

It was a very tiring exchange. I got rid of him by agreeing to meet him in my office in three days' time. He was to give me a ring at my office the next day and fix up the time.

Meanwhile, I asked Ram Niwas to update me on him and made further enquiries at and around his old rented flat. But these efforts did not yield any new information about him and his family. His wife had left the flat a few months after his sudden disappearance, and had either joined him or gone back to her parents or to some unknown destination.

And now this reckless fugitive wanted to see me, and I was waiting to meet him after I had more or less finished with my office work.

I am by nature impatient of wait. And this fellow made me wait for more than half an hour. When he finally came in, he just wished me and sat down quietly. He must have attributed the scowl on my face to my annoyance at some of my office fellows' stupidity or dereliction of duty.

'Are you beyond all time calculations, Rajneesh?'

'Sorry?'

I focused my gaze upon his confused and curious face.

He felt there was something wrong and said: 'Sir, I haven't understood what you said about time.'

'Oh, you haven't?' There was a lot of sarcasm in my tone.

'Please tell me, sir, what you meant.'

'What was the time of your appointment?' I asked him rather sternly.

'Four o'clock, sir.'

'What's the time now?'

'It's only 4:40, sir. Sorry, sir, I'm late by a few minutes because. . . .'

I didn't let him continue with his usual habit of giving lame excuses and bluffing without limit. But he did succeed in squeezing in two of his trademark sorry's.

'What brings you here,' I said matter-of-factly. 'Tell me quickly what I can do for you.'

'Sir, I wanted to share with you some of my new experiences in the last few months.'

'We could do this kind of sharing some other time. Why don't you tell me first what exactly you've come here for?'

'I need some money, sir. But I assure you, sir, I haven't come to you for this.'

'Have you, then, come to meet and seduce Sheila? Haven't you been making funny calls to her a little too often?'

'No, sir, not at all, sir,' he said very emphatically.

I was not interested in extorting a confession from him. So I changed tack.

'Where's your wife? You've abandoned her and your children?'

'I haven't, sir. She walked out on me.'

'How could she have walked out? She was very much there in that flat for a month after you'd left her?'

'Sorry, sir. She was a very . . .'

'And your first wife who you'd dumped at the cruel mercy of your shrewish mother? Was she also very bad or unfaithful?'

He was red in the face now since he was exposed beyond the security of his bluff screen. My gestures did not leave him in doubt that he was required to leave. When he was on his feet, he lingered a bit and said: 'Sir, I had a mind to share with you my interesting experiences of the past few months. When can I see you again, sir?' I did not want to say a straight no and evaded the question.

'But I must see you, sir.'

'It could be possible in a few days.'

'Say, ten days, sir?'

'You could give me a ring in about ten days, yes.'

When he was leaving, I surveyed his back. It was this strong and broad back, I thought, which had backed him up in all his backdoor and bad deeds. I was wondering why he was not turning this big back of his upon me so that I could rid myself of one recurring source of my neck-pain.

I do not know how Sheila came to know what had transpired between him and me. She very solicitously asked me why I had agreed to meet him again in ten days' time. When I asked her how she knew that, especially the exact number of ten days, she just flashed a smile and went to the kitchen to fix me a cup of coffee. Obviously, as she could not have eavesdropped on us in my office, she must have switched on her sixth-sense button to divine things in order to keep me from harm.

Two days later, I came to know that Rajneesh on his way out of the office had run into his cousin, Ram Niwas. This had come as a shock to him because he had least expected him here. He tried to get in touch with Ram Niwas a couple of days later. The latter did not like the idea and told him so in as many words. Yet, he had to receive a call or two almost every day. Because he knew I did not like that man, he asked Firoz to let him meet me. Standing in front of me, he was so scared that he was not getting proper words to apologize. I made him speak up and he told me everything. I sent him with a warning that he should not waste the office time on responding to private phone calls.

At home that evening, I felt unusually relaxed. I listened to Beethoven's Symphony No. 5 and then inserted another cassette randomly into my old Philips music deck. I was thrilled. Mehdi Hassan was rendering a Qateel Shafai's *ghazal* in his rich, mellifluous voice. The transition from one *ghazal* to the next was seamless despite vast differences of melody and meaning. When the cassette clicked to a stop, I kind of touched down at the runway of reality. Sheila had brought me coffee and told me that she was preparing a special kind of dinner. Some candles and a cake were also ready to celebrate my birthday! I did not remember my birthday and had never celebrated it before. Thus, I was rather mystified. As she was the last person on earth to keep me in suspense or in any other kind of strain-causing state, she told me with a bewitching glint in her eye that she had got to know of my birthday from my age certificate, which one of my files in my study had spilled out.

At 8 p.m., the two of us were sitting face to face at the dining table to celebrate a long-forgotten birthday. Though the table was duly laid with all the paraphernalia necessary for a birthday 'bash', yet to me it seemed to be one of the weirdest parties I had ever attended: the birthday boy in the glitzy company of a mega cake, an ivory-handled serrated steel knife, colourful candles, glazed crockery and spoons and knives and forks as his honoured guests! Sheila, my inclusively multiplied host-guest, wished me the amount of happiness, spread over many many happy returns of the Day, that a million guests together could not have wished. It was a moment of transcendence: I was at a wondrous point in my long memory lane. I could hear music and melodious voices and see steps beating down rhythmically . . . When I descended, I found myself trying to rationalize Sheila's ability to arrange a birthday party with such a consummate skill. She had, after all, come from an orphanage, where the inmates were not taught even the bare basics of life. Kapila needed a slave and had 'bought' her for 500 rupees when she was a child of about seven years. She needed her all the 24 hours and made her do all the tiring chores and errands. She would not let her rest and sleep and eat enough. She was good at housekeeping, and Sheila might have learnt a few things, but she could not because Kapila would rather she did not learn anything lest she should become independent.

But the birthday party showed that her training and taste were no worse than Kapila's. It was not at all the case that all the time when she was being made to work like a slave, she was subtly imbibing the art and aesthetic of housekeeping. Thus, I could not but attribute her uncanny skills of housekeeping to her native intelligence.

Sheila found me too preoccupied with my past. To drag me out of it, she once again wished me a happy birthday. I realized that I had not thanked her enough for her great effort and her wonderful taste.

'Sheila, words simply fail me to thank you enough for all this. Come to my side of the table, my dear.'

She came to me at once, and I kissed her on the forehead and the cheeks. Her eyes misted over with tears of joy. She said 'thank you for everything, saab', pressed my head to her warm breast unabashedly and kissed me very affectionately.

The next day, there was a blind call to Sheila again. She did not respond, for she was sure it was from nobody but Rajneesh. She was now expecting another such call and was, therefore, armed with a defence weapon. There was a peal of rings at 3 p.m. She let the phone ring for some time more to tire out the caller. But the caller had, obviously, more perseverance than she had expected. He kind of prowled for the right time, that is, a few minutes before my return home. When the phone rang again a few minutes before 5 p.m., Sheila knew who the call was from and blasted the caller without bothering to identify him.

When I reached home a few minutes later, she told me about the phone call. She was not upset at all, and I was quite sure that she could not have made any mistake about the identity of the caller.

There was no blind call to Sheila for the next few days. But after a few days, I received a call from this man. He wanted to know whether he could meet me on the following day. I said yes and fixed 4:30 p.m. for the meeting. He thanked me over and over again for my 'great kind gesture'. But when the appointed time came, he was not there. He was late by at least half an hour and came in, casually mumbling something about his being late by 'a few minutes' because of a traffic snarl on the way.

'What's your meaning of "a few minutes", Rajneesh?'

'Sorry, sir,' he mumbled as nonchalantly as he had mumbled his 'a few minutes'.

'Anyway, let's come to the point. What's it you want to "share" with me?'

'Yes, sir, I remember I wanted to tell you about my experiences at Lucknow.'

'But what were you doing at Lucknow?'

'Sir, I have a friend there. I needed some money for a house I'm constructing at Sujangarh. But that's not important, sir. You wanted to buy some land, didn't you? I've found a beautiful plot and paid some money in advance to an estate agent. That's why I'm here, sir.'

'But you've come here to "share" your great experiences in the last few months?'

'That's there, sir. But let me first tell you about the plot of land and the amount I've given to . . .'

'Let's cut this crap,' I snapped, 'and talk about your memorable experiences at Lucknow or wherever.'

'I'm sorry, sir. I thought I might as well talk about the money first.'

I was now very clear about what he was up to. I had collected enough data on his antecedents and his colourful exploits in the matter of cheating people, both individuals and organisations, and therefore I was determined to keep him off the subject of money.

'I'm not interested in your money matters,' I said rather curtly, and he got the message and had no option but to talk about Lucknow.

'Okay, sir, I'll tell you about my Lucknow visit. I was staying with a friend, Mohan Tripathi, who lives near the Nazeerabad market. He had promised to lend me some money for my house but needed two to three days' time to arrange the amount. At the same time, he wanted to make my wait seem anything but wait. He treated me to an unforgettable evening of wining and dining at a gorgeous restaurant. To say the least, it was an evening the like of which I had never experienced before. But the following day had a much more happening occasion in store for me. The whole town was being dolled up like a bride. Ratna Devi was going to celebrate her great birthday at Dasharath Bal Park in the evening. And do you know, sir . . . ?'

'What?' I blurted out just to give myself a little break from his nonstop gossip.

'Mohan had wangled an invite to her great party—a solid four-page glazed card with the great lady's stunning picture splashed on the entire first page. I was told that a great artist, Karim Hussain, had designed this card.'

'Why're you so gushy over the card? I'm not interested.'

'You want me to tell you about the party, sir? All right, sir. But I thought this card thing would prepare you mentally for one of the most amazing birthday parties I have ever attended?'

'Okay, fine. I'm quite prepared now. You may proceed direct to the party.'

'Yes, sir, I will. I'm thrilled even at the thought of that grand jamboree. Because of Mohan's contacts with big people, I had along with him a ringside seat. A huge cake was invitingly staring at us. Can you imagine, sir, how big and beautiful that cake was?'

'I reserve my imagination for . . .'

'Sorry, sir,' he said, 'I'm carried away when I conjure up the shape, the size and the surface of the cake. It was about 60 feet from the north to the south and all of 40 feet from the east to the west. It had been so made as to resemble the shape of India. Madam Ratna Devi was, after all, no different from India! And people were shouting "she is India!"'

I fidgeted but let him continue. I wanted him to gush freely and let off all his gas.

'The table on which the cake was placed had been specially ordered for this purpose. Scores of tiny bulbs were twinkling over and around the cake like fireflies. And, sir, I needn't describe to you the colourful canvas walls and the exquisite snow-white gate leading into one of the largest marquees ever pitched, perhaps, in the whole long history of feudal India.'

Firoz popped in to know whether I needed some tea or coffee. I said yes and he disappeared. Perhaps, my office was waiting for me to call it a day. But I was in no hurry because I wanted my guest to exhaust all his ammunition so that I could rid myself of him for ever.

'Perhaps, I'm taking too much time, sir. I'd cut the matter short now.'

'All right,' I said a little dismissively.

'I'd leave the rest of the splendour to your wonderful imagination, sir.'

I couldn't quite hide my irritation at his insincere lapse into flattery. And he understood my mind.

'I come to the main part, sir: the arrival of the madam. There was a long-standing ovation, followed by deafening slogans and hundreds of "Long Live Ratna Devi Ji's!" '

'Did you also shout?'

'Yes, sir, I enjoyed repeating all those delicious slogans and Long Live's. I couldn't resist that. She was so beautiful! Her dress was gorgeous! She was bedecked with the most beautiful and the most expensive ornaments I or anybody there had ever seen. Her diamonds alone must've cost her 75 to 80 crore! Amazing! She shone like Venus in the firmament!'

'Venus in the firmament?' I repeated in irritated disgust.

It was a signal to him that he should now wind up his yarn.

'And do you know, sir, who splurged all the money on the party?'

'Some millionaire friend of hers, perhaps.'

'No, sir,' he said triumphantly, thinking he had at least once beaten me hollow in the matter of general knowledge. 'It is the state, sir. The state is obliged to her for her great sacrifices and her magnificent deeds. How else would it have reciprocated her great services if it hadn't spent a pittance that it had spent on felicitating her on her great birthday?'

It was six o'clock now, and he still had a few things to say! But because my staff was waiting to leave, I had no choice but to end the meeting. When I stood up, he pleaded for some more time with me.

'Why more time, Rajneesh? Haven't we talked enough?'

'Thank you for that, sir. But I had to tell you about your plot, sir. And also about my money problem.'

'This plot thing is utter nonsense, I'm sure.'

'No, sir. It's there, sir.'

'In you imagination, I'm sure. Let's not talk about it any more.'

'Okay, sir. My money problem is still there, sir. Mohan refused to lend me any money. I'd gone to him all the way for help. My house is under construction, sir . Can you suggest some other source, sir?'

I know this was his habitual way of cheating people of their money. He could not have been constructing any house anywhere except in his imagination. I told him to suspend the construction and pray to God, who would certainly come to his rescue.

He understood my meaning and begged 'my kind leave', which I granted more spontaneously than anything I had given him so far. When he was leaving, he turned his face towards me and cast a lingering glance at my not-too-convivial face.

At home in the evening, Sheila congratulated me before I told her anything about this meeting. I had not done anything great or extraordinary? Well, she liked my being tough, which was not quite typical of me. She knew that several people had earlier taken advantage of my softness. Kapila was one, who had denuded me of almost all my bank balance before she had run out on me. Among the rest of my defrauders was Kapila's younger brother, Satish, who had borrowed three hundred thousand rupees from me and later declared himself bankrupt to con all his creditors. The others got a percentage of their money back, but I did not because I could not chase the matter to its end.

All these bitter memories and several others came into my mind in an unbroken sequence, and I felt very bitter indeed. Since the trigger was Sheila's congratulations, she cursed herself no end. Before I could protest that she was unnecessarily hard on herself, she had darted to me, pressed my head on to her breast and was caressing me by weaving her soft fingers through my eager hair.

PART TWO

ONE

Surprises, pleasant or unpleasant, make things appear vibrant. I had a string of them in the space of just one week. Sheila had gone to her 'mother' orphanage to meet her 'parents' and 'siblings' there. She was reluctant to go, but I helped her make up her mind because I had sensed a hidden desire in her to go and meet 'her people' once. Alone in the house after the office hours, I was feeling rather listless and also a trifle helpless. Not only because I felt lonely without Sheila's aura floating in the house but because I could not do many things which she had been doing for me for a long time. In this kind of situation, I very much wished something new would happen to enliven things, if not to help me out of my helplessness.

Bang at this time, I heard the doorbell play a tune. I opened the door to nobody else but Robert Darwin! He sported a greying beard and a few new wrinkles on his face. I did not ask him any questions as if I had been expecting him and was now meeting him at a mutually appointed time.

He was not apologetic that he had not bothered to be quite in touch with me these years. I did not feel bad about this since I had more or less cut him off from my interests. He was now to me just like a waft of gentle breeze, or a gust of wind, that comes and goes on its own.

He stayed with me for two days. I was as hospitable as usual, though he had to do a little more work than me in the kitchen and in keeping the house in general. But I seemed to be too obviously uninterested in him. He wanted to tell me so many things and waited for me to show interest. Since he did not find me inclined either to say anything about myself or ask him any questions about him, he chucked formality and turned on the tap. It did not take him long to get me interested and, to his relief, I was a quiet listener for the better part of two hours. When he finished with this story, he had told me all that he wanted to tell me and edited out all that he did not want to reveal.

For the first time, there was no dialogue between us. He was recounting his episodes and experiences, and I was listening. Even when some of his narratives sounded interesting to me, I tried to camouflage my interest by putting on a dead-pan face, though at the same time my alter ago was censuring me for my duplicity.

Some of his well-articulated experiences stand out in my mind. He had been in Orissa for two years immediately before he visited me, and so several of his stories encompassed the horror of poverty, starvation and death in the southwestern districts. He called this area Orissa's 'death belt'. But people, he said, were free to choose the manner of their death: they could starve to death, or eat what they could lay their hands on and die of food-poisoning.

Most of these people, he added, who exercised their 'free choice' or wielded their 'free will', were among the lowliest of the lowly of our death belt. They gobbled weeds and roots to their heart's content and thus technically were not considered to have died of starvation. His 'twisted' look at me had a triumphalist sarcasm in it when he described this most 'imaginative' spin that the authorities there had put on the semantics of death. The most macabre part of this story was also its climax: many of these malnourished, starved, emaciated skeletons were compelled to mortgage their government-provided below-poverty-line certificates (known as BPL certificates in the official jargon) to their village moneylenders, and thus the rice, that could have kept these worn-out creatures breathing for some more time, found its way to wealthy rice-millers, who sold it back to the Food Corporation of India, from which it had come!

He recounted to me many more stories of starvation deaths to underscore the point that most of the time it was made to appear that the victims had died of anything but starvation. The official line was simply 'disarming', he said: for example, how could those 30 children, who had died in a village in the Kalahandi district, have been taken to have starved to death when they were getting a *roti* or a quarter plate of boiled rice each every two days?

Some of these stories related to grisly murders, gruesome tyrannies and bizarre rapes; still others pertained to rampant corruption in private and public life. All his stories appeared to be true because of the plethora of graphic detail he provided in each case to support them. And though he was not too explicitly judgmental this time round, he left me in no doubt as to why he was recounting all these stories to me. But I did leave him in doubt about my attitude to his favourite hypothesis, though I listened to him for hours without cavil or question.

He still had several more stories to unfold, but could not continue because I invoked an important preoccupation. He understood my inability to share any more of his 'precious' experiences and wound up his visit with a promise to come again and with his parting comment upon the Convention of Religions, which I had attended several months before. He had followed the proceedings of the Convention through the newspaper reports from day to day, and the conclusion that he had drawn was that 'Faith TODAY breeds nothing but violence'. He particularly emphasized the word *today*, and that is why I have put it in capitals.

Though I was not manifestly participating in the monologue, yet I could not resist the temptation of asking him this question: 'What did faith breed YESTERDAY?' He did not dismiss it as a rhetorical question and felt compelled to answer it:

'Faith did breed violence occasionally, but it also brought out . . .'

I knew what he was going to say and cut him short rather unceremoniously.

When he was gone, I found it more difficult to part from him. However, his absence was a relatively less disturbing presence to me and let me reflect on him somewhat dispassionately: He was probably not an impostor. He felt deeply about things, reacted to them very sensitively and expressed himself 'honestly'. He held on to his crackpot philosophy of antievolution but only implicitly. The best part of him was that he no longer sounded even tentatively judgmental in his descriptions and statements.

An hour or so of reflection gave me a new perspective on him. He was now to me somebody who gave me food for thought rather than disturb me. I had a feeling that if and when he visited me again, he would, perhaps, not be unwelcome.

Two days later, I felt very bad that I had nobody to share things with. I missed Sheila very much—for the first time since she had left. I very much wanted her to come back, but I hesitated to call the orphanage because in no case was I prepared to curtail her holiday.

That afternoon, when I was making myself a cup of coffee in the kitchen, the doorbell announced a visitor, and, to my pleasant surprise, I opened the door to Sheila herself.

'What a surprise, Sheila! I didn't expect you back so soon?'

'Sir, but you wanted me to come back?'

'Wanted? Come back? Oh yes, I did!'

She knew I had understood what she had said. Which means she would have come back earlier if I had missed her so much a day or two before.

When I told her about Robert Darwin's surprise visit, she was not surprised. I told her what he had told me about his experiences in the last few years and what I thought about him now. She listened to me quietly and said: 'He is a bit of a cynic. But cynics are wise people.'

I was rather surprised at her remark as well as her use of grammatical language. She had a serious problem with her use of tense and subject-verb agreement, which she had been trying to get over on the sly, perhaps to give me a surprise in good time. My reaction to her remarks was in the form of the raised eyebrows and a puckered forehead, and her response was a beautifully modulated 'Thank you, sir(.)', which added more to my delight than to my surprise.

TWO

The deadlined project had reached its near-deadline, and my boss had left its formal wrap-up entirely to me. His general guideline was that it should come to completion in style. In those days of high decibel publicity for products and projects that manufacturing and service companies mounted day in and day out, we needed to execute a real blitzkrieg to attract attention to our not-too-earthshaking project.

Before that, I had to give the end part of the project an appropriate finishing touch. To this end, I planned a visit to Lucknow to obtain the help of a renowned chartered accountant and finance wizard. He was available only during the weekend. This suited me very much because I needed all the working days to work in the office in order to tie up the remaining loose ends of the project.

When I was getting ready to leave, Sheila offered to accompany me to Lucknow. Her offer puzzled me, to say the least. Obviously, she had no desire to romance me there. For that, she had opportunities galore at home. I could not quite hide my irritation when I said no to her. She cushioned my annoyance with her very caring but anxious smile. I realized there was something on her mind, which was worrying her and which she did not want to explain to me. With this thought, my irritation gave way to curiosity, and I turned my eyes to her rather tense face.

'Sir, I know you cannot take me with you to avoid a scandal this might create. But I will not let you go alone if you are leaving tomorrow.'

'Do you want me to take some office assistant along with me?' I asked very eagerly.

'No.'

'Then?'

'If you must go tomorrow, I have to go with you. On any other day, you can go alone.'

I could not help believing that she had foreseen something, which obviously I could not. Therefore, I left on Saturday morning instead of Friday evening. And that made all the difference. The Friday plane crashed mid-way and not a single person survived.

I got the news of the crash when I reached Lucknow. I took the cell phone out of my left jacket pocket and called home. Sheila's throat choked with emotion when she tried to utter 'Sir, God bless your life(!)'. For more than a minute, she could not control her sobs. The only sound I could understand was: 'Come back soon, sir. I wan—t se—you.'

Prior to my Lucknow trip, I had begun to believe that I owed her several things—such as sympathy, care, selfless love. But post-Lucknow, I started to believe that I owed her my very life. From that point on, I never looked back on my life. There was nothing comparable to my present life. I never after that thought of marrying again. The present Vigyan-Sheila relationship was the best 'marriage' ever. A new kind of love developed in me—the kind I had never experienced before. Kapila had married a rowdy parvenu, Roshan Puri, without bothering to divorce me. I did not need to file a divorce suit. I was free but did not need to remarry.

Sheila was the mistress of the house and I was its co-master. I realized for the first time in my life that any individual's love need was much more powerful than their sex need. Before this, I was all for our great friend, Freud.

This was how I looked at things. But what was her point of view? I started to speculate: She had just turned twenty-one and had all her long years of womanhood before her. She had her physical needs and would certainly need a permanent relationship. Therefore, one day, sooner or later, she would leave me and . . . These and such other thoughts coursed through my mind. But I left them at that and let them press on me a little more forcefully for a few days.

Then, one day, when I found them putting too much strain on me, I talked to her. She knew beforehand what was going on in my mind and was prepared for this dialogue. Her stand was the same which she had very clearly expressed at the time when I had pulled her over to myself during one of her caring-cum-massaging sessions with me and later again when I had proposed to her. When she was reiterating it, I saw tears of joy in her eyes and could hardly hold back mine. A timely cup of coffee came to our rescue.

THREE

Kapila's parvenu, Roshan Puri, was a very crude and cruel man. His newfound wealth had made him all the more heartless. His marriage to Kapila was a nine days' wonder. On the tenth, there was a real fight. They just stopped short of beating each other. I cannot say for sure why they had married at all. She was looking for a rich living and, perhaps, he was looking for a sexy doll. She did get her riches, but she was not sexy and selfless enough to give her unstinting best. Somewhere, during these unequal bouts of banging, there was a clash of two overblown egos, leading to a real crash. Perhaps, she acted a frozen slut, and he proved an uncouth, uncultured brute, forcing his macho prowess too much and too often on her delicate desire. Post-tenth day, Kapila had a separate bedroom readied for herself and enjoyed the luxury of having spurned him; and he was happy to go back to his old pleasures.

A few days after the bust-up, he found out that she had not divorced her former husband. He exulted that he could now exploit this woman the way he would like to, or throw her out without causing himself any harm. He had used some of her mistresses to manipulate his business deals. His real business was smuggling. He smuggled narcotics mainly and had an army of well-groomed men and women tasked with specific jobs. A string of beauty and massage parlours fronted for his real business. It was in these snazzy places that dolls like Kapila were used to their full potential. They not only doubled as beauticians-masseuses and sluts but also as conduits for his real business.

Roshan was planning to slot Kapila into one of these places when he found out that their marriage was legally null and void. Meanwhile, she had also discovered that he had committed the same crime: he had not divorced his last, umpteenth wife, Sulekha, before marrying her. So, when he confronted her with his ultimatum, she was ready with a befitting reply.

'You didn't divorce Vigyan Verma before marrying me, you cheat,' he thundered.

Her eyes were riveted on his face. Her brows were mysteriously knitted. He was sure she was searching her mind for a tenable excuse. But she was trying to whip up enough anger to emote suitably. As he was about to utter his most damning final 'verdict', she exploded: 'Have you divorced Sulekha, you pimp? She's still your eighth legal wife, who you're now using in your beauty-cum-sex parlours, and you had the audacity to marry me, you brute!'

At this, he was enraged and darted towards her to hit her. Before his hand moved to swipe her, it was in the iron grip of her right hand raised vertically towards the sky. As soon as his hand was let go, he stormed out of her room, shouting the filthiest of abuse and dreadful threats.

After this violent fight, it was all quiet in the Roshan Puri household. If it was a lull, it lasted a bit too long for it. He was rather scared of her and would do his best to avoid her. She had her freedom back. Her bedroom was her exclusive turf, where she lived in luxury and planned and plotted against him with impunity. She was determined to teach the 'bloody criminal' a lesson of his life. He pretended to be very busy with his upfront business, but he was actually preoccupied with forging a foolproof scheme to eliminate this 'conceited slut'. Neither could take recourse to a lawsuit because, legally, they were not husband and wife. Both, therefore, were thinking up a plan to get the better of the other or, more precisely, to worst the other. But this seemed a long drawn-out process to both. So, they decided on a short cut. He had no dearth of money. He hired a contract killer for two *crore* rupees. She too had acquired some money, but could not have laid hands on crores. So, she used both her feminine charm and money to hire an assassin. Both killers prowled around to hit their targets. But a comedy of errors intervened, and the targets survived their hitters. But for some inexplicable reason, she all of a sudden felt very scared of him now and thought of seeking my help to save her life.

I had long buried her under thick layers of time. Back from my office one afternoon, I was waiting for a cup of coffee when I heard the doorbell ring. Sheila opened the door to her old mistress. She announced her and went back to the kitchen. Kapila came straight where she expected me. I was much too surprised to welcome her. She stood there facing my stupefied face and then asked my permission to sit down.

'Have I disturbed you?' she asked to thaw the frozen situation.

'Yes, you have . . . Anyway, what brings you here?'

'I'll tell you.'

'You could've called first. You're now Mrs . . .?'

'I'm still Mrs. Verma, legally I mean.'

I found the ground fast slipping from beneath my feet. But when I was told that she had no intention of rejoining me without my 'clear and kind' willingness, I tried to look normal. I listened to her and agreed to protect her from Roshan Puri's ire, if she was willing to leave the town and go to live with her relations at Indore. She asked me with her put-on politeness whether she could stay with me till the danger to her life was over. I had no option but to say unambiguous 'no'.

Because of my social status, I had lots of clout in the police department. A phone call to a senior Superintendent of

Police evoked the right response. Since Roshan Puri had long been under the police scanner, it was not too difficult for the police to protect her from him.

I thanked my luck that I acted smart and strong enough to keep the woman away. What a relief it was! Sheila shared it. Her reassuring look was in a way a pat on my back. Standing in the kitchen all the time, when our face-to-face was going on in my bedroom, she was arming herself with a strategy to come to my rescue in case I floundered.

The SP had liked my advice. In a few days, he understood its soundness too and acted on it. He advised Kapila to leave for Indore. She did not like the idea. He acted a little tough, and she had no option but to pack up. It was good riddance, but not my total deliverance. To avoid any future repetition of this kind of quirky encounter, I filed a suit for a divorce.

As I was not a social nonentity, my divorce suit became a media sensation for quite some days. As a result, I saw a few raised eyebrows in the office, but they soon lowered. After all, they all had known that Kapila had run out on me and married a mafioso. I found out a few days later that most of these eyebrows were stumped as to why I had not applied for a divorce all these years.

Anyway, I was under no obligation to give any explanation to anybody. I was answerable only to myself and I could not find fault with what I had done or not done in respect of Kapila. Sheila had been my conscience-keeper for quite some time and her 'informed' view was that I had done the right thing vis-à-vis her ever since she had fled me. She particularly stressed that I had all along acted as a gentleman by conscientiously avoiding to be cruel or even rude to her even in the face of numerous strong provocations.

FOUR

In my office a few days later, Firoz was briefing me about my engagements in the day. I asked him to cut down on them because I was to be much too busy for the whole day with the final meeting convened to put the seal of completion on our deadlined mega project. To my annoyance, he popped in again in less than half an hour to say that Rajneesh was waiting in his cabin and insisted on seeing me immediately. To be fair to him, he had tried to little avail all his public relations skills and powers to dissuade the latter. Anyway, I asked him to send him away at any cost.

When the meeting was over, Rajneesh, who I had kept waiting at the entrance of my mind, came rushing in like a gust of dusty wind. This fellow appeared to me to be the worst of all the human and other happenings in my life. Some of the other happenings included Robert Darwin's recurrent epistolary and personal encounters and Kapila's unexpected disappearance and reappearance. In view of these happenings, a thought had been trying to take root in my mind for some time. It surfaced a few days after Kapila's reappearance. I could see a pattern emerging: My life tended to revolve round these three figures. When one was gone, the other peeped in. They were, of course, very different from each other and were creating different kinds of problems and challenges in my life. At this point of my thought chain, however, my focus was not on the problems they had been creating for me. What troubled me was that these three 'insignificant' individuals were defining the very ambit of my life. I very much wanted to break free from these confines and give my life a much wider scope and meaning.

Sheila knew what was to follow. After Kapila's exit, it was time for Rajneesh to enter. The stage had been set by her to its minutest detail. She even knew the time when the Director would signal him to enter. Exactly at five o'clock in the afternoon, she anticipated a ring at the door and was ready to open it. As if the door were transparent, she opened it before Rajneesh's hand reached for the bell button. He had a shock of sudden surprise and was virtually dumb for a moment. When he found his tongue, he asked her if I was home. She was for a second or so tempted to misinform him, but this kind of thing was so much against her nature that she asked him to wait at the door. After receiving a positive signal from me, she went back to bring him into my study. He wished me 'Good afternoon, sir' and I just nodded in response.

It was obvious to him that he was not too welcome. He had just barged in at a time when I was busy planning for an important meeting slated for the next day. And I knew he could not have anything to talk about but his favourite old wants and needs and indulge in his favourite hobby of boastful bluffing. His house was permanently under construction, and he was always in need of money. Plus he always had some imaginary sop to offer to me as a prelude to his request for money.

His shrill 'sir' snapped my thought chain, and I looked at him. He had a pineapple in his hand, which he had pulled out of a polybag.

'What's this, Rajneesh?' I said.

'This is a little gift for you, sir. I know you're fond of it.'

'A rare gift indeed. But whenever was I fond of it? It appears you know more about me than I do myself.'

'Thank you, sir,' he said, pretending not to understand the unsubtle sarcasm in my words and tone.

'Let's come to the point, Rajneesh. What can I do for you?'

'Nothing much, sir. I'm here just to say hello and to find out how you are.'

Sheila brought in the tea trolley and started pouring us tea. He looked at her straight once and then cast a few furtive glances. She winced a bit when she spilt a few drops of scalding tea on his left-hand fingers. But she composed herself immediately and left the room. She never took tea with me when there was a guest, and Rajneesh in any case by her own decision was out of bounds for her.

I waited for him to leave, but he was not even half way through. This time, it was a Sohan Panwar, instead of a Mohan Tripathi, who had backed out of his promise to lend him money for his half-constructed house, which had moved mysteriously from the Sikar district to Sujangarh in Rajasthan. And the plot of land he had almost 'bought' for me was also near his aborted house.

'I've paid almost half the price for your plot, sir,' he said, acting a benevolent smile. If you could spare just a small amount, sir, the plot would be yours. I'll pay the rest.'

It was with great effort that I controlled my temper and continued the conversation.

'You can keep *my* plot . . . You'd better sell it and spend the money on completing your half-constructed thing.'

'But, sir, I need money to complete the deal for your plot.'

'So?'

'I was wondering whether you could suggest some way out of this pressing money problems, sir.'

'I'm afraid I can't suggest any solution that you might like. But I can tell you one way of solving this painful problem for ever.'

'What's that way, sir?'

'You shouldn't construct a house at all.'

'But, sir, I've already constructed half of it.'

'Don't bother about it. When you go back to it, it'll not be there!'

'What do you mean, sir?'

'You know what I mean, don't you?'

He understood my meaning better than I myself did. But he feigned that he was not upset at all. In fact, he acted as though he was very happy with my 'advice'.

It was getting on for seven o'clock. Sheila was at the door to ask me if I needed a cup of coffee. Before I could say anything, he said a big yes to coffee and added he would prefer cream coffee. The coffee over, I hinted that it was time for him to leave. But he lingered. He wanted to fix another meeting in order to share his 'new' experiences with me. I asked him to say his say at once, regretting that I would not find time for another meeting for quite some time. Just at this moment, Sheila managed to peek at me furtively, and I changed my decision automatically.

'Sir, I'm ready to wait as long as . . .'

I cut him short and told him to give me a tinkle in ten days or so.

After he left, she came in to explain her furtive peek at me.

'Can I disturb you, sir?'

'Now, don't tease me, Sheila!'

'But I am not teasing you, sir. He was with you so long, and before he came, you were working on some file. That is why I . . .'

'Okay, sorry. Now tell me what you wanted to say.'

'I wanted you to give him some other time and not to let him continue to say his say.'

'Why, Sheila?'

'I have something very important to tell you.'

'What's that?'

'This fellow killed his second wife a month ago!'

'What? I thought he had only one wife. Second wife? Killed her?'

Her eyes were all empathy.

'How do you know all this?'

'You know how I know, sir.'

'And where's his first wife?'

'I do not know that for sure, sir. You told me she had gone back to her parents?'

'But what's your news?'

'I am not sure. I have a feeling she eloped with one of Rajneesh's second cousins and has been living with him.'

'Then, why didn't you let me be with him for a few more minutes and then dismiss him for ever?'

'Well, I did not want you to spend any more time with such a dangerous person. And as for another meeting in ten days, you could refuse to meet him.'

In my heart of hearts, I trusted Sheila and the information she gave me. And yet to satisfy my curiosity, or, maybe, more to reinforce my faith in her clairvoyance, I asked my private detective, John D'Souza, to find out the real truth about Rajneesh.

More than Sheila's clairvoyance, it was her rapid transformation from an illiterate housemaid to a perfectly literate housewife that was continually raising the level of my surprise. Her language had almost completely shed its rusticity. It was now indistinguishably the language of a formally educated person and was showing clear signs of evolution towards accomplished speech. It was certainly not by accident that she used 'you could refuse', and not 'you should refused' or 'you can refused', which she might have used not more than two months before. Second, her love and loyalty towards me were unrecognizably different from what they were just a month or two before. They had morphed towards a level of refinement I had never experienced in anyone. Her love had all the richness of lyrical romance minus the passion and possessiveness of libido; her loyalty had the quality of care and concern never seen or heard of in any servant towards their master. Perhaps, I now was able to appreciate why she had declined my proposal of marriage. Marriage possibly conjured up in her the image of Kapila. She must have felt that she could not be a Kapila and a Sheila at the same time.

The detective was ready with a preliminary report. Most of the things Sheila had told me about Rajneesh were true. But because he was still looking into some new leads, I asked him to take a few more days and hand in a complete dossier on the man.

Meantime, I received a very brief note from Darwin, telling me that he would like to visit me in about a week's time. Since the letter did not contain any fixed date, I sent him an immediate reply to ask him to put off his visit to a later date. I regretted my inability to spare any time for about 15 days because I was extremely busy with winding up my deadlined project.

His reply to my regret letter was not too kind. He complained that I was trying to avoid him. In reply, I regretted that he was not fair to me and assured him that we would meet before long.

The detective handed in his findings on Rajneesh on schedule. All that Sheila had said was absolutely true, but it was a very small part of the whole truth, which was far more damning and dreadful. The fellow had become a total beast. When he killed his second 'wife', she was six months pregnant. The postmortem revealed that the foetus was a girl. This fuelled speculation among the police and the public as to why he must have killed his wife.

That he had cheated more than a dozen people of their hard-earned money was a minor thing. Much more serious felonies were being attributed to him. He had become a dreaded extortionist in the last two to three years and had brutally assaulted several people for refusing to pay their regular extortion amounts. One of his victims, who had defied his heavy demand, died when he was hit repeatedly with an iron rod.

The report also mentioned a few unverified rumours. One such rumour had it that he had killed a number of other people for defying his crazed whims and vagaries. Some of these murders, according to this report, 'appeared' to be true. He was not less cruel to women. One view was that he hated them very deeply. He had raped many and killed some of them when later they had tried to be difficult. His sexual habits were bizarre, to say the least. He preferred minor girls and boys and plied them hard, sometimes for hours together, getting them to do all kinds of kinky things. Even worse things, kinkier even by the most cranky sexual standards of any society, formed part of the report. But I ignore them here not because I am too squeamish, but because the picture of his sexual life is already too dark to accommodate any more black paint.

The stories of his thefts and robberies were many. Even if half of them had been true, he would have been a man of great wealth. But the report did not say that he was extremely rich. He was described as a man of moderate means. Perhaps, he had splurged on wine and women much too often and also on controlling the forces of the law. Or, maybe, he had hidden away his wealth in some secret vault and his moderate facade was to keep the authorities off his trail.

Why he persevered so doggedly to keep up his equation with me was now totally beyond my comprehension. It appeared quite unlikely that every time when he came to me, he intended to borrow some money or share his great experiences with me.

I particularly wanted to know about his perennial 'half-constructed' house. The report said he had several big houses in different villages and towns in Rajasthan and several more were under construction at any time of the year. It did not say how he used so many houses and why he was still building so many more. The only explanation given was that either he had become insatiably greedy or the irredeemably corrupt politicians around him had taught him that unlimited real estate was a sure gateway to power.

The last pages of the report were only a summary of the findings. I skipped them quickly to make a mental evaluation of the whole thing. It appeared to me that only a part of it stood to reason. The part based on speculation and hearsay did not pass muster with me.

The next two hours were dedicated to a postmortem of the report with Sheila. Visitors were to be kept off. She listened to the whole thing so coolly. I could not see any emotional reactions suffusing her face or gestures. I felt as though she had known everything. But she said she had known only the part she had told me. I looked at her a little quizzically. She 'divined' what my question was and explained that she had not focussed her mind on his entire history. Perhaps, some stimulus had accidentally attracted her mind only to his second-wife-killing spot, and thus she had told me only about that. I had no doubt now that if she had tried to expand her focus, she would have seen the whole thing. This was quite evident from her response to the report now. Now that she had 'scanned' the entire foreground and background and had a clear perspective on him, she said that not all the things in the dossier were true. There were quite a few things which she found wildly exaggerated or simply fabricated, and I could not agree with her more.

Anyway, even the picture emerging from this 'rationalized' report was much too dark for a person who any respectable individual could afford to associate with. So, the decision was that I would keep the man at an arm's length, if a greater distance was not possible.

FIVE

The report of our project was now complete. My boss was very pleased, though there was a few days' delay in its submission. In less than two days, it was thoroughly examined and assessed. The First Secretary to the boss, who was an honest and fastidious bureaucrat, praised it in glowing terms. Since this gentleman had never praised anything in such terms before, the boss thought it prudent to make his own assessment. He could not have disagreed with his secretary less.

And then what followed was quite on expected lines. There was a very heavy pat on my back, so much so that I almost 'smarted' under its pleasant though tingling impact. A party was thrown by the boss to felicitate me. I was lionised by him and all his senior staff. Other colleagues and the staff in my section of the Company practically queued up to shake hands with me. I was too euphoric inside to decide whether I was reacting properly to the mood of the occasion, that is, whether I was modest enough, or at least not too immodest, to use 'proper' words and gestures in response.

In the evening, when Sheila opened the door, her face was a mirror in which I could see a video of the day's happenings. She did not have to congratulate me. She had a little treat ready for me as a wonderful non-verbal response. The table had been laid with varieties of sweets, snacks and dry fruits. When the cover was removed, I had a taste of her entirely new sense of taste and occasion. When we were eating, she congratulated me on my 'promotion'. I knitted my brows in incomprehension. She was quick to react and explained her use of the word in a deadpan tone. She was not excited because she thought that my promotion was long overdue and that I deserved much more than this.

The very next day, the boss summoned me to his office. When I entered it, he stood up and congratulated me! I found it difficult to control my emotion. To hold back my tears, I started reading the letter of promotion, which had just the opposite effect. It said what I had not expected. I had been moved two steps upwards. I was now a senior vice-president!

I do not know whether I was too modest or too rigorous in my standards at that time to have assessed my 'achievement' in terms used by my boss and his hierarchy above me. My rather overemotional response was perhaps to do with this. Sheila would not quite agree with my assessment of my work on the project. And her opinion was more reliable because it was not based on not-too-infallible inductive criteria: it was based on her 'gut' feeling.

I need not hide the fact that this recognition of my work and my big promotion marked the happiest moment of my life up to that point. Logically speaking, my happiness could not have gone further up; nor could it have stayed at this level for long because change, or in this case up-or-down movement, is the law of nature.

Just a week after this climax of happiness, I had a brush with unhappiness. Sheila had gone out shopping at four o'clock as usual. When she was returning with her heavy shopping bags, somebody sneaked up on her from behind and threw a thick black cloak over her. A gag was about to go over her mouth when she 'saw' everything in the abduction plan and its execution. A mysterious superhuman strength (which I call 'power') suddenly coursed through her limbs, and she threw her heavy bags back over the abductor, who ran for his life and vanished into the narrow lanes behind the crowded shopping centre.

A little after five o'clock, when I returned home, her face did not show that something ugly or dreadful had happened to her. Later, when she brought me coffee, she related to me very calmly what she had escaped. I had never felt so disturbed before, nor had I ever seen her more composed. She had to work very hard to bring me back to my normal self. When I asked her whether she had been able to see the face of the criminal, she said she had visualized it but could not place it. The only course open to us was to report the matter to the police. But she wanted me to wait for some time without giving any reason for it. Perhaps, she was mulling over the whole incident and trying to match the face with all the faces she had seen till that time. Suddenly, she said it was certainly not Rajneesh. Who could it have been, then? She had no answer. But I had one. In view of all that the dossier had said about Rajneesh, he could not have been kept out of the circle of suspicion. He must have hired somebody or ordered one of his minions in his mafia gang to commit the crime. Sheila did not completely disagree with this line of thinking, but she was not worried at all. Said she would catch the hoodlum one day and also assured me that nobody could take 'my' Sheila away from me.

My promotion entailed many privileges. I was moved to a much bigger room with plush furniture, carpets, curtains and hangings. Its overall inner décor was organized by an upmarket professional. A simple man like me felt like a beggar in a royal palace. I was provided with two independent telephone lines and a separate peon to run errands for me. Plus I was given a brand-new chauffeur-driven air-conditioned car. And these were only the more important of the privileges that the promotion automatically conferred upon me.

The project I had turned out 'so successfully' had to do with the United Nations. The World Bank Chief, Robert Whitefield, was slated for a visit to India in a fortnight's time, and my Company very much wanted him to read it and express his appreciation of it.

Naturally, I was assigned the job of presenting the project report myself to Mr Whitefield. Since it was based on my extensive research on the evolution of new social structures addressed to the amelioration of the living conditions and living styles of the common people in India since Independence, I prepared a synopsis for presentation, which highlighted the structures that had been meticulously developed to deliver on amelioration. My presentation seemed to be quite impressive. It evoked appreciative response from most people in the audience. Whitefield asked for a copy of the project report. He wanted to give it a good look and make his objective comments on it.

He had a number of engagements in the following days. He had to visit some of the World Bank-funded development schemes in the city and in the national capital region. He was to deliver an evaluative lecture on the working of all these schemes in India, and my project report was supposed to provide him with one of the more important inputs. My boss and other senior and junior colleagues were not worried. They were convinced that I had done a really good piece of work. But I had to keep my fingers crossed till the D-day.

'Whitefield' suggests that the bearer of this surname was a White. But, actually, he was an Indian, who had been born and brought up at Whitefield in Bangalore. He had a complexion as dark as a person in South India can have. But he had been in the West so long that he had forgotten that he was an ethnic Indian and that there was a bond of blood and (cultural) belief between him and his country. It seemed to me that he had been consciously cultivating a Naipaulesque condescension towards it. This was reflected in some of the off-the-cuff remarks that he had thrown up here and there.

So, my trepidation was not without reason. I was the only ruffled entity in a perfectly organized seminar room: sleek noiseless furniture ergonomically placed; a cultured white-board smartly hung behind the rostrum; a most sophisticated OHP and a slide-projector with an air of aristocratic nonchalance about them; and men and women in a fulfilled pose as if they were fixed pixels of a still picture. In short, I was the only real audience in the midst of decor and ergonomics.

The speaker stood dwarfed behind a rather tall designer lectern. The near-ovalness of his face suddenly reminded me of Robert Darwin. But the very next moment, I forgot the latter. It was now only the face behind the lectern, and me. It opened into a mouth and started to speak:

"Ladies and Gentlemen,
I have several functions as a United Nations man. One of them is to survey and assess the impact of the various developmental schemes and projects being run under the aegis of the World Bank. Over the last fortnight, I've looked into the working of a cross-section of the entire developmental work funded by the Bank. I'm afraid I'm not satisfied. As a matter of fact, I'm deeply disappointed and in some cases even disgusted."

The feeling of disgust poured forth from each lineament of his face. To me at least, his face looked darker than its original shade. Even the 'fixed pixels' responded. Some faces and limbs were astir. My crossed fingers also stirred a little in an effort to separate.

"I can't see anything working properly. All these schemes look pretty as they sit on paper, but very ugly in implementation. If I may say so, they are being implemented very clumsily or not being implemented at all. On the ground, I can't see any sign of development. The sections of the people who these elaborate projects are addressed to remain as undeveloped as they were twenty to twenty-five years ago: ignorant and superstitious; malnourished and sick; depressed and miserable. You Indians are, perhaps, the cleverest statisticians in the world. In fact, you're great magicians of numbers. You trot out figures at every drop of a hat, and when you have to present them in black and white, they stand neatly and tidily in snazzy columns and rows. And what do they actually present? Nothing! Absolute nothing!"

The pixels now showed some signs of animation. Some eyes were blinking, like those of cartoons in animation films or clips. Perhaps, some doubts or even questions were struggling to pop out of their sockets. I was almost on my feet, but the speaker did not like any interruptions at the moment of his rhetorical peak. He continued in his cavalier style:

"I don't find even a fake connection between these figures and the reality on the ground. And the project report that this office has prepared is no exception. In fact, in certain respects, it is the worst of all such reports: it tends to cheat the reader most effectively because of its extremely deceptive style of composition and rhetoric. It talks about the evolution of new ameliorative social structures. What are they for? What have they effected on the ground? I don't find any correspondences whatever between these structures on paper and their impact in the field. It's a shame that almost all the figures so ornamentally placed here and there are false!"

I was now fully on my feet. I protested both his tenor and tone. He tried to shout me down, but I refused to sit down and challenged him either to prove his point or withdraw his 'irresponsible' remarks. He took umbrage and I made a befittingly firm response. The situation would have taken an uncontrollable turn but for my boss. He coaxed me to sit down and let the speaker first complete his presentation. He then persuaded the speaker to resume and subtly suggested that he speak in an 'academic style'.

His 'academic style' turned out to be worse than his unacademic style. He was all spite from now. Everything in my report was a fabrication. And he was saying all this so crudely and callously. I was seething with anger and the MD and some of my senior colleagues were palpably agitated. But he was allowed to let off his steam till the last puff:

"What're your 'social structures addressed to amelioration' doing? In the first place, where are they? I can't see them anywhere except in your meretricious project report. Twenty-five per cent of the entire world's blind people live in your country, and yet 40 hapless poor people lose sight at one go at a 'free eye camp' near Madurai! Twelve million of your people are deaf and dumb, 24 million mentally retarded and six million orthopaedically handicapped, and your great structures are fiddling or boogieing somewhere in a discotheque! I have all these frightful figures staring at me from all directions. You have such a diversity of these disabled creatures like your great cultural diversity! I'm too disturbed and scared to reel off these diverse statistics separately. And also to spare you some embarrassment, I throw all of them at you at once and rid myself. Your largest-democracy-in-the-world has *only* 90 million disabled people, which works out to all of 9% of your huge population! And your greatest democracy 'sports' about 30% people living below the 'poverty line'. Whatever this hygienic phrase might mean in your official jargon, I understand what it actually means. It means that these 30% 'individuals' are worse than cattle in a famine-cursed region: They live in the most appalling conditions ever; they have no food, no clothes, no shelter; they either starve to death or shiver to death or swelter to death."

Here he looked only too pleased with himself to be able to feel the impact of his sweeping oration. Almost all faces in the audience were red with anger rather than embarrassment. To them as to me, all the figures seemed blatantly exaggerated, if not totally false. Anyway, none stood up to protest because he appeared to be wrapping up his nasty and painful polemic:

"So, ladies and gentlemen, to cut the long matter short, I'd suggest you either dismantle the ameliorative structures you've raised on paper, or build real solid structures on real solid ground that may really and truly improve the lot of the 90 million disabled and all of the 300 million 'able disabled' people. Thank you."

When he was leaving for his seat with a colourful file, I looked at my boss, who nodded promptly. I do not quote my speech here. I just recount in a few words what my riposte comprised. Rising above the love of my voice and words, unlike this World Banker, I took him to task on every count. I told him in as many words that if he had come here to pour vitriol on everything Indian and demolish every structure we had raised, he had no business to continue to be here. Our picture was a lot better than the one he had painted. And a person, who could not make an unbiased, dispassionate assessment of things, was not qualified to be representing the United Nations and recommending schemes and disbursing funds for 'amelioration'. I told him finally that my report was as honest as possible and certainly less 'meretricious' than his long and loaded tirade.

I was not looking at the audience when I was speaking. I was being swept off my feet by the force and flow of my words and intonation. When I found myself coming to a halt, my eyes automatically turned to the audience. My boss's eyes had an unusual glint in them. Obviously, he had approved of my reply with all the harshness about its edges.

Whitefield blew his lid. But no one was bothered. The formalities were cut short, and our great 'Indian' left without extending any warnings or making any commitments. The boss could understand what was going on in my mind and assured me that my project was not at all a fiasco. He was a very clear-headed and strong man and knew how to get round the likes of Whitefield.

And, yet, it took me quite a few days to get the whole thing off my head. I did get over the anguish that Whitefield had caused, but not Whitefield himself. In hours of introspection that followed the Whitefield effect on me, I tried to separate his person from his statistics and his heavily loaded remarks. And I saw some sense in what he had said and could make plenty of sense of what he had not said. He had talked at length about our 'physical' disability and touched only briefly upon our 'social' disability. He could have said a hundred and one things more about our poverty line and some alarming things about our starvation deaths, weather deaths and our ever-rising graphs of crime rate. He could have sadistically reeled off, like our meticulous journalists, rapes-per-minute, murders-per-half-a-minute and other-felonies-per-second statistics. But he did not do that. My tentative conclusion was that although he had ruffled our feathers a bit too hard, he also left behind for us some solid food for thought.

I tried to finally clinch this conclusion with the help of Sheila. After listening to me, she was happy with me, but did not speak up. No, I was not quite mystified. Perhaps, she was thinking that we should introspect more often than we usually did?

SIX

Robert Whitefield again put me in mind of Robert Darwin. Both were cynics? Not exactly. Whitefield, it seemed, hated India and everything Indian and strongly believed that nothing could change for the better because everybody here, from top to bottom, was dishonest and corrupt. Darwin, on the other hand, did not involve himself in these controversial problems of Indian character. He claimed to be an antievolutionist and did not believe that human beings were evolving into better social beings.

Of late, Darwin had been gaining a new space in my perspective on life in India as well as in the world. I was not exactly veering round to his view of things, but was becoming more tolerant of it. I no longer believed that what he believed was the crazy philosophy of a zombie or a crackpot. I rather started to believe that his approach was something, which could possibly enrich, or at least broaden, one's perspective.

A few days after the Whitefield blockbuster, two letters were waiting for me when I went home after the office hours. One of them was from Kapila. It was a letter of complaint, ending in a request for help. Her brother and his family were allegedly ill-treating her, and thus it was becoming increasingly unbearable for her to stay on there. She described the conditions there in detail and in the end very humbly requested my permission to return to Delhi.

This put me in a quandary. I did feel for her despite my doubts about what she had said. At the same time, I did not lose sight of the fact that she could not help being a perennial source of nuisance. For two days, I did not share this problem with Sheila. When I put it to her, she said that Kapila's problem was not genuine and that she wanted to be in Delhi only to live life in her own way. The solution we agreed upon was that I should straight away warn her that if she moved back to Delhi, I would not be able to protect her either from Roshan Puri or from anybody else.

The second letter was from our Robert Darwin. It was a very intriguing letter and therefore I quote it here verbatim:

> Dear Vigyan,
> This letter might surprise you, though I have no intention to do so. You would remember how my wife, Elizabeth, had run out on me, leaving me disconsolate for days. You would also remember how I was able to reconcile myself to this loss: partly because your Kapila had also ditched you in a similar manner and suddenly and we shared a bond of deprivation and anguish. And you certainly cannot forget the way we tried to get over this unbearable pain: by pretending that we hated these faithless women and swearing an oath that we would never let them come near us.
>
> The surprise is that today I'm bleeding for the same Elizabeth. After she left me, she lived in an illegal 'wedlock' for over four years. And this 'husband' of hers got sick of her and sold her off to a hardened criminal, who in turn sold her at a big profit to an 'upscale' advertising and modelling training centre, which actually fronted for a number of illegal trades, such as drug-smuggling, arms-trafficking, prostitution and what have you. Now, can

you believe that what I want to do to her today is not only to save her from exploitation but also to reclaim her and take her back as my wife?

I know this kind of attitude is a breach of the oath I swore with you, but I confess that this is how I feel today. I am writing this to know your reaction. It will be very helpful indeed if we could meet within the next few days and decide what I should do.

Kind regards,
Robert Darwin

He was right. I was more than surprised. I suddenly felt there was a strong bond between us. Elizabeth's fate put me in mind of Kapila's present condition, which might in time be worse than Elizabeth's. And I found myself searching my mind to see whether I had any soft feelings for Kapila. Fortunately, I did not find any. But this did not diminish my sympathy with Darwin's desire to save Elizabeth.

Sheila did not say anything about the letter. But she was strongly in favour of a meeting with Darwin at my convenience. So, I wrote to Darwin, saying that I had no objection to his intention to take back Elizabeth and that there was no breach of promise or agreement involved in the matter. I also said that he would be welcome to come and discuss the matter with me if he still thought this was necessary before he took the decision.

I had never seen Elizabeth. Thus, my sympathy with her was of a neutral kind, based on my sympathy with the principle of human rights. I had nothing against her as such; in contrast, I had so many things against Kapila. Therefore, what applied to Elizabeth did not necessarily apply to the latter.

This kind of logic removed from my mind the apprehension that she might return and decide to live with me as my wife.

Darwin's reply was unexpectedly prompt. He said he definitely needed to come and meet me and that he would let me know of his visit as soon as he could.

The next few days saw a few disturbing happenings in our office. Amjad Ali, a senior assistant in my office, had gone to Patna in connection with an important piece of work relating to my Whitefield-crossed Project. On the third day of his arrival at Patna, his dead body returned on an Indian Airlines flight. All of my staff and I were at the airport to receive the body. His wife, Jahan Ara, was asked to come to the office to receive an important piece of news about her husband. She was all nerves when she arrived with her nine-year old son, Irfan. When she entered my office, I used all my power of self-control to keep my composure. I was supposed to administer a preventive psychological palliative so that she could cope with such a great tragedy. Despite all this cushioning exercise on my part, when she saw the body, she collapsed then and there and was declared dead as soon as the stretcher carrying her reached the emergency ward of our Company hospital!

Ajmad Ali had been killed in a crossfire between two rival gangs supported by the Rajvir Sena and the Leftist Sena. He was on a visit to a shopping mall in the downtown area. The report of his murder could not be lodged with the Delhi Police because of our obsolete Criminal Procedure Code. I sent a senior officer, Arjun Singh, to Patna to lodge the First Information Report. A pompous SHO at a police station in central Patna fixed his stern gaze on Arjun Singh, most probably to browbeat him into keeping his mouth shut. When the latter persisted, he broke into guffaws, which were multiplied by half a dozen of his Assistant Sub-Inspectors imitating him dutifully. Our poor Arjun Singh, woefully ignorant of the ways of the Patna police world, had the 'audacity' to ask him: 'Sir, I don't understand all this. Why're you all laughing so loudly? Do people here laugh so loudly and boisterously together at such murders?'

The SHO's eyes emitted fire. He had possibly never been asked such an 'impudent' question.

'We're laughing at your crass stupidly, officer from . . .'

'Delhi, sir.'

'Yes, Delhi. We're laughing because we haven't come across such foolishness for years. Such murders here are a dime a dozen. Who'd bother about such triflings? Do you think we're idle and silly people like you and have nothing better to do?'

Arjun left the police station in great despair. As he had to return on the 8 p.m. flight, he thought it wise to explore alternative ways of reporting the murder. An old friend of his, who he called on to pass his waiting time, advised him to tell the whole thing to the press. Our great SHO got the wind of this and sent two of his dreadful-looking assistants in the garb of professional hoodlums to warn him to leave the town at once. The poor fellow went straight to the airport and passed his weary waiting hours there.

Amjad Ali's child stayed with me for a few days. I was planning to make a permanent arrangement for him. Till that time, I thought it wise to keep him with me rather than send him to an orphanage or a boarding school. With Sheila as my backup, I could do any such thing for anybody.

In less than a fortnight, the child's luck smiled on him. Jahan Ara's parents, who lived in Toronto, got to know of the tragedy and contacted me immediately. I consoled them and assured them that Irfan was quite safe with me and being taken care of very well. They asked me to send him to a boarding school till they came to India to take him with them.

He was very happy with Sheila and loath to go. Therefore, I told them that he would stay with us till they came to India.

Darwin's next letter did not bring me the news of when he would be coming but informed me of Elizabeth's escape from the advertising and modelling centre. She had tried to befriend Darwin so that she could use his help to escape this horrible dragnet. Darwin had suggested to her three ways of giving the slip to the mafia centre and also assured her that he would hide her and protect her after she had fled them. From that point of time, he tried to keep track of her but lost her footprints after some distance. The woman had escaped everybody, including our great Darwin. His latest information was that she had eloped with a young handsome member of this mafia gang.

I wrote back to him to express my sympathy with him. I desisted from using harsh words against Elizabeth, though the tone of my letter must have made my feelings very clear to him. In my heart of hearts, I felt grateful to him as well as to Elizabeth for their indirect help to me in deciding my response to Kapila's request.

My mind was now made up in regard to Kapila. I wrote her a firmly worded letter and warned her not to move to Delhi under any circumstances. She had always been a foolhardy type, and therefore I did not quite expect her to heed my warning. By seeking my permission to move to Delhi, she was only trying to keep the door to my possible help in her future emergencies open. When I said an emphatic no, she had nothing to lose but this faint hope of contingent help. Thus, I was prepared for any move on her part.

My brief sympathy letter to Darwin did him a lot of good apparently. His response letter did not reflect any sense of despair or pain. He had, it seemed, bounced back to his usual philosophical self. That is why he did not make any mention of Elizabeth whatever and breezily rode his hobbyhorse in a celebratory tone of triumph. He closed his letter with a promise to meet me soon.

I was back to my post-Project routine and my usual musings over my personal life, my ambient society and life in general. These musings did sometimes disturb me when they seeped through to my soul's aquifer. But, more often, they played around my outer self and its relationship with its environment—that is, individuals, state, society—leaving me relatively tranquil, if not at perfect peace with myself.

This state of tranquillity in me was almost always short-lived. This time, I was rather surprised that it was outliving its wonted span. But this pleasant surprise, like any other surprise, proved transient. Kapila's violent vibes soon disturbed the placidity of my musings and scattered them helter-skelter. One fine morning, when I came to know of her presence in Delhi, she had been there for over a week. I pretended to ignore the fact, but Elizabeth's latest escapade did not leave me alone. I was worried and my musings were entirely gone. But I did not start to brood. I was determined to face the problem if and when it challenged me. And it did challenge me before I had my boxing gloves on.

Kapila called to fix a time for a meeting. She was staying with a friend in a YWCA hostel. She said she was quite safe there and did not need my protection any more. When I asked her why, then, she wanted to meet me, she said she needed to discuss a very important matter. I advised her to discuss such matters with better-informed people like lawyers, counsellors or some mafiosi and rang off. Two evenings later, she rang me up again and pleaded for a meeting. I put her off by saying that I had to be out of town for a few days. She knew I was telling a lie to avoid her. So, she gave me a buzz the next day and insisted on a meeting. This time, I just blew my lid and she backed down, but only to prepare for her next move. When I asked Sheila what she could have been up to, she replied without a second's lapse that she was planning to wrest her old place as my 'life partner'. For the first time, I felt a whiff of irony in the manner she uttered the words *life partner*. A minute later, I realized it was anger rather than irony. Anger against Kapila because she was without doubt plotting to bamboozle me into taking her back.

After I shot down Kapila's request, I just bided my time with my eyes and ears wide open. I knew how to deal with hustlers like her when it came to the crunch. Meanwhile, I had much more necessary things to do. Amjad Ali's place was still vacant and, therefore, my share of work had increased. I was also going through my Project tome again in the 'light' of Whitefield's uncharitable comments on it. By and large, I had confidence in my general abilities and in my acumen to judge things rightly. But, this time, this World Banker had shaken me a bit, and I thought it prudent to take a second look at my findings and suggestions in the Project.

Darwin's next letter sounded funny rather than serious. It had a heading like a schoolboy's classroom essay: 'The Right to Life in Democracy.' During his last Bharat Darshan itinerary, he had travelled through parts of UP, Jharkhand, Bihar and Uttaranchal and was brimming over with stories of 'success' there. Almost everyone had a gun there to protect their Constitution-blessed right to life. No other part of the world, whether ruled by democracy or dictatorship, could boast of such a 'foolproof' right to life. He had statistics of arms and factories where they were made; of big wholesalers and small-time traders of these creations; of *senas* and political satraps patronizing them.

The letter was, no doubt, interesting but not so the news that he would be landing in Delhi on Sunday, which was five days away. I had been awaiting him after the Elizabeth episode, but now the heading of the letter followed by a few things about his itinerary served as a preview of his coming meeting with me, and thus made its tenor highly predictable.

When he finally landed, he had so much to tell me about this 'right-to-life' matter that his letter seemed in retrospect not even a faint outline.

'Why did you go to these parts, Robert?' I asked with a tightly puckered forehead.

'I'm fond of travelling, Vigyan.'

'But why did you have to travel to these God-forsaken regions?'

'Well, I wanted to see whether God ever visits the places He has "forsaken",' he replied to outsmart me.

'Should I take it that this big tour of yours was part of your mega experiment to test your philosophy?'

'Yes, of course. A part of it only. And, that way, anything I do is part of that experiment.'

I was silently looking at the changes his face had undergone since we had met last.

'And you must remember, Vigyan, that my basic interest is to observe things, to study life, and not to verify my philosophy or thesis.'

'Oh.'

'And there's nothing sacrosanct about my philosophy, dear.'

My ears pricked up.

'I mean I'll give it up if it proves wrong, and I wish it'd prove wrong.'

'Do you think it may prove wrong?'

'It doesn't seem likely.'

He had put up at a guesthouse. His plan was to stay in Delhi for less than a week. When I asked him to stay with me, he politely refused. The explanation he gave was that he was a man of very independent habits and did not want to have to make even the slightest adjustment in them.

Over coffee, we indulged in small talk. I expected him to bring up the subject of Elizabeth. But he did not. It seemed he was at pains to avoid it and I did not have the heart to touch him on the raw.

I made a passing reference to Kapila and then flinched from talking about her because it could have led to Elizabeth. So, I directed my curiosity towards his recent long tour and asked him if literally 'everyone' in that vast 'right-to-life' area had a gun.

'In a manner of speaking, yes,' he said nonchalantly.

The way I looked at him propelled him to say what he had actually intended to convey in his letter but had not done so.

'Every one of the haves, Vigyan. About thirty per cent people in these regions don't get even one *un*square meal a day. How can they have guns, or even kitchen knives?'

'Do you mean all the haves possess guns or some other arms?' I asked just to understand the exact conditions there.

'Yes, almost all. I hope you don't want to question my "almost", Vigyan?'

'No, not at all. But where do they get all these weapons from? And, then, we have more than one Arms Act. How do they get round them? I mean, how do they buy these things and keep them?'

'You've asked so many questions in the same breath. Let me answer the first one first.'

I tried to look more serious than I was.

'Have you heard of a place, called Munger?'

'No.'

'It's a celebrated district in Bihar, a state where a female Bharat rules on behalf of a modern-day Ram.'

'Why is it important?' I was curious.

'At a score of places in this district, there're several mini-factories, producing guns of all kinds. The British set up a gun factory at Munger to exploit the gun-making skills of the local people. Since then, dozens of gun-making units have been producing guns on a large scale.'

'But where do they sell so many guns?'

'Where do they sell? Everywhere, Vigyan. That's why "everyone" has a gun.'

'Oh!'

'And, now, these armourers here and in the neighbouring districts and states are great experts. They can now produce all kinds of arms: machine guns, sten-guns, even AK-47 replicas!'

'Do they export arms?'

'Export arms? They're not enough even for the domestic consumption. They'd rather import some if they could.'

'You mean they're not yet enough to go round?'

'And they'll never be enough. The population outstrips every other kind of production, you know.'

'Despite the fact that these arms kill enough people to control population?'

'Yes, and they also control poverty in a way.'

'How, Robert?'

'Now, don't be naïve. These gun-toting haves kill more have-nots than they kill other gun-wielding haves.'

'Why?'

'It's easier, man. The right-to-life haves are all well balanced against one another. They're all armed to the teeth. So, they often kill those who can't defend themselves.'

'I never thought things could be so bad in these regions!'

'They're worse in certain other areas. Kanpur is one such area. More murders are committed in this area in a month than in all the rest of Uttar Pradesh.'

'Oh, that's horrid!' I exclaimed.

'Yes, and in certain rural pockets of this vast district and its neighbouring ones, life's still cheaper. Ransom-grabbing goons can kill a person just for a few thousand!'

'How do you explain this, Robert? Are arms factories the main cause?'

'Yes, of course. The armourers here, no doubt, aren't as great experts, and arms aren't manufactured on the same scale as in the Munger region. But the right-to-life sentiment is much stronger here, and that compensates for any lack of arms.'

I am a well-informed, open-eyed man, and yet my eyes were opening wider and wider at every revelation about arms and murders and other heinous crimes in these parts. Darwin obviously anticipated my question.

'No, the law's ineffective. In fact, it's dead. Why? Because it conflicts with the haves' right to life. The police is in collusion with criminals and politicians, and these politicians will fail if this collusion fails.'

Darwin was interested in continuing with the subject, but I wanted to change over to something else. Sheila's entry with her coffee-trolley was very welcome. She had overheard snatches of our long conversation and wanted to participate. But she hesitated in the presence of Darwin. I goaded her on to open up, partly because I wanted Darwin to see how fast she had morphed into not only a literate but accomplished person.

'Sheila, would you like to know of Darwin's experiments with truth in our "dark" continent?'

'I needn't, sir. I've heard your conversation in parts. It's a horrible picture indeed.'

Darwin seemed to be much less surprised at what she was saying than the way she was saying it. I could see a sense of delight suffusing his face.

'You wanted to say something more about this "horrible picture"?' I asked to prompt her.

'A true and full knowledge of these things is necessary,' she said somewhat shyly, 'but . . .'

'Yes?'

'But we should do something to change this picture rather than . . .' She stopped short again.

'Yes, we *should* do something, but *can* we?' said Darwin very sadly.

'Yes, we can,' she said very confidently. 'We can do *something* at least.'

Darwin and I both looked at her face with a degree of unintended respect.

'We can educate public opinion, which will change things . . . in the end.'

Educating public opinion about social evils is one of the most difficult things—certainly more difficult than shooting down evildoers. I did not quite know Darwin's present approach to social evils or even social problems. But so far as I was concerned, I had never thought about such things: fighting social evils, or bringing about social reforms.

After coffee, Darwin wanted to go back to his guesthouse. The following day was a Saturday. We decided to spend the whole evening together at my house. Sheila promised to provide at least two special dishes for dinner.

In the morning, as I was leaving for office, a courier brought a letter from Rajneesh. I prised it open with an angry hand. The fellow wanted to come to see me again! It was now not difficult for me to tear up the letter and throw the pieces into a garbage bin. What was difficult was to understand how this fellow could have the temerity to write to ask to see me.

I returned from office somewhat early. I expected the evening to be lighter than the last one. Hopefully, we were not going to discuss any heavy stuff like that sombre picture of those dark regions. And Sheila was going to add some spice to the evening with her surprise dishes.

Darwin was late. He was held up in a traffic jam. Meanwhile, I disposed of half a dozen necessary phone calls to

Bombay and Chennai. When he came, he looked haggard. He said he had been thinking about Elizabeth and could not sleep well in the night. Inadvertently, he brought in the dominant theme for this evening. He wanted Sheila to be around. Sheila too was somewhat keen to be part of the evening in a fuller way and thus she wheeled in the coffee trolley promptly.

From Darwin's account of Elizabeth's collusion with crime and of her multiple elopements, she emerged as a totally irredeemable case. And yet, it seemed, he 'pined' for her. I was finding it very difficult to square this side of his with his intellectual engagement with our crucial social issues in particular and his theory of antievolution in general.

He was waiting for me to ask questions about Elizabeth, it seemed. Because the moment I tried to unobtrusively sympathize with him for his suffering, caused mainly by her irresponsible and callous behaviour, he started to write, as it were, a biography of her irresponsible and immoral doings from the very first day of their married life. He had by now unearthed her premarital adventures also, and what he was telling us now was a story from the beginning of her life.

Sheila was almost on the verge of tears, and I was trying to play the role of a macho male, though I was feeling equally lachrymose inside. He had narrated most of the story and was continuing with his sombre account in a most gloomy tone. I wanted to stop him at this point, for I could easily predict what was to follow from that moment onwards.

'Why did you want to reclaim and adopt such a person, Robert?' I asked

'I loved her, dammit!'

I did not know what to say.

'And I still love her, very much.'

'Even after this latest elopement?'

'Yes. And my biggest problem at the moment is how to get over this stupidest of all my failings.'

'We'll find a way out of it, sir,' said Sheila, her eyes misting over with tender sympathy for him.

He turned 45 degrees to look straight at her face. His attitude was that of a credulous adolescent, who wanted to believe her wholly and expected her to spell out her 'way'.

Now we both were focused on her face. I mentally saw an oracular look playing on her mien as she was preparing to open her mouth.

'Sir, you stay with us in this flat for 15 days, and you'll overcome this pain of pining . . .'

I did not understand why she had not completed her sentence, but I suddenly noticed her eyes riveted on Darwin's face. To me, her suggestion appeared to be a bit of a letdown, though Darwin was more oriented to her now than before.

'But staying here might be rather . . .'

'You have a choice, sir,' she said very confidently this time, having by now overcome her feeling of embarrassment in suggesting remedies to a superior person.

'Yes?' Darwin was very eager.

'If you can't stay here for a few days, you could go back to your first love.'

'My first love?' he said, with his eyes and mouth going wide open with surprise.

'Yes, your first love. Elizabeth is not your first love. Your first love was a far better person, and she's still pining for you, more intensely than you are pining for Elizabeth.'

Both of us were listening to the 'oracle' with great respect. Even my momentary disbelief was gone.

'The moment you go to this person and embrace her with an open heart, Elizabeth will have vanished from your mind without leaving a trace.'

'Thank you very much, Sheila,' he said in the tone of a new convert.

Darwin had fallen for Faith in his college days. A daughter of one of his teachers, she was a tall girl with a very bewitching face. Her slightly chubby cheeks added to her charm, though her rather figureless body detracted from it. Finding no response, Darwin had reconciled himself to the situation and kind of fallen out of love. She had pined for him all the time since, but had buried her emotion inside her as most girls of her class and time did.

Sheila's peep into his past put him back in time, and he started working towards this aim from that very moment. When we met again the next evening, he told us he had already sent out his message of reconciliation through a sure means of communication. No doubts in this regard remained in our mind, and we treated this evening as a special time for our relaxation.

Darwin left for his newly decided destination the next day. Sheila felt relieved, but I felt rather sad. I missed him for the first time and even looked forward to hearing from him, especially about his 'first love'. The solution to the Elizabeth problem contained in it, in a way, a solution to the Kapila problem. Though I had no 'first love' to go back to, I had an equally important reason to throw her off for ever.

A few days later, when Kapila phoned for a meeting between us, it did not take me even a second to shoo her off. No amount of pleading on her part was able to move me. At the end, she rang off in a huff, which suited me well.

With her and Rajneesh being off my head, I thought life for me was smooth from now on. We all like such momentary illusions and they often come to cheer us up at the end of one dark lane or another. Sheila enjoyed my freedom from cares very much. In fact, she suggested private celebration between the two of us. When I suggested (I think I was serious?) that we should toast our relief with a glass of wine or whisky each, she said she would do anything with me that I should not regret later. Since she had never tasted any alcoholic drink before, I did not have the heart to violate her unwavering faith in me.

SEVEN

There was a new wave of rapes and murders in and around the walled area. The police was placed on red alert, and yet the mayhem continued. Since some of the victims belonged to the Muslim community, these crimes were predictably being blamed on the Hindu communalists. When some Hindu boys were murdered in cold blood near the old Sabzi Mandi area, these bloody acts were taken as reprisals by the Muslim hoodlums living in the walled city. These recriminations, fanned by some of our 'incorrigibly objective' print journalists, reached a pitch of incandescence. The police was now warned to be on ultra-red alert. Section 144 Cr. P.C. was promulgated. The criminal elements got back into their secret rooms and plotted for avenging the death and dishonour of their near and dear ones. And then, suddenly, one day seemed very ominous. Things were very quiet. One feared something eerie about this unusual lull. The time was moving smoothly into the night. At the stroke of midnight, when half the world was asleep, we had a tryst with our national destiny. There was bloodshed over a large area. An indefinite curfew was clamped. There were wholesale violations of this order. We had full faith in our police, and therefore our sacred army was still not asked to be on the ready. The remaining impure blood drained out fully and the flow stopped.

Naturally, a commission of enquiry was appointed to look into the causes of the riot. This was the 35th big riot in the country since Independence. The findings of all the earlier enquiry commissions were more or less the same: religion and history were the main causes. The differences consisted in slightly different immediate provocations and slightly different goons initiating them. Because the times had changed, this commission was 'expected' to come out with entirely different findings, which would possibly suggest some miracle-producing ways of ending such riots for ever and establishing permanent harmony between our great communities.

This umpteenth war of independence was fought on two levels: on the ground between our heroes; in our press between our pampered, prejudiced and opinionated journalists. The war fought in the media was far more lethal than the ground war. The public memory is short. Even the most gruesome murders are forgotten after some time if there are no motivated agents of disharmony around to wake up the sleeping dogs. But our scribes and anchors keep reminding people periodically that they have scores to settle with their foes.

Darwin had kept track of this riot. In fact, he had prepared a whole file of clippings on this 'war'. With his first love, Faith, around, his understanding of things was fairly balanced. His antievolution angle was intact, but his sympathy with the human predicament in our 21st century multicultural India was a bit broader and deeper than before. He did not blame the individuals squarely; he placed them in a milieu which, being a result of historical and social forces itself, was responsible for reversing their moral or social evolution. Ironically, his theory did not quite apply to himself: his changing perspective on man and his condition was a proof that he himself was evolving in the 'positive' direction.

This is my understanding of the main part of his long letter that he wrote around the time the enquiry commission was appointed. The remaining part which interested both Sheila and me spoke mainly about Faith. He was deeply in love with her.

He acknowledged very gratefully Sheila's contribution to the resurrection of his relationship with Faith, who, he said, justified her name more than anybody else had ever done in his experience: she was not only perfectly faithful herself but inspired his faith in her fidelity and in the improvability of things in general. He cherished fond memories of our last meeting and had many words of praise for our warmth and hospitality. Though he ended his letter with that old cliché, 'I'm looking forward to . . .', he seemed to convey something more than the words did. Sheila was sure that Faith would soon write a letter, without waiting for a reply to this letter.

I wanted to write a long letter and, therefore, I waited for the weekend. Meantime, Faith's letter came as though to prove Sheila right. Sheila hurriedly read it out to me on the phone. I quote here just its main part:

Dear Sheila,

I've never met your 'husband', but I seem to have met you at some place, some time. I have only a blurred memory of the meeting, though I can recall somewhat hazily the lineaments of your face. I can see through the haze of time a tiny mole in the middle of your left cheek.

Anyway, I'm writing this brief letter to thank you for sending back Robert to me. Not that I can ever thank you enough. But I can at least try, can't I? I feel so deeply for you, Sheila. The degree of gratitude I feel for you puts me utterly out of my depth. I shouldn't say more— in fact, I can't say more. How's your husband, Vigyan? He must've inspired you to suggest the great idea to Robert. Would you thank him on my behalf, my dear Sheila?

Love.

When I reached home that evening, Sheila presented this letter to me with a flourish: tied with a red ribbon and placed on a platter. When the coffee trolley was wheeled in, my eyes were irresistibly drawn towards the ribbon. When I read the letter, I turned to Sheila to see her reaction. She had not found it unusual, it seemed. A tiny mole on her left cheek was very much there, and she could not understand when and where they could have met. Perhaps, they were kindred souls. That is why she had told Darwin that his first love, Faith, was pining for him. Pondering over this mystery, I was more and more mystified. I did not even remember that I was still reading that letter and Sheila was waiting for me to say something. She gently nudged me, and I found myself reading the rest of the letter. I was not much surprised by Faith's assumption that Sheila and I were man and wife. Anybody could have taken us as husband and wife in the situation in which we were placed. What really surprised me was that she could 'see' a tiny mole on Sheila's cheek, but could 'not see' our real relationship.

We were now sipping coffee, but I was still too preoccupied to be chatting with Sheila, who was, perhaps, communing with my preoccupied self. Thus, she was possibly witness to my thought that Faith had actually 'seen' us as spiritually married rather than physically married. And spiritually married we really were: how else can one describe such a warm, selfless, complementary mutuality? As though to interact with my thought, she began: 'Thank you very much, sir.'

'For . . . ?'

'For affirming our real relationship. I wish this "marriage" would last for ever, sir.'

'It has to,' I enthused, 'because it's based on love and only love. Because desire and give-and-take and possessiveness don't debase it.'

'I am extremely happy to hear that. But, sometimes, I feel bad, sir, that I do not do anything for your desire.'

'What more do I need, Sheila, when I'm so fulfilled? I don't know where my desire's gone. Perhaps, you've satisfied it.'

This fulfilling dialogue would have gone on for some more time but for the doorbell interrupting it.

I opened the door to a courier, who delivered a multi-coloured envelope. I was too impatient to wait. So, I tore it open without a paper knife on my way back to my study. It was from Robert Whitefield, out of all people. Its contents were quite unexpected, if not exactly amazing. His daughter was getting married to a White, which perhaps accounted for such a funny envelope. The invite was an excuse for breaking the ice between us and conveying an important message.

Dear Mr Verma,
This is mainly to invite you to my daughter's wedding, which will take place in the marriage hall of Krishna Hotel here. My wife and daughter are very keen to meet you and your family. I hope you will be kind enough to accept our invitation and reach here a few hours before the wedding. My daughter, who has been working on 'Enabling Social Structures', has read your great Project Report and is extremely impressed by it.

I also take this opportunity to apologize to you for what happened between us during my lecture in you Company's seminar hall. I had no intention to offend you. I was just carried away by a slew of preconceived notions. I wish I had had the time to read your Report very carefully before talking about it. I felt so sorry for the

```
happening soon after that, but I was wait-
ing for an opportunity to say so.
   I look forward to hearing from you
soon.
   Yours sincerely,
   Robert Whitefield
```

Sheila did not understand part of the letter. I explained it to her. She listened without reacting. I had never seen her so expressionless. I was happy that Whitefield had at long last understood the value of my research and also apologized for his extremely arrogant behaviour. It was for the first time that she was so immune to my happiness. On all earlier occasions, my happiness or even pleasure was her happiness or her pleasure even as my pain was her pain. I was still looking at her face, expecting it to break into expression, when she blurted: 'This is a trap, sir, a very well-laid trap!'

I jumped out of my skin. My head was spinning like a top. How could such a big man have thought of laying a trap? The very next moment, I looked to her only to find myself veering round to her view. And, yet, I made bold to ask her: 'Sheila, are you sure?'

She shot a rather enigmatic glance at me, and when she saw my puzzlement, she beamed a smile. My illusory mood of triumph that the letter had generated was gone.

I was convinced now that the letter was a trick conceived to entrap me. But I wanted to find out why this man had thought out this trick and what he was going to gain out of this trickery. After all, we had no personal animus. Whatever had happened at his lecture was only a professional discussion, and only he was responsible for creating bad blood between himself and my colleagues and me.

I hired John D'Souza and tasked him with finding out everything about this man, plus the plot he had thought up to trick me. This man was still in Bangalore even six weeks after his visit to our Company. I briefed D'Souza about him in detail and asked him to start his work straight away.

On receiving no response to his invitation, he sent a hurried email, reminding me of the invitation and asking after me and my 'family'. In reply, I sent him a prompt email accepting the invitation very gratefully and apologizing for my inability to reply earlier. This mail was very cautiously phrased and expected to put him off the trail of my counter-plan to checkmate his deception.

D'Souza was on course to execute the plan. He put a tab on Whitefield a full week before his daughter's wedding date and pumped information out of all the conduits leading to and from him. His report was more or less ready two days before Whitefield could have expected me to land in Bangalore 'with my family'. He was now waiting to find out only the name of the person who had been assigned the main task of blackmailing me or enticing me into the mousetrap that Whitefield had ordered for me. He succeeded in finding out well before the zero hour that it was the latter's son, Matthew, who was going to cast the net. So, the report was on my desk a good twenty hours before the countdown for my arrival in Bangalore was to begin.

And, so, I was now going to nail the man who had been plotting to ensnare me. The report was foolproof. Every point made in the main body was supported by unquestionable evidence. The speculative part was added as an appendix.

I showed this report to my boss. He not only approved it but also 'ordered' me to proceed against that man without a minute's delay. I had his permission to involve anybody in the Company to help me towards this goal.

When I was making out a case against Whitefield, a new thought crossed my mind like a flash: he could be a fake, a total impostor. Sheila was not too clear about this angle, nor did she seem to show much interest in this line of enquiry.

Anyway, this did not dampen my effort to probe all possibilities.

My main basis, of course, was D'Souza's findings. I used them very judiciously, plus I supplemented them strategically with all the eccentricities, wiles and guile that he had indulged in during and after his lecture to do us down. And, finally, I added to this complaint all the unfair comments he had made on my Project Report.

When the file was ready, I placed it before a plenary meeting of my colleagues. They approved it in toto. And then the boss had a look and okayed it immediately. The packet I finally dispatched to the World Bank included my Project Report as well as the letter of invitation Whitefield had sent me from Bangalore. A great burden was off my head and I could relax now. I was not at all worried about what the Bank might say in response to this whole exercise. The only thing left to be done was to send Whitefield a letter of 'apology' for not being able to make it to Bangalore on the eve of his dear daughter's wedding.

Within a month of my complaint reaching its headquarters, the World Bank acknowledged my work on social structures as a great contribution to society. The Chief of the Bank congratulated me on the phone personally. I was a celebrity overnight, and messages of felicitation flooded in. I was given a fabulous cash reward and a fat grant to get my 'thesis' published under the title 'Structures for Social Evolution'. The book sold a hundred thousand copies within a month of its publication, and its demand increased manifold in the following few months.

Whitefield became utterly irrelevant in the light of my recognition by the World Bank. And, yet, I was a bit curious to know of what had happened to him. He had been summarily dismissed and dispossessed of all that the Bank had given him.

PART THREE

ONE

Celebrity entails added responsibility. The Company wanted me to go to Karachi to do some preliminary exploratory work for setting up a marketing unit there. I was unwilling to go, but as a 'celeb' I could not afford to set a bad example by saying no. This time, Sheila did not insist on accompanying me. She only said that it would be helpful to me if I took her along. When I told her that I would need the assistance of my secretary and a clerk in my office during my tour, she said she would rather stay back.

On the third day of our stay in Karachi, the air was thick with rumours that the Shia-Sunni riots might break out in the ghettos not far from our hotel. Since our work in Karachi was more or less over and we had a plan to visit Muzzaffargarh, we decided to leave Karachi a day in advance. The taxi in which we were travelling broke down about 30 kilometres before Muzzaffargarh. We were near a village, called Meerwala.. We passed the night as guests of a petrol-pump owner, Abdul Rehman, who acted like a good host. We were flattered to hear that he liked Indians very much. We also reciprocated his sentiment by saying that we too liked the people of Pakistan. In the morning, we wanted to leave, but he wanted us to stay with him for a day. Apart from getting an opportunity to exercise his hospitality to the full, he wanted us to be witness to the village *Panchayat* arbitrating in a case relating to a sexual aberration. We were tempted by this offer because I was very interested in understanding how the traditional juries of village elders arrived at their verdicts in different societies. I was sure there would be something in the event that should make a contribution to my work on social structures.

We were seated on the stringed beds meant for the important village men and guests. The atmosphere was hush-hush, indicating that something serious and sacred was to follow. We must have waited for all of 40 minutes when five bearded old men dressed in white skull caps and long *kurtas* came out of a room in the Panchayat House. They had perhaps deliberated on the case in question in private and were now going to arbitrate in public. The complaint before the judges was that a handsome boy had had an aberrant sexual relationship with a girl of a high tribe. Women's presence in such gatherings was forbidden in that society. But the entire family of the alleged criminal, including their women, was obliged by the Panchayat Law to be present there. We could spot three black *burqas*, which meant that three women were present there.

All eyes were fixed on the judges, and the silence was getting more and more curious every minute. Then a gavel-like thick-headed stick struck a steel pitcher, and the senior-most judge rose to say something—perhaps, to pronounce the verdict. But he did not do anything of this sort; he ordered Raziya, the oldest of the three burqa-clad women, to get up and move to a room on his left. We were told that Raziya was the only pubescent girl in the alleged criminal's family. The other two burqas contained minor girls of ten and nine years of age. The girl whose neck was on the block knew what was going to happen to her. She resisted the verdict. The father and the uncle of the girl pleaded for mercy most piteously. The blind mother of the girl was on her knees praying to the Allah-mighty above for the safety of her poor daughter. But Allah traditionally resided in the Five Judges rather than on the *Arsh*, the Eighth Floor. The heart-rending cries of the family for help went unheeded, and no one from the crowd of about a hundred 'respectable' people of the village as much as raised a finger.

Suddenly, we saw the girl being dragged violently by four strong mustachioed men in their early thirties. She pleaded, cried, shouted for help. She was being pulled by the left hand, and her right had was raised as high as it could go till she was sucked into the verdict-execution room.

We were the only people who did not know what precisely was going to happen inside. After all, to our knowledge, she had committed no crime whatever. But we had no way to decode this mystery. Our neighbours' eyes were downcast and their lips sealed.

After one full hour's suspenseful wait, which experientially appeared infinitely longer, we saw the battered and tattered Raziya limp out of the dark execution room. After what she had gone through inside, she had thrown the burqa rule to the winds. What had she to hide and secure now, after all?

The boy for whose 'sexual crime' his sister was sentenced to one hour's rigorous toil as a punishment by four macho men turned out to be an 11-year old boy!

We went back to Abdul Rehman's hospitality utterly shattered. Our host was no less devastated. He apologized many times over as though he had caused great offence to our delicate sensibility himself. This gesture helped us partly get over our anguish, and we considered it our duty to help him be at peace with himself.

As we were taking leave of him, a second cousin of his, Nasir Khan, came in. So, we had to stay over for some more time. The hangover of the Panchayat verdict still lingering there, the subject came up spontaneously during the introductions in spite of us. Khan was full of praise for the wisdom of the judges, who had pronounced such a 'fair' verdict. The word *fair* was too much for my nerves. With all my inherent prudence, I could not resist the urge to join the issue.

'You call it a 'fair' verdict, Mr Khan?'

'Yes, it's very fair. Somebody had to be punished for that abominable boy's horrid crime!'

'But they should've punished the person who'd committed the crime.'

'No, that wouldn't have met the ends of justice. Justice in our tribe is based on the principle of tit for tat, that is, a tooth for a tooth.'

'Which means?'

'It means that rape must be punished with rape. But since rape can't be committed on a boy, the judges very rightly picked his only adolescent sister.'

'This is bizarre, extremely disgusting, Mr Khan!'

'What's bizarre . . . ?'

I did not let him complete his sentence. I felt like tearing him to shreds, but I stopped short of that for the sake of my host. All the same, I did not want to give up on this very important issue.

'In no society of the world, is a woman raped as a punishment for another person's crime. *That's* bizarre.'

I wanted to have the last word, but Khan would not let me enjoy that luxury. He knew I was an Indian and wanted to hit me where it hurt most: 'We can't rape a woman even as a punishment *under* our law, and you're free to rape women of any age, at any place, at any time, *without* the sanction of your law?'

'At least you admit that our law doesn't sanction rape whereas yours sanctions it, though as a form of punishment.'

'But behind the law, you keep on . . .'

'No, we don't,' I cut him short.

The argument was now degenerating into a bitter fight. He was very agitated and frantically searching his large shirt pocket for something as though he had been looking for a strong rebuttal lost somewhere in it. Then, suddenly, he whipped out a piece of paper.

'Now, look here, Mr Verma. Here's a record of some of the recent rapes and other heinous crimes committed in your great-big country.'

'I've never said we have no crimes or no criminals there,' I said, to avoid any more exchanges for more than one reason. But it seemed I had caught a Tartar. Without waiting for me to complete my reply, he started reading out from the paper he had taken out.

'On the 7th of July last year, a father rapes his own six year-old daughter in your New Delhi; on 30th July, a 14-year-old boy rapes a 2-year-old neighbour, who dies from over-bleeding; in the same month (the exact date not given), a 12-year-old minor is gang-raped by three men. And all these rapes took place in your great national capital before the nose of your mighty government, which always claims to be on the moral high ground.'

Listing crimes is not an argument, Mr Khan. I can produce a much more dreadful list . . .'

'You're free to produce it, but let me first complete mine.'

Since there was no way to stop him, I just let him let off his steam.

'Here's a tally of rapes committed outside your national capital. On August the 5th, villagers in the Hazaribagh district of your brand-new province strip and rape a 50-year-old woman and her 26-year-old daughter, then parade them naked, and then force them to swallow human shit . . .'

I got up to leave, but he wanted me to stay on for a while.

'A minor girl,' he continued, 'after having been raped for months in Trivandrum by about 200 great film celebs and other VIPs, falls into the hands of a few vicious videographers, who force her to pose for hard-porn films.'

I chafed not because the incidents he was listing were wrong, but because he was reading out the stuff to take revenge for my comment on the Jury's verdict and thus to humiliate me. Even Abdul Rehman felt embarrassed that his cousin was laying it on a bit thick. He asked the latter to stop it because I had to attend a business meeting. But Nasir khan was a tide that could not be turned.

'One's mind boggles at the variety of rapes,' Mr Verma, 'that your country provides. Here's an example of a "socially sanctioned" rape: a mother-in-law in north Delhi gets into a dowry-related quarrel with her 20-year-old hapless daughter-in-law on the 8th of August and gets her assaulted and raped by her 17-year-old son.'

Just one example to illustrate the variety was obviously not enough, and so he was citing another bizarre case of a rape in a hospital.

'On the 3rd of September, a senior doctor in charge of a surgical ward in a prestigious hospital rapes a 19-year-old comatose girl.'

His lists seemed to have no end, but my patience was certainly limited. So, I excused myself. I did say good-bye to him, who silently responded with tightly knitted eyebrows. Abdul Rehman accompanied us to the petrol pump where the taxi was parked. He gave me a powerful hug and waved a do-come-again kind of goodbye when our car purred into action.

It did not take us much time at Muzzaffargarh. Our contact had got everything ready. We left for Karachi soon after signing the papers, though our host wanted us to stay there overnight. The road was unexpectedly good and our driver was driving the car very smoothly in order to let me have a good nap. About midnight, we broke journey at a beautiful motel. This motel had a 24-hour restaurant. Because we had skipped our dinner, we had some snacks and coffee. We had booked a suite in advance. I preferred to occupy the room on the back.

The next morning, we were in for a big shock. The news channel of Zee TV was reporting a terrible sectarian riot between the Sunnis and the Shias. The Sunnis had exploded a powerful bomb in a huge Shia mosque in Quetta, and more than 100 people saying their prayer were roasted alive and another 100 odd were seriously wounded. The result was a bloody riot, which spread to the city and over a wide area around. The Sunni police was conveniently ineffective in stopping the bloodbath and only Allah knows how many more hapless Shia men, women and children were done to death. The Zee TV footage showed grisly scenes of gore, numerous dead and dying humans scattered everywhere. The PTV, however, blanked out such nauseous scenes of gore and blood in order to spare the delicate sensibilities of the ruling class and the well-heeled the horror of so much blood flowing, of so many underdogs dead and dying and of so many convulsed with pain and crying for help.

My mind was convulsed with agitation. I could not bring myself to eat breakfast in this mood. Firoz and Lokesh were, however, able to wash down some bread and butter with very hot coffee. On the way, the Zee TV footage was re-playing itself out on my mind's screen. It was more vivid now than when I had actually seen it on TV. I became a flow of thought, and then an impetuous flood of powerful thought-feeling currents. Instantly, I was a spectator watching these currents. I saw all those rapes and exploitative abuses being washed up and down; immediately following were that big bang in the Shia mosque, countless dead and dying bodies, consequent carnage everywhere; finally, rapes and massacres flowed and ebbed together, one above the other, the other above one.

We reached Karachi rather late. We were just in time for the flight back to India. Firoz was sitting next to me. Sitting so close to me and seeing me stuck in the marsh of a stagnant moment, he tried to get over his official distance from me and made bold to bring me out of myself. He did not quite succeed. However, I realized the folly of being so deeply involved in life's tragedies and farces, which in any case kept on happening everywhere, all the time. I was now surfacing towards excogitation, towards rational thought, which bore its own cross: I could not decide which of the two was the worse crime, a father violating his 6-year-old child, or a mob of frenzied fanatics murdering thousands of their own people in cold blood.

I was back home at 7 p.m. It was Sunday. Sheila had been waiting for two hours flat. Everything, she said, was ready in my room. A change of clothes was on my bed. She wanted me to have a quick wash and come to the dining table for coffee and snacks. She knew I would not take lunch. She had not taken lunch herself. When she saw me getting a little annoyed over this, she immediately helped me unwind.

There were, of course, other reasons why I could not relax. I tried to act out a smile, but my face betrayed me. Suddenly, I found her eyes penetrating my mind. She must have seen what was going on in it. She suddenly said: 'Oh, that is not an uncommon occurrence in that part of the world.'

'What isn't uncommon, Sheila?' I was astonished.

'Those four macho men raping a hapless teenager, sir.'

'But it wasn't just rape, Sheila,' I protested. The village judiciary ordered the rape as a barbaric an-eye-for-an-eye punishment! And do you also know, dear, that her brother for whose "sexual crime" she was thrown before the wolves was an 11-year lad, who could've been doing anything but raping an 18-year damsel of a higher tribe.'

'I can understand that, sir. But nobody can do anything. That's the way of life out there. People have been seeing this kind of thing for centuries. They are used to it.'

She was absolutely right. But *I* was not getting 'used to it' like those 'wise' people. She 'saw' that horrid Zee TV footage rolling out on my mind's monitor. A mysterious hand switched off the footage, and I found myself looking to her. My eyes caught a fleeting glimpse of a hand swishing down to her chair.

'That's too much blood, I know, for a single place and for a single moment of barbaric frenzy. But my answer is the same, sir. This has been happening like clockwork in those dark regions. It would be a freak if it did not.'

'But . . .'

'Now look at the list of rapes and other kinds of abuse of women, sir, that Nasir Khan was reeling off so triumphally.'

'Yes, that list is true,' I said with a deep sigh.

'And these crimes too have been happening like clockwork. And you are right that we cannot decide which kind is the worse. But nor can we stop the clock. It must go on . . . ticking and ticking and ticking.'

'And we should go on watching and watching and watching,' I snapped. I was irritated, perhaps, because she had said something which was so irrefutably right and to which I was finding it so difficult to reconcile.

'No, we need not go on watching idly or unconcerned,' she continued very calmly.

'What should we do instead?' I felt helpless.

'We should do what we can towards improving things—in our own little ways, of course.'

'How?' I said rather unconvinced.

'By educating common opinion, by fighting evil in whatever way we can.'

'In spite of Robert Darwin's belief that . . .'

'Yes, very much,' she said with a little glint in her eyes. 'In fact, to prove him wrong.'

'To prove him wrong' helped me snap out of my Pakistan visit hangover. I needed another cup of coffee, perhaps, to stabilize in my normal way of thinking and living.

Sheila wanted me to rest for some time. When I said I did not need any rest, she literally forced me into bed and pulled a bedsheet over me. Perhaps, she had some special dishes in mind for dinner and needed a lot of unencumbered time for that.

When I woke up after two hours, a letter that a courier had delivered half an hour before, was waiting for me. It was from Darwin. Elizabeth had killed the man she had eloped with and was now in police custody. A lady Assistant Sub-Inspector helped by two hefty constables was using the third degree to pump her. She had proved too tough for these women in uniform. Therefore, the Station House Officer was now going to set his crack male policemen upon her to break her spirit. And our dear Darwin was in panic on account of this.

Sheila had finished her cooking. When I read the letter out to her, she became very serious. It took me some time to understand this change. She was actually focussed, but for a much longer time than usual. And, finally, when she defocused her attention, she was not able to throw any light upon the letter. So, we mulled over the letter together. Our tentative conclusion was that he could not have been pining for that depraved woman again. He had possibly a normal feeling of sympathy with an old associate, a woman who was once his wife. He had panicked most probably because she might fail to bear the physical torture and blurt some wicked lies to involve him and even Faith.

We expected another letter from Darwin. It came within three days of the first letter. Our conclusion was right. She had involved both him and Faith. She had alleged that they had killed her paramour in order to frame her and thus get her sentenced to death. Her history of the last few years, however, came to his rescue and he was exonerated. Faith in any case could not prima facie have been blamed for any such thing.

This news was great relief to me. Sheila shared it fully. But she still looked a little anxious on account of Faith despite her knowledge that the latter had not only her sixth sense but also her spiritual strength to protect herself.

The third letter gave us a perfect lowdown on the whole episode. I quote the most important part of it here:

> I am sorry, Vigyan, for writing you another painful letter. But this one should give you as much relief as pain.
>
> The Elizabeth problem is more or less solved now. We cannot be entrapped any more. The police investigation has brought out everything. Elizabeth did kill her paramour, Abu, and did the 'right' thing for the first time in her life. He had tricked her into a fake marriage and honeymooned with her in his stage-managed posh house for quite some days. She was deeply impressed and vowed lasting fidelity to such a 'wonderful' man. But hardly had she pledged her love and loyalty when an equally 'wonderful' friend of Abu, called Padam, landed at the house. She was to be a call girl from now!
>
> She understood everything in a flash: the marriage, the posh house, the honeymoon, the dedicated lust. The first person she was to sleep with was our friend, Padam. She acted as a paragon of virtue that night under a viable pretext. His job in any case was to initiate her into the

call-girl business rather than sleep with her. For the next few days, she went on her calls but used her guile and charm every time to escape without having sex. Abu had now full faith in her and started eating out of her hand. On the decisive might, he cancelled one of her important visits and wanted her all to himself. And, thus, Elizabeth got her life's chance to prove her lasting fidelity at dead of night!

She is now in judicial custody and will spend half her life waiting for the final trial. Lest you should worry about me, I want to assure you that I am not in love with her, though I cannot help sympathizing with her present plight. I am in love with Faith and will love her 'till death do us part'.

This letter was great relief to us. However, Sheila still had a tiny bit of apprehension lurking in her mind. She was not clear about it but felt that it had to do with Faith.

TWO

The World Bank's award had raised my official status by two notches. I was now next to the MD in hierarchy. My office décor did reflect my status, but my general behaviour with the staff did not show this. One day, I felt I was becoming popular at the cost of my boss. To retrace my steps a little bit, I started acting tough. But this whole show seemed so clearly put-on that I had to retrace my steps again. My boss was too shrewd not to have noticed this back-and-forth somersaulting on my part. I was summoned and was expecting a bombshell. A feigned frown on his face suddenly broke into a broad smile and then into an office-decorum-controlled laughter. He would have got me promoted, but that would have meant either his or my leaving this office.

I had now higher and heavier responsibilities to discharge, which would have bogged down a less resourceful and experienced man. That I had become so efficient and innovative administratively never dawned on me before this moment, when suddenly new complex responsibilities devolved upon me. I did not quite understand myself how everything was falling into place without any hitch or hiccup. I tried to rationalize all this and attributed most of this success to the unqualified cooperation from my staff. But such unstinting cooperation gravitates only to the centre of a gravitational force.

As soon as I snapped out of this mood, I hated myself for this narcissistic streak. All of a sudden, I pierced a thick wall of time and saw on a peeling wall fading black letters glaring at me: 'Self-praise is self-deception.' I also saw how a teacher who was so full of himself had filled every schoolboy with dislike for him.

This chastening time-warp was necessary, and I did feel chastened, though I did not know who I had to thank for this: my inner self, nature, God?

The 'inner self' reminds me: Many days before, I had an uncanny feeling that my inner self was expanding. It was just a momentary illusion. Several days later, I had a similar experience, but this time it lasted a shade longer. I thought I was, perhaps, hallucinating. The third time, I saw Kapila sleeping with me and snobbishly telling me of her glorious premarital past rather than making love to me. This was a clear case of hallucination, in which I was reliving a bit of my past.

I talked the whole thing over with Sheila. She kind of agreed that the Kapila bit was a case of reliving a past experience. But the feeling of my inner self enlarging or expanding was an entirely different thing to her. Her eyes were blinking very fast now. I thought she was trying to 'see' things. But soon she was rubbing her eyes hard as though some dust or particle of grit had attacked them.

Apparently, she had no explanation for my experiences, but she did convey a feeling to me that my consciousness was undergoing an evolution. I looked at her and had a sudden but fleeting impression that she was responsible for it.

Two days after this revelation, a very funny thing happened. Two hours after lunch, I was at my desk clearing the day's files. I found something happening inside me. The column of files in front of me morphed into a human shape, which suddenly became sentient and mobile. I clearly saw Rajneesh walking through the office door towards me. 'Good afternoon, sir,' he said in his usual loud and excited way.

'What brings you here at this odd hour?' I said angrily. 'I'm too busy at the moment. Come some other time.'

My voice was a bit louder than my usual volume and pitch. Firoz came rushing in. He did not understand who I had been speaking to in that loud, angry voice. He did not dare ask me what had happened and went back slightly embarrassed.

Just a day later, Rajneesh was very much in town. He phoned me several times to fix up an appointment. I did not want to see him, yet I wanted him to come to my office. I had a mind to compare the two editions of him walking towards my desk!

I consulted with Sheila. She said I had nothing to fear, though this meeting would do him great good, which, of course, was not my aim.

Anyway, I let him meet me a few days later. At 4 p.m., he was supposed to meet me in my office. He entered on the dot. He was zooming in on me the way that phantasm had done. I did try to sham a smile, but I think I did not quite succeed. He wished me his usual ebullient good afternoon, and I motioned for him to sit down. He sat down with his usual noisy, gabbled 'thank you, sir'.

An attendant knocked and peeped in. I ordered coffee and biscuits. My eyes were fixed on Rajneesh's face, and his were downcast. I did not know, for the first time in his presence, where to begin the conversation. I was very disturbed inside and found it extremely difficult for a few seconds to fight the urge to show him the door. But I had to begin somewhere: 'Now, what did you want to see me for, Rajneesh?' I asked in a feigned neutral tone.

'I just felt a strong desire to meet you, sir. I hadn't met you for a long time.'

'Let's come to the point, Rajneesh. Do you want some money to complete that half-constructed house?'

'No, sir, I don't need any money or anything, sir?'

'Then?'

'I just wanted to share with you a few things about the social work I've done since I met you last.'

'Social work? What kind of social work?'

I was too upset not to want to reel off the entire dossier to him and order him to get the hell out of my office. But just at this moment, Sheila peeked into my mind, and the entire mood changed. I was ready to listen to his colourful tissue of lies.

'Lots of social work, sir. All kinds of social work.'

'But you need lots of money for your social work. Where do you get this money from?'

'I have my own exim business. I make quite a bit out of that. And, then, there're quite a few kind-hearted millionaires in this country, who are willing to help the poor, the destitute, the hapless.'

'But these kind-hearted people are generally close-fisted. How do you . . . ?'

'I know how to work on their minds, sir. I have now a highly developed public relations skill. I can make anybody dance to my tune!'

He was sure he had enthralled me completely. His tone now had a ring of over-confidence, and his diffident face at the time of his arrival had waxed bright with an air of triumph. This cocky air turned me on and I gave him, perhaps, the worst time of his life. I gave him a full rundown on his whole gamut of crimes against humanity: his mafia, his murders, his rapes, his robberies, extortions, you name it. He was flabbergasted. He had never thought I could have even dreamt that a man of his 'integrity' and 'character' could commit such heinous crimes against society. Obviously, he could not have said anything in defence of his 'social work' any more. He rose abruptly. His face was blood red, and he was shaking from head to foot. For a split second, I feared he might attack me and was prepared for the worst. But he suddenly turned and without saying his usual 'goodbye, sir' stamped out of the office.

I had a hunch he might go to my house to 'meet' Sheila. But I warned only a forewarned person. The doorbell went on ringing, and she knew without looking out through the peep-hole who the caller could be. While leaving, he phoned her and told her that he only wanted to 'express his sincere regret' for what he had become in the last two years and a half.

For two long days, my mind was overshadowed by this degenerate character. His 'evolution' was complete. He had fallen off the brink of the precipice. Sheila was silent, though she knew what was going on in my mind. A few days later, she told me that it was no use crying over spilt milk. Which meant that criminals like him were irredeemable? No. Her cryptic reply meant that only some of them could be redeemed. Why did she not interfere when I was so obsessed with him? She said with her face suffused with overwhelming care and affection that she wanted my obsession to run its full course and peter out naturally. At the end of this 'silent' dialogue, this fellow was completely gone.

And, yet, I wanted to talk to Darwin about him. Fortunately, he had now a phone connection. One did not have to wait for ages to get a reply by post. But he was not available for two days. And when he finally was, he did not take much interest in Rajneesh. When I persisted, he said rather mysteriously that I should learn the art of forgetting forgettable things. As a result, I had no choice but to leave the whole thing to time.

THREE

Kapila had lain low much too long, it seemed. She calculatedly maintained a low profile in the YMCA hostel and quietly cultivated new relationships. Within about three months of her returning to Delhi, she was thick with at least three important government functionaries. One of them was reportedly a keyman in a section of the Home Department. All this I came to know about from John D'Souza. He also told me to my great dismay that this woman had been spying on me through a detective she had engaged ever since she had set foot in the hostel. A few days later, he revealed that she knew everything about me, including my latest encounter with Rajneesh.

But he was a little bit behind time. She had covered up some of her footprints. So, he was finding it rather difficult to update me on her. For example, I did not get to know one very important thing about her till much later: that she was now very close to Rajneesh and had been conspiring with him to do me in. When I came to know of this, I asked D'Souza to find out the exact plot they had hatched against me. Their plot had two strategies: first, I was to be trapped in a trumped-up charge of buying and selling narcotics; second, I was to be knocked down and killed by a vehicle driven by a 'rash drunken' driver. The second strategy, according to this plot, was to be carried out only if the first failed. This information was very helpful. I informed my police contact and at the same time lodged a regular report with the police station to forestall the trap. The police intelligence was on the red alert. It was not long before two shadowy characters were seen prowling around my house. They were caught with two bagfuls of smack and heroin. Only a few minutes of the third-degree treatment was enough to force them to open their mouths. Within the next two days, Kapila was behind bars. Another three days, and our great mafioso, Rajneesh, was also in the police lock-up.

My brush with death was not too great a price to pay for sending these two extremely dangerous criminals to jail. Sheila said I had no danger to my life from now on even if the prosecution failed to secure their conviction. She added rather nonchalantly that they would not have succeeded in harming me even if their wicked plot had not been unearthed in time.

Darwin came to know of this imbroglio from a newspaper report in *The Hindu*. I received a frantic telephone call in my office. He wanted to come at once to see me safe and sound with 'my own eyes'. I had never seen so much emotion in him. In the evening, we called him. Sheila allayed his fears by assuring him that I was as safe and strong as before. However, we invited him to visit us at his convenience.

His life had always been a permanent itinerary before he met his Faith. Post-Faith, it alternated between home and his special personalized anthropology. Most of the time, Faith accompanied him on his 'study' tours. But, sometimes, she stayed behind alone to look after a business venture they had started lately in order to supplement Darwin's dwindling income from his fast depleting inheritance.

After the Rajneesh-Kapila plot, Darwin's plan was to fit Rajneesh's lock-up at Jaipur and Delhi into his itinerary. He wanted to see that 'devil' in the 'hell' with his own eyes. They had met once before at my place momentarily. Rajneesh was coming in when he was leaving. So, when their eyes met across the lock-up bars from a distance of 10 feet, it was a different view for both of them: Darwin saw in Rajneesh his theory in flesh and blood, and Rajneesh saw in Darwin a friend of a friend-turned-enemy. They stood like stills for quite a few seconds, then their eyes blinked fast and then glowered, transmitting a mutuality of a frightful kind.

The spookiest thing was that when Darwin was leaving with his eyes still fixed on Rajneesh, the latter raised his left hand and wished him 'good luck'. The sinister tone of the words was unmistakable, but Darwin, quoting his own words, was 'the last man on earth to get scared' of such things. His only regret was that with all his attitude and ocular eloquence in that face-off, he had failed to put the fear of God into him.

He had two more stopovers on his way to Delhi. For some time, he had been studying some nomadic tribes in central India. And now he had a chance to study such tribes in the north-central region. He knew beforehand where these nomads would be camping. He found the first group near Kotputli. They had pitched their improvised tents a little off the National Highway. Some families had extended their bullock carts into their dwellings. The children went about almost naked. Some girls had a fig leaf on. Men, women and their children upwards of about eight years were busy forging agricultural and domestic tools and sundry articles of daily use. This was one of the several groups of nomads in Rajasthan, popularly known as *Gadrua Lohars* or 'blacksmiths on wheels'. The popular belief in that area was that they sold their young girls, who came back at their earliest opportunity to be traded again, and that their women folk freely indulged in prostitution and generally pandered to the truckers who stopped by for their usual fucks. Darwin's understanding was that, for the most part, these and other such popular views of these groups were untrue. They were typical of the views any society holds of the people at its margins.

When Darwin was narrating the details of his visit at these nomads' camp, he found me more interested than he had expected. Therefore, he felt encouraged to tell me of his second stopover too.

This time, he had had to make a long detour. A different kind of nomadic group was camping near Narnaul, some 40 kilometres off the National Highway. This group was part of a small nomadic tribe, called *Sansis*, who were generally considered 'dangerous criminals'. It was believed that their main occupation was thefts and burglaries. They usually pitched their tents not far from busy places so that they could commit these crimes without being detected. To Darwin, these people were not very different from the blacksmiths on wheels, and yet nobody accused them of flesh trade or human trafficking. His perception was that they did not have any recognized trade or professional skill, such as blacksmithy, to front for their livelihood activities, and therefore they were branded as an irredeemable tribe of criminals. What he found difficult to understand was why the mainstream society was not doing anything whatever to absorb them rather than callously treat them as the 'other' people.

We had had two long meetings since he had arrived. I was particularly interested in what he told us about his 'glowering' face-off with Rajneesh. I tended to believe wishfully that what he said was going to happen to the latter. He was confident that this vicious character would in no case escape the dragnet of the law. Sheila respected his confidence but did not seem to agree with what he said about Rajneesh in view of the latter's long arm, leveraged by his enormous resources of men and money.

Anyway, we wanted to forget him for the time being, and like all normal people (Darwin sometimes called them 'lazy' people), we decided we would cross the bridge when we reached it, forgetting that we might never reach the bridge at all.

Darwin's interest in the nomads was quite informative, but he was certainly not going round just to satisfy his idle curiosity; he always flew on the magic carpet of some of his hypothesized premises. This time round, it was not quite clear to me how these nomads fitted into his mosaic of pre-patterned ideas or assumptions.

In our third long session, I sounded a bit sceptical about the purpose of his meeting his 'flotsam'. He was eagerly waiting for such a provocation, it seemed.

'No, Vigyan, I'm afraid you've got me wrong?'

'How?' I was very doubtful.

'When I was looking at these people, my focus was on our mainstream society.'

My forehead tightly creased into curiosity.

'I mean my eyes were studying these people, and my mind was focused on the society.'

'Does this mean that you were trying to explore how far the society was responsible for their present state of marginalization?'

'Yes, of course.'

'And what's your conclusion?'

'Well, I haven't reached any definite conclusion as yet. It'll take me some more time, Vigyan, to say anything definite. And I'll need more data too.'

'Anyway, can you say something now,' I asked, 'by way of a tentative statement?'

'Okay, if you insist, I'd say the society has played a big role in not only keeping these people on its fringes but also pushing them further away from its hub.'

'And what's your theory to do with this, Robert?'

'I think we'll talk about that later.'

We could not meet after this interesting tete-a-tete. He left next morning. There was an urgent call from Faith. Some shadowy character had been prowling around their house for two days. She had informed the police, yet she wanted Darwin at home as soon as possible. Within three days of his return to Hyderabad, the prowler was caught by Darwin himself. He handed him over to the police and requested them to find out if the fellow had any connection with Rajneesh or his mafia gangs.

I was rather worried about Faith, but Sheila told me that Faith was capable of defending herself against anybody. Anyway, perhaps anticipating our anxiety, she called to say that there was nothing at their end whatever to worry about.

A few days later, Darwin gave me a ring. He suspected some link between this mysterious prowler and Rajneesh. Therefore, he was looking at the whole thing from that angle: after that face-off across the Jaipur lock-up bars, this fellow could have hired a small-time criminal to frighten them

FOUR

Kapila was one of a hundred undertrials in a Delhi jail across the Yamuna. She had learnt a lot about the underworld ways of life during his Roshan Puri days. She was equipped with more guile than all her jail-mates. Besides, she not only possessed more charm but also knew more about how to use it to advantage than anybody else there. Soon, more than one officer could be seen paying her more attention than to any other young prisoner.

All these undertrials had been herded into two barracks. Life was really very hard. As it happens in overcrowded places 'infested' by starved and deprived creatures, there were regular scenes of raucous fights over space, food, lesbian infidelity. Our Kapila was very different and managed to stand out. Her face had that innocent lewdness, and her figure a rare magnetic pull. Her eyes spoke the language she very much wanted them to speak. After acting a coy mistress for a few days, she started playing her well-rehearsed real role. She was taken out almost every night. The two junior officers, who took her out for the first few days, could not have possibly monopolized her. So, they occasionally fobbed her off as a brand-new piece to a senior warden, G.L. Dagar, who to her great delight was a chronic bachelor. Once she reached that height, she did not look below. She kicked the juniors in their pants and started to play the role of a most faithful wife. Dagar was very pleased with her ministrations and allotted a separate cell to her near those barracks. This cell was equipped with certain facilities due to a junior jail employee. The justification for this allotment was that she had a rare manipulative skill to control a few difficult young criminals in Barrack No.1.

Kapila could not have asked for more. This dream situation was a sure door to freedom. The only thing to do was to take the next step in the right direction, and that she did before long. Her next few visits to Dagar's residence endeared her to him more and more. She tended him, nursed him so tenderly, more than anybody had ever done. She massaged him everywhere, arouse-tickled him on his most sensitive points and made love to him more often and in more ways than he could have imagined. And he was almost sold on the idea of keeping such a treasure for ever, but she did not buy him.

One Sunday morning, when Dagar was in his deep blissful sleep after a nightful of booze and lust, Kapila unlocked his car and drove out in the male guise of a cousin, who had stayed overnight.

When Dagar woke up and tried to reach for her to take her into his last warm embrace before leaving the bed, he found her side of the bed 'untreasured'.

The print media went gaga over this 'wonderful' piece of news. The national dailies competed with one another in claiming that they had had their special scoops on this great scandal. They published their peculiar scoops in as colourful a manner as possible with the result that each version turned out to be substantially different. So much so that they seemed to have been reporting entirely different happenings.

And TV news channels would not be left behind. One footage was as different from another as chalk from cheese. All these pictures were a complete sham: perhaps, mélanges made up by mixing together some old file pictures!

Darwin had his own take on this 'great drama'. To him, Kapila was irrelevant; GL Dagar, who according to his information had been dismissed from service within 24 hours of

Kapila's escape, was the central character. His view was that Dagar could not have deserved a better deal.

Our relevant subject, however, was Kapila, not Dagar. We were curious to find out where she could have gone. My detective, D'Souza, told me casually that she was headed for Indore, which to me appeared to be the least likely of all the places she could have decided to go to.

Sheila felt that I was right but could not say anything beyond this. We were getting a bit worried now because Kapila had proved herself capable of hatching dangerous conspiracies in collusion with any criminal. Then, all of a sudden, Sheila got focused and 'saw' Kapila heading towards Jaipur, obviously to join Rajneesh.

When I tried to apprise the police station of this fact, the Station House Officer would not buy it, saying that my information could not be true. He also gave his twisted reasons for his stand.

In less than a week, one of my office clerks drew my attention to a boxed news item in a Hindi daily. It was about how a notorious undertrial, by the name of Rajneesh, had escaped a Jaipur prison. A very fair deal was struck between him and the warden, who *took* one million rupees and *gave* in return a cutter for the bars and a ladder for climbing out. Early next morning, a siren sounded a security alarm, and the crack policemen of the jail security fanned out in a matter of minutes to catch the culprit.

The essential part of the news was true. I came to know from another source that there had been a jailbreak a few days before and Rajneesh had escaped. As it happens in all such cases in this country, the police was totally clueless in this matter for days on end. There were a hundred and one hiding places in his home district, and he must have been sure that he would never be caught.

My suspicion was that there could have been a regular contact line between him and Kapila when they were in jail. It was not just a coincidence that they escaped to freedom around the same time. Sheila agreed with me and said that she would not be surprised if we got the news in a few days that they were living together in one of his *havelis* around Sikar.

In his hideout, Rajneesh was using his freedom, it seemed, in reorganizing his mafia gangs in order to strengthen his old empire and to prepare to settle his old scores.

One proof of this was a trial assault on Darwin's house in Hyderabad. Darwin had been living in an old high-ceilinged bungalow in Begumpet. It had big ventilators, whose shutters were operated by strings tied to pegs below. One evening around nine o'clock, Faith was alone in the house, expecting Darwin very eagerly. Suddenly, one of the ventilators opened and a big piece of stone fell down upon the floor with a very loud thud. She was more surprised than frightened. The trajectory of the stone falling down proved that it was thrown with a calculated force to make it fall down on a pre-decided point.

When Darwin came home, he tried to guess what could have happened. His first aim was to find out the goon who had been hired to strike. He hired the services of a private security agency, which provided him with a 24-hour camouflaged vigilance around the bungalow.

I had been constantly in touch with Darwin. He knew everything about the jailbreak and Rajneesh's dramatic escape to freedom. He also knew where Rajneesh could be hiding. So, when he hired the security agency, he told them who he suspected and where they should look for him.

Sheila felt very bad that the Darwins were suffering because of us. After all, it was because of Rajneesh's hostility to us that he was targeting the Darwins. Darwin had challenged that fellow at the Jaipur lock-up because of his sympathy with us. Now we had to fight the enemy unitedly with all our forces and resources.

The word *forces* referred to the combined spiritual energies of Faith and Sheila. They were in constant touch with each other, spiritually as well as telephonically. They were trying to ensure that every evil move by Rajneesh and his mafiosi was to be forestalled even as it was being planned. Faith was capable of seeing surreal images in a subjectively delimited field, and Sheila saw clearly what was happening at a place or in an area when she focussed on it. A little later, I came to know from Sheila that Faith was developing some occult powers which sporadically expressed themselves and that she was trying very hard to tame them so that she could harness them to work to our advantage, when necessary.

Anyway, my aim was to use all my resources, including these spiritual powers, to get both Rajneesh and Kapila arrested and jailed so that they could be prevented from doing any harm to anybody. Darwin's aim was the same. We were now on a kind of hot line.

FIVE

The general elections were approaching. The political parties were drafting their manifestoes. My *Structures for Social Evolution* was a rage. Every piddling little party, not to mention the proud pan-Indian ones, wanted to make 'use' of it according to their election planks and according to their lights. I knew for sure that most of its findings and recommendations would be misinterpreted or misused. But I was feeling helpless.

As expected, I soon found some of these parties reading their favourite meanings into the misusable parts of the book. My 'structures' were taken as a licence for evolving any kind and number of organizations to cater for their favourite vote banks and to create new vote banks.

One important regional party, for instance, set up an organization to grant *mangal sutras* to the election-eve brides, belonging to the fence-sitting sections of voters in the society. The funds, of course, were to come from the state exchequer.

A national party put together a Social Justice structure, whose job was to get the economically backward upper-caste sections reservations in government and public sector jobs. Its aim was to make a 'big dent' into the upper-caste votes and swell its vote bank, traditionally consisting of religious minorities, *dalits* and backwards castes.

The same pan-Indian party had earlier invented an amazing political gimmick. It had created a partisan body, fully funded by the government, whose task was to provide free midday meals to the below-poverty-line school children. The scheme partly worked for some time with a twofold downstream result. The free-meal eaters started to be looked down upon as beggars, and the members of the partisan body in charge of running this all-Indian free kitchen fattened at the cost of the starving innocents, in the inaccessible far-flung areas of the country, whose begging bowls remained extended and ever empty. Even when the siphoning of the massive free-kitchen funds was going on full throttle, the party was tom-tomming the great social revolution that they were bringing about. I heard one wag commenting in a public meeting organized by another party that history would one day find time to pay tributes to this 'great social revolution', which was teaching children that begging was a self-respecting act and that the traditional notion of human dignity was nonsense. Anyway, whatever meaning one might read into this social revolution, it certainly took the shine off my humble 'evolution' in my *Structures for Social Evolution.*

The important parties were running neck and neck in making promises of all kinds. One said it would provide free electricity and water to all farmers. One north-India party promised it would further increase subsidies on quality seeds and fertilizers; and one south-India party declared that it would give two *sarees* each to every poor would-be bride during the period of its rule. All these parties and some others had already established faith-enticing structures to deliver on these promises.

I was very worried that my recommendations were being grossly misinterpreted and mutilated so that they could fit into preconceived political agendas. I talked the matter over with some of my colleagues. My MD realized the seriousness of what was happening around and summoned me. He suggested two or three ways of countering the misuse of my thesis. He asked me to present the real intention and meaning of my book to a few important academic, social and political audiences across the country. He assured me that he would sponsor these presentations and try to ensure the presence of the press in full strength. The first place where I was invited to make a presentation was the Indian Habitat Centre in New Delhi.

It went off very well. The pressmen were agog over the structures described and the possible social evolution resulting from them. And when I quietly added a few remarks, praising their possible contribution to social progress, they all went mad about my 'revolutionary' ideas, which were at the same time so eminently practicable. A colleague, later on, said tongue-in-cheek but without malice that my presentation was better than my research!

The press that I got at the Habitat Centre was enough to get me invitations from intellectual clubs and political organizations all over the country. I made a strategic selection from these invitations in consultation with the MD and two other senior colleagues. It was decided that if I continued to get the kind of press I had got at the Habitat Centre, presentations at only half a dozen places across the country would be enough to disabuse the literate population of the disinformation that the political parties were inflicting on the public in the name of my UN-applauded *Structures*.

In less than a month, I visited seven politically important places and made my presentations with increasing confidence and aplomb. Every presentation was significantly better than its immediate predecessor and, as good luck would have it, got a proportionately better press. My *Structures for Social Evolution* was now well known among the people who mattered and was now much less liable to be misused.

Darwin kept track of my entire tour and avidly read through the press reports of all my presentations. At Hyderabad, which was the last point of my lecture tour, he managed to be present at my lecture along with Faith. He had 'wangled' the invitation through an important political contact and kept it a secret from me till my surprised eyes spotted him in one of the front rows among the audience.

Despite the importunate requests of my hosts that I should accept their hospitality and stay overnight, I spent the night with the Darwins. Their dilapidated bungalow in Begumpet was as I had pictured in my imagination: it had that old-world aura about it and was romantically frayed at the edges. Sitting on their front verandah, we talked and talked and talked. It was rather weird that I did not feel even for a moment that I was meeting Faith for the first time. And she was the first to say, not Darwin, that our get-together was incomplete without Sheila. She even said she missed Sheila very much. And then we all began to miss Sheila together. We wished she had been with us. Then, suddenly, we all became rational: after all, she was only a phone call away. And then we talked to her turn by turn, again and again, until she had to say that she too missed us very much. She missed us also because she had to break a piece of news about Rajneesh. He had written to say that he would like to come to see me! Immediately after receiving the letter, she had focussed and 'seen' him somewhere in Rajasthan. And yet she had been taking care to see that she was not accessible to any surprise attack or attempt on her life or liberty.

The next morning, I flew back to Delhi. Sheila was waiting at the door. She showed me that letter as soon as I made myself comfortable. Her reading was that he was very keen to make it up with me, but she advised me against it. My view was that he was trying to play a trick on me rather than make up. Either way, it was advisable, to my mind, to help the police to catch him. Sheila, however, was of the view that we should wait for some time before we took the final decision. Perhaps, she was prescient of what was coming. In the evening, there was a phone call from that fellow. The caller ID on the phone clearly showed that he was calling from Gurgaon.

He insisted on seeing me. When I put my foot down, he heard the loud tap on the marble floor and quieted for a while. I rang off and thanked God for getting rid of him. But I had thanked Him a little prematurely, perhaps. The telephone rang again within minutes. This time, he made an extremely humble request. I almost saw him going on his knees as he used to do every time he implored me to do something difficult for him in the past, but I did not relent. To turn him off from wherever he was, I threatened to get him arrested if he continued to pester me. This time, he lost his precariously held balance and threatened to 'teach me a lesson' if I did not agree to meet him within 24 hours. My thundering voice in response cowed him down a bit, and he went on alternating between cowering entreaties and veiled vulgar threats. In utter disgust, I put down the receiver.

That evening, the telephone did not ring again. Perhaps, he was planning his next move in his hideout. And I wanted to have my own counter-move ready. Sheila suggested that we did not need to do anything because she was sure in her mind that he would be arrested very soon without our intervention. And this was what happened within a week. Kapila was not with him. Either she had not joined him at all, or they were hiding in different places so that they might not be arrested together. The third, least likely, possibility was that they had agreed on a live-in arrangement but busted up before long in a sudden clash of their overblown egos.

Within a month, we found, to our surprise, that the least likely possibility had turned out to be a fact. Kapila was most probably behind Rajneesh's sudden bust: she had colluded with one of his rivals in his mafia gangs and cemented her relationship with the latter with a marriage contract.

Kapila's new partner, Abdulla, was a ruthless gangster. Rajneesh had selected him out of a hundred dreadful macho men. Abdulla had a clear edge over every other candidate for the post because of his *brutality* and *utter fearlessness*.

Rajneesh had five gangs under him, each assigned to a different slew of tasks. Abdulla was in charge of two crack gangs tasked with the responsibilities of kidnapping for big ransoms and extorting huge monthly amounts from the rich. He was also very handy when somebody was to be maimed or eliminated. Lesser tasks were under the charge of lesser criminals. All these chiefs were called 'leaders'. His own designation was 'overlord'. The overlord paid them big salaries plus a fixed commission from the successful execution of a task. He did not execute any task himself. He was 'above crime' in this sense and was sure in his mind that he would go scot-free if any of these gangsters, leaders or cadres, was caught red-handed. He was very proud of his imaginative 'policy-planning' and his perfect blueprints, which he passed on readymade to the leaders with the instructions that they be executed exactly as they were.

The leaders and the cadres had complete faith in their 'great' overload. Only Abdulla was not too happy. He harboured an ambition to supplant him one day. Rajneesh's dependence upon him had turned his head, and his self-image now was that he was second to none in bravery, hardiness and prowess. When Rajneesh was in the Jaipur lock-up, he got his much-desired chance to test the qualities and skills that he was proud of having in abundance.

When Rajneesh escaped from the lock-up, he needed to find a safe hideout within the limits of his empire. To his great surprise and chagrin, he found the terrain changed. He summoned Abdulla to ascertain what exactly was going on and was surprised to see a noticeable change in his demeanour. But he studied him cannily and calmly and then let him go with a pat on his back. To multiply his eyes and ears, he strengthened his favourite spy network. He had now three different cadres that had to keep an eye not only on whatever was happening in his entire domain but also on each other. The innermost cadre doubled as his crack security group and his nodal intelligence group.

After this new set-up was in place, things seemed to work smoothly for some time. But when Kapila escaped from her NOIDA jail-cum-home and arrived on the scene, everything began to change for the worse. Possibly, Abdulla had contacted her in jail, thinking that she could be a great help in his scheme of grabbing Rajneesh's empire. She apparently joined Rajneesh as a deputy leader of one of the gangs and chose to stay in a separate house not far from his hideout. This arrangement was ideally suited for Abdulla's plan, who gave her whatever she needed and wanted, plus the assurance of security against the police as well as Rajneesh. Two of Rajneesh's intelligence groups had been infiltrated by Abdulla's men, but the third group remained fiercely loyal and told him one evening that Abdulla and Kapila had informed the police of his whereabouts and he could be arrested any time. Thus, he fled the place in the middle of that very night with his crack group of spies and security men to give him protection on his way to Gurgaon, where he was arrested a few days later.

His re-arrest was welcome news for us. At least for some time, I did not need to worry that the fellow would pester me with his worrisome requests for a meeting or threaten to teach me a lesson. Since I was now thoroughly aware of his powerful resources of money and man power, I could not afford to be complacent. Another danger still loomed. Kapila was a little more dangerous in that a lot of mystery surrounded her intentions and movements. Everything about her had, therefore, to be demystified as early as possible. So, I asked my detective agency to assign D'Souza to the task.

The Darwins felt quite relieved that they were rid of any immediate threat from Rajneesh and Elizabeth. But like us they too were rather anxious on account of Kapila being at large. I assured them that I would have her put behind bars within a month at the latest. Then, we all agreed to meet in Hyderabad or Delhi to find a permanent solution to the problem posed by these three criminals.

SIX

It was a Sunday afternoon. I was sitting in a restaurant with an old friend from my schooldays, Amit Sarkar. He had discovered me in Delhi some months before and promised to meet me before long. He was a professor at Patna University and was now in Delhi to present a paper on 'Breakdown of Social Institutions in India' at JNU. We were sipping coffee and looking across the haze of years into our distant adolescent past. We alternated between delicious nostalgia and painful angst induced by the present. On the whole, we were in a relaxed frame of mind, when suddenly a shrill sound of 'Bihar is burning(.)' disturbed the sound waves. It came from a table not far from ours. Two young men were discussing politics, it seemed. This one-liner was a quote from a Patna High Court's judgement on an extortion case, in which three men and a young girl had been done to death on a busy road. The court had also directed the chief secretary to file an affidavit, stating the steps being taken to prevent such crimes.

Both these young men were apparently from Bihar, though they were from two mutually hostile castes. One belonged to a caste generally at the 'receiving' end and other to a caste often at the 'giving' end. It was on the whole a session of virulent recriminations, though towards the end, perhaps because of two tall mugfuls of foam-topped coffee cutely smirking at them, they had come to terms.

Before the espresso silenced them into a 'we-couldn't-care-less' rapprochement, they had given us a lot of food for thought. Kidnapping for ransom was a highly lucrative industry and was flourishing like weeds in a long neglected field. The young men's heated discussion had touched Prof. Amit Sen on the raw. One of his teen-aged daughters had been abducted, raped and killed only three years before. So, when they were leaving after partially purging themselves of their caste-induced animus towards each other, he had an accidental peek at them. He recognized the young man belonging to the 'giving' caste. Years before, this man had been a student at the university. He remembered teaching him economics and having him punished for his rowdyism. His daughter was a victim of a mafia belonging to his militant caste, and he was more or less sure that this young man had been very much involved in the crime.

Immediately after the man left, Amit Sen could not blink back his tears. When I tried to counsel restraint, he started crying like a child. A waiter two tables away heard the unexpected sound and rushed to us to ask if he could help us in any way. I told him that my guest's eyes were very sore and ordered him to bring us two bottles of chilled beer. By the time he returned with the beer, the professor's eyes were safely hidden behind my dark glasses, and his mouth was closed to the outcoming sound.

'Cool it, dear,' I said very sympathetically. 'I can understand what you're going through, but . . .'

'I'm very sorry I couldn't control myself because of this criminal. This fellow not only touched the raw nerve in me, but also reminded me of a hundred and one other tragedies, even more heinous and harrowing.'

'Oh.'

'What the Patna High Court said is a gross understatement. Bihar's not burning; it's burnt to cinders. Some say to "embers" only wishfully. They think the sparks hidden beneath them will one day kindle big fires of revolution and . . .'

'You don't believe that, Amit?' I was rather depressed.

'Yes, I don't. Dead people don't bring about revolutions. They only wait to be cremated or buried.'

'We shouldn't lose hope like this, my friend. Otherwise, we'll all die before our death.'

'We're already dying, Vigyan, without the help of death!'

He was very agitated. I did not know what to say. But I wanted him to talk as bitterly and furiously as possible to purge all that had distended his psyche to the bursting point. I looked into his eyes, signalling support to his desperate stance, and he burst into a storm:

'The situation is utter mayhem, Vigyan. Half the society's organized into the caste and class mafia gangs. The other half's their safe playground, where millions of milk-white sitting ducks lay eggs or feed their chicks in mortal fear of instant deprivation or destruction.'

I went on looking at his face, waxing more and more distorted with a mix of agony and anger. I also felt his breath quicken into a rasp. My face was now a perfect picture of my inner turmoil in spite of myself.

'And these groups of predators most of the time prey on their soft targets, these poor sitting ducks. Thus, they are increasing and the ducks are decreasing in numbers.'

At this point, I could not but ask a question:

'But these mafia gangs do fight between themselves. Their number should also decrease?'

'I wish it were so. But their number will never decrease. The moment one gangster is killed, five join in his place! I wish they'd fight among themselves and finish off one another, these ghouls.'

'But what about the government?'

'It's a weaker government, which runs on selective tax collection. It avoids coming into conflict with the strong "government" of the mafia gangs; quite often, it's in cohoots with these gangs, whose ransom collections together add up to twice the revenue collection of the weaker government.'

'My, this picture is a bit too dark even for Bihar!'

'No, it isn't even half as dark as the reality is.'

'You mean the reality . . .

'Yes, it's very much darker. Half the stalwarts of the weaker government are with them, aiding and abetting in their extortions, abductions for ransom collection, vendetta killings and caste-inspired carnages.'

'Where will all these lead to?'

'The fear is that this mafia *raj* might spread to the entire country, and then . . .'

'And then there'll be a revolution?'

'Yes, there *will* be one, but it might take a century or two to materialize!'

There was not a ray of hope in this absolutely gloomy scenario. I wanted to pull him out of his pitch dark mental cave without shining any flashlight through its opening. I ordered two cups of coffee. The waiter responded very quickly, and when he came, he lingered for a while. This drew Amit a bit out of his cave, into the hustle of the restaurant. Two curiously dressed, or better undressed, dolls from our capital's fash frat passed by us, wafting a strange aroma over us.

As though this aroma worked as poisonous fumes on his respiratory system, Amit rushed back into the safety of his cave. He had seen similar dolls accompanying a terribly handsome middle-aged overlord, who ruled over at least one-third of the states of Uttar Pradesh and Madhya Pradesh: In Uttar Pradesh, the latter's domain extended from Chitrakoot Dham to Allahabad, and in Madhya Pradesh, he ruled over vast areas between Rewa and Satna. His name, which people in his domain uttered only in panicked whispers, was Baruwa. As ill luck or good luck would have it, Amit had been among the crowd at Satna that he had addressed. He sat in a diamond-studded high-backed upholstered chair, flanked and backed by half a dozen dazzling dolls with velvet-covered mega fans in their graceful hands. The audience were motionless eyes and ears but still respiring. He thundered and scared the daylight out of one and all. When they were dead to the last man, he lowered his volume to a winsome tone and gave a brief speech. Every syllable was lapped up without their frightened tongues making even the faintest of noises.

At the end of the speech, the dolls deposited their fans with the attendants behind them, trooped over to the space in front of Baruwa and sang a worshipful chorus in praise of their great lord. The ceremony over, the retinue packed everything up in minutes, and one could see a dusty cavalcade of cars zooming off.

The restaurant had vanished from the cave in which Amit had relocated a while before. He was now with Baruwa and his men and women. From this vantage seat, he told me all that he could see first-hand. Baruwa was the unchallenged lord of these realms. He ran a parallel government with the help of nine trusted lieutenants, who he proudly called 'my nauratanas'

His tax collection from his favourite sources was enormous. Among his 'illegal' sources of revenue, such as extortions and ransom collections, were his 'legal' (he called them 'honest') strategies of collections. He would 'charge' huge sums of money for key transfers and postings. And from numerous rural development projects, he would get his 'legitimate' 40% cuts. Through his great good offices, anybody could get a posting of their choice. Through his sure-fire clout at appropriate echelons, any go-getter or NGO could get any profit-making project sanctioned.

One of his nicknames was 'Mr Elusive', which was obviously a misnomer since it was the police that eluded him rather than he eluding the police. He was *wanted* for 231 cases of murder, dacoity, extortion and kidnapping. But he would never be caught because every politician *wanted* him to help them in their elections. He helped everybody running for *gram pradhan* to MP. This got him huge sums plus a permanent guarantee against arrest by any authority.

His parallel government was in a way supportive of the other government. It did not matter if he committed a few score rapes, kidnappings and murders a year provided he helped the socially recognized respectable criminals in pursuit of their pelf and power.

From a professor, Amit had morphed into a wimp. He was not crying apparently; but, inside, he was all anguish and tears. The same waiter came again, but he was disappointed to see Amit in total control of himself. I was surprised that Amit was able to change in less than a minute, chameleon-like, from a weepy baby to a picture of poise. But the very next moment, I could rationalize this change to myself as a defensive mechanism of the defenceless in their seriously destabilized regions.

Since he had himself come out of his cave, I did not need to pull him out. I just kept him above ground by a bit of small talk and a reference to Sheila and her saintly clairvoyance, which awakened his curiosity, even his interest. It was no longer necessary to invite him. We just went home. When the door opened before I pressed the doorbell button, he was all agog. The degree of respect in Sheila's folded-hands welcome reduced at least a part of his doorbell-induced excitement. Everything had been readied to welcome the guest. Coffee was served even before he thought we really needed it. Sheila sat with us all the time, giving him the wrong impression that some maid or cook was working in the kitchen to keep the coffee table supplied with everything.

He did not know anything about my relationship with Sheila. And he had no reason not to presume that we were man and wife despite our age difference. I stole a glance at Sheila and we agreed out of sheer naughtiness to let the illusion remain till he visited us again.

He stayed with us for two days. He became more and more curious to know about Sheila's 'psychic' powers. Neither she nor I was able to blunt his curiosity. That she had been born with them or she did not know when or how she had come to possess them did not satisfy him. To be fair to him, he did not press the matter beyond a point, and the subject changed by a quirk of circumstance and veered round to Patna. There was a phone call from Patna, out of all of places in the vast world. It was from Darwin, who needed some information about my *Structures for Social Evolution*. The effect was that I 'lost' Amit. He was now back in Patna brooding over the vagaries and perversities of the region. Sheila could draw him back, but she waited till he was willing to escape the torment of memories. When the moment came, she veered towards him, and their eyes met in a long communion. And, then, in a few minutes, we were chatting normally as though nothing had happened. The rest of his stay was eventless except that Sheila's cooking and care kept him too pleasantly surprised to let him relapse into Patna. Before he left, there was another phone call from Darwin, but this time, thank God, it was from Lucknow.

Darwin was looking for something in Patna and thereabouts. Elizabeth had escaped from jail and was reportedly hiding somewhere near Patna. She had made common cause with Kapila, who had been at large since she had escaped from the Delhi jail. Darwin wanted to prevent any nefarious plan on her part to attack Faith and him. He found some clues, and his subsequent visit to Lucknow was addressed to this aim. He was relieved that he had made a 'foolproof' preventive arrangement with the help of a senior police officer.

I wanted him to come over to Delhi. I was keen to share Amit's problem with him. But he was in a hurry to get back home because he had not yet got over his worry about Faith. To Sheila, his worry seemed pointless. But she did not mind his over-cautiousness.

There was no news form Amit Sarkar for over two weeks. I was rather anxious to know what had happened. There was no response to my repeated telephone calls. Then, one evening, his answering machine was suddenly working and I left a loud message. He had been out of town for several days, it appeared. As soon as he returned home, he called me. His Vice-Chancellor had been abducted by a Danveer Sena gang. Because this VC was one of the few people he trusted and drew his interest in life from, he was utterly distraught. He had sent his family to her parents in Kolkata and had himself left home for the dual purpose of staving off immediate danger to his own life and searching for clues to where the VC could have been taken.

I was absolutely shaken. I insisted upon his either going to Kolkata or coming over to Delhi. But he did not want to leave the station till he had traced and assured the safety of his VC.

I was in this frame of mind when Darwin called. He straight away asked me the reason of my being so distraught. When I told him that the immediate reason was Amit Sarkar, the first impression I got was that he was shocked. But, not unexpectedly, he said he was sad, but not at all surprised. He had seen much worse things, he said, in that region and even at other places in the country. We were jolted so easily, he added, because sometimes, much against our better judgment, we refused to prepare ourselves to face such eventualities.

A few days later, when the telephone rang, strangely enough, I knew who the call was from. Darwin was speaking from Amit's home at Patna. He used Faith's help to help

Amit and Co. save their VC. Was he not disproving his own theory that everybody helps only themselves? No. If there were a few stray individuals of his kind in this world, they were not actors in the play on the life's stage. In fact, he was a little miffed this time that a person of my calibre and experience could ask him such a naïve question. However, he assured me that he had not lost all hope for this hapless planet. His hope lay not in those silly, facile, romantic notions of the perfectibility of man, but in the recent strides in the field of genomics. I rang off on the note that we would talk about his interest and faith in genomics when we met in Delhi shortly.

SEVEN

Rajneesh was now lodged in a relatively obscure but strongly guarded jail outside north Delhi. Abdulla had tightened the screws on the gangs still swearing loyalty to Rajneesh and ensured that no help from them reached the latter. This information came to us from my detective agency. Snippets percolating to us from some of my other sources confirmed it. But this did not make the Darwins immune to Rajneesh's miasma. Nor did it make Sheila and me cosy and complacent. Darwin's dictum was that 'constant vigilance is the price of security in the present state of man's social evolution'.

As though to prove that no amount of vigilance could ensure freedom from danger, there was a letter from Rajneesh within a fortnight of his arrest and imprisonment. The letter was beautifully typed and bore his real signature. That he was able to have this letter typed and posted indicated that he had already bought more than one person from the jail staff. The next step was quite predictable. The contents were innocuous: he only wanted to meet his former teacher out of 'pure love' for him. If I had complained against him or the jail staff involved, the letter could have been used against me rather than against them. I chose silence and realized later that it was a good decision. External silence invariably heightens internal vigilance.

A few days later, there was a cryptic letter from Kapila. Every word denoting 'love' connoted 'hatred'. This did not surprise me. But it did rattle me with its inscrutability. What on earth did she want to convey? Wanted me to be perpetually on tiptoes? Wanted me to repent that I had lost a gem of a woman? Or wanted me to take her back and embrace her with all the passion at my command only to be stabbed in the stomach or Bobbitized?

Sheila advised silence in response to this letter as well. Silence was our best defence till we found out what place she had written to me from. The post mark, which was difficult to decipher at first, yielded its secret at last. The woman was at Jaipur or somewhere in that region. My detective promised he would ferret her out in less than a month. But even after three months, he was in the dark, though he feigned confidence through his embarrassed face.

Anyway, we increased the level of vigilance rather than worry about her next move. Two more letters came. One carried a veiled warning and the other a naked threat. Our response was silence again. Meanwhile, D'Souza called on us. The smile on his face showed that he had something positive to convey. I had alerted the police a few days before. They swooped on her in her hideout near Sikar and sent her to jail.

I wanted to celebrated this occasion. But, on second thoughts, I found the idea much too puerile. Sheila suggested a peaceful retreat with the Darwins to a quiet sylvan place. The Darwins wanted to spend a few days at Naturoville, a spa town near Haridwar.

The place provided a marvellous background for our meeting. Sheila and Faith were face to face for the first time. I had heard a 'quack' say several years before that when psychic powers met, they just added up. So, when these two ladies met, I was expecting most irrationally some fireworks or, at least, scintillations. Nothing of the sort happened. Together, they were much more quiet and innocent than they had been separately. As they were glued to each other, Darwin took me aside and told me to watch unobtrusively how they were communing: the air between them was not disturbed by any palpable sound waves, and yet they were talking. When he saw my puzzlement, he gave me a nifty set of headphones that Faith had given him. I not only heard but also 'saw' what was going on between the two 'great psychics'! I removed the device, and they seemed to be sitting quietly facing each other.

We had come to the edge of the town. It had rained heavily for a few days before we arrived here. The trees were greener than in paintings. The roads were fringed with lush green grass. A cool breeze wafted heavenly aroma across us. Our nostrils automatically expanded to take in as much as possible. It was 6 p.m. and we were at the tether's end. Beyond this point was nothing but untamed nature: thick foliage, squat bushes, big trees, then tall trees, all backed by sloping hills merging into sky-kissing mountains. *Breathtaking* was the word I understood for the first time. Everything was an irreplaceable word in an exquisite poem.

Faith and Sheila were behind us. We were walking like snails. Suddenly, we stopped to turn back. Darwin wanted to stand here for ever. Faith and Sheila were in transports of double bliss, it seemed they were in communion with each other as well as with the magic of nature.

I let them merge with the environment. I stood there as a mystified spectator, unable to separate the three figures from their ambience. They seemed like flower buds blossoming gradually in response to the gently seductive caresses of the fragrant breeze and the dimmed sun rays. I felt like plucking them and taking them back to our guesthouse suite. Suddenly, I felt something coursing through my blood, and I became part of the scene.

Everyone of us had taken in enough of the bliss around and was now ready to move back. On our way back, we saw a godman, clad in ochreous robes, preaching a communal agenda in a subdued way. The devotees were lapping up the 'delicious' fare. Darwin stood there like a lamp post. His ears were focussed on the godman's discourse, and his eyes were fixed uncannily upon me. I, of course, understood what he wanted to convey through his unbroken ears-eyes line.

I did not know why we were returning so circuitously. We had hardly taken 20 minutes to reach the edge of the town. Was this due to God or Darwin? The answer to this question did not matter when we saw on a small patch of bare land a circular crowd of people. Inside the circle, two cocks, with their blood-red combs straightening up to reflect their rage, were fighting like hell. After several bouts of attacks and counter-attacks, one of them lay defeated. The owner, furious perhaps in his first humiliation, pounced on his bleeding rooster and twisted its neck till it squeaked to death. Darwin looked at me, and I looked at Faith and Sheila, who were calm as ever.

The last episode was very off-putting. Our suite had been burgled. Most of the things of everyday use had been taken away. We were left with only what we had on us. The guest-house staff and the police were excitedly busy looking for clues and trying frantically to pin down the culprits. But we knew like everybody else in this land of promise and hope that only one per cent stolen and robbed goods were recovered and just one per cent of the recovered goods were ultimately restored to the original owners. So, we returned to Delhi immediately without bothering to leave our addresses with the guesthouse or the police. We had gained much more than we had lost.

Faith wanted to stay with us for a few days. Darwin had to attend to some business at home, but he did not want to go back without Faith. Sheila decided the matter for them. They were now to stay with us just for two days. This was the best time of our togetherness. In a few hours, we had forgotten our Naturoville experience. I had no option but to take two days' leave from office in order not to miss the indescribable joy of our stay together. The kitchen was Faith's domain for the first day. She wanted Sheila to be with us all the time. And her speed of cooking and doing all other kitchen chores was amazing—twice, three times, many times that of Sheila? In a few minutes, she was with us to complete the foursome for a game of cards. She teamed with me, and we won every game without any convincing fight from the other side. Darwin was rather upset, but Sheila enjoyed her defeat more than she had ever enjoyed anything before! Possibly to make him feel at ease, Sheila subtly suggested the change of partners. And now Darwin was winning every game, and Faith had one eye fixed on her fanned cards and the other on Sheila's face. My eyeballs were violently fleeting forward and backward to scan what super game was being played over and above the cards. To my surprise and delight, I was visualizing a subterranean line of communication between the ladies. Sheila was making Faith win. Or was Faith making Sheila lose? The latter seemed less likely. But I was rather confused. Why, then, was I made to visualize the line? To help me understand that we were only playing—not winning or losing?

Darwin said he was hungry and asked Faith how long it would take her to get the lunch ready. Even Sheila joined in a burst of applause when she told us with a poker face that the lunch had been ready since morning. To satisfy ourselves that she was not joking, we went to the kitchen to see half a dozen dishes and a pot of rice ready! Had she prepared them at night and hidden them away with the connivance of Sheila? No. She was ready to cook our supper in our presence and claimed that she could do it even faster!

The next day was Sheila's time. She never left us alone even for a moment, and we were treated to breakfast, lunch and dinner with a clock-like precision. And in between, there were teas and coffees for the asking.

I did not understand till a few months later why Darwin and I had not quite grasped such uncommon proficiencies that Faith and Sheila so spontaneously wielded. We had, by habit, clung to our little rationalities in spite of several chinks in our psychical armours.

We had never seen Darwin shorn of his antievolution philosophy. Darwin plus Faith was a new equation clamouring for realization, it seemed. Sheila was non-committal on this point. Faith was a petite beauty, an epitome of grace, charm and love. She was perfect faith incarnate, the aura around her reflecting the contrastive opposite of what was fickle and false. She resonated to Sheila because of her responsive frequencies and to Darwin because of his integrity.

Being of little faith comparatively, I was rather apprehensive that Darwin might find his philosophy slipping through his fingers and end up like some of us believing blindly that man was moving towards perfection and human society was crawling, however slowly, towards utopia.

It was time for the Darwins to leave. It was sad to part. For two days, we felt 'lonely', Sheila and I. We had been so complementary before. Faith had done something? For two days after they had left, Sheila seemed to be preoccupied. I felt I was alone. On the first day, when I returned from office, I had to ring the doorbell twice. When I asked her the reason, the answer was a distracted face. On the second day, the things had returned to near normal. The door opened before I pressed the button. After our usual cream coffee, I tried to look into her mind. It was blank. I probed her gently over the next two days, but she would not open up. On the third day, when I was absorbed in a lilting Lata Mangeshkar melody, she suddenly rushed to me and burrowed her head into my chest, and then her arms tightened round my waist as though to prevent me from eluding her grasp. I framed her head in my hands and turned her face towards me. Tears were flowing in two uninterrupted streams. The anxiety on my face elicited a smile through her tears like a lightning flashing through raining clouds.

She missed Faith so intensely. She had reminded her of her beautiful over-loving mother, who had died saving her father from a fierce assault on the family by a band of marauders in her native village.

I wiped her tears, caressed her and kissed her, her eyes being all the time fixed on mine.

'Don't cry, my dear. I can understand your pain. And . . .'

'Yes, sir, you do so very well. And you are everything to me.'

'Everything?'

'Yes, you are my mother, my father, my lover, even my Faith, everything.'

'You rushed into me to meet every one of them?'

'Yes, yes.'

I looked into her eyes, with two glistening tear drops still lingering on their corners.

'I have always felt like that, though I did not cling to you like this every time I remembered my home.'

I stopped my tears with great difficulty.

'This time when I missed Faith along with my mother and father, my emotion swamped me. When I pressed myself into you and clasped you tightly, my love for you had unshakable Faith in it.'

To hide my tears, I smiled tenderly. She gently placed her palms on my eyes to coax the tears back.

The office work next day frightened me. I had never seen such a high column of files on my desk. Firoz told me that the work had accumulated because I had seemed to be 'much too preoccupied' to my officials. Before Firoz left, I felt a strange spurt of energy in me, which pushed the pendulum to the other side. By lunchtime, my desk was as clean as my mind.

When Firoz peeped in again a little before lunch, I was 'too unoccupied'.

Firoz left as soon as Ram Niwas called to say that some lady wanted him to put her through to me. I routinely said yes and had a bit of a jolt when I heard Kapila's rather harsh voice at the other end. She was still 'willing' to give up her life of crime and join me as my 'faithful' wife! I controlled my temper for a while to let her say her say uninterruptedly. Her words and voice changed from rational to emotional to frantic. My impassive response was a red rag to the dormant bull in her, which got enraged and charged towards me. The superman in me took it by the horns and hurled it back through the air. It was much too mauled to rise and charge back.

The very next day, there was another unexpected call. The caller identified himself as Manmohan Desai and wanted to be put through to me without delay. But to my great annoyance, this fellow was actually Rajneesh. He was 'very keen' to meet me. He 'would not survive' unless I 'granted' him permission to come and see me. No, he had not escaped from prison. It was obvious, however, that he was planning to escape before long. He was mentally prepared to receive my outburst. The more angry I got, the more pleading and flattering his voice became. In sheer disgust, I warned him not to cross the barrier of the bars and banged the telephone.

It was not a coincidence that Kapila and Rajneesh phoned me one after the other. They were either in regular touch through their jail touts or were in the same jail and planning their next devilish move. I did what I could through my police contact to ensure that they did not escape to freedom.

EIGHT

One Saturday afternoon, I was in for a series of big surprises. I received unprecedented commendation from my boss for the work I had done in the last few months. And when I went home that evening, bigger surprises were waiting for me on my desk. One was a huge cheque from my publisher: my *Structures for Social Evolution* had been on the best-seller list for the second consecutive year! The second surprise was a beautifully got out slim volume, titled *The Structures for Antievolution.* The blurb was extremely striking. I eagerly thumbed back to the title page to find out the name of the author. It was Robert Darwin! I had missed it because it was printed in an unusually fine font size.

He must have been writing it for over a year. But why had he hidden this fact from me and persuaded Faith too not to talk about it. To spring a surprise upon us? Or to forestall my objection to his authoring a book, which was an apparent antithesis of mine? No. He knew me too well to fear that.

I finished reading the book by Sunday evening. Most of the time when I was reading it, Sheila made it a point to sit by me as though to take in the contents by a process of osmosis, if not by a kind of psychical transmission. Strangely enough, when the reading was over, she did not ask me any question. But I did want to talk about the book and when I started to attempt an exposition of its main points, she reacted as though she had read the book before me.

Anyway, the structures that this book mainly expounded had no connection with the structures for social evolution that I had propounded in my book. The first important structure was Religion, and the second was Plutocracy. These were the hubs of all ancillary systems and structures, which did not matter much on their own. He, therefore, focused on the roots and stem rather than waste time on the stalks and leaves. "Religion is the most fundamental form of politics. The number of its followers is its brute strength: the larger the number of followers of a particular religion, the greater its bargaining power and manoeuvrability against other religions."

Marx's 'opium of the masses' was a rather incomplete, if not shallow, exposition, which implied that these doped or opiated masses could be 'ultimately' woken up. Robert Darwin's 'religion', on the other hand, sent one and all, not just the unthinking masses, to sleep for ever. It pre-doomed everybody at birth to antievolution, or regression to a kind of social atavism.

"Its grip is so strong that nobody once in it can ever escape it. It rakes in more victims and lets go none. The result is the present-day inner darkness in spite of the powerful outer lights that sometimes dazzle everyone.

"Even the blind can see the symptoms of blind faith that religion has spawned. A tooth relic of one Bhagwan is worshipped as a sure way to salvation; a hair relic of another Bhagwan is preserved as the most precious possession of human civilization. There are virgin holies having immaculate conceptions, and worthy saviours rising after they are well dead and making definite promises to come back one day. There are exalted gods incarnating as ideal men and sometimes even as animals to save the good and destroy the bad.

"Imagined forms of God—animals, half-animals, inanimate objects—are imbued with divine powers and worshipped in a most abject manner. Most dreadful and grisly forms of man's surreal imagination—a revengeful god disembowelling a sinful human, a most horrible-looking, bloodthirsty goddess mangling a cruel antisocial and lapping up their warm blood with her gory tongue—are taken as incarnations of justice-dispensing powers of the Almighty.

"Small-time 'saints' are worshipped alongside the traditional gods. Actors are deified and worshipped blindly in specially raised temples; dreadful criminal politicians are apotheosized as gods and receive floral tributes from their prostrate acolytes; and big-time politicians are eulogized in most obsequious doggerels, called *chaleesas*.

"With the result that man is now a mere robot, programmed to perform certain functions and utter pre-recorded words. And what will the forms of Religion, which are thirsty for each other's blood, do except to cause endless bloodshed and destruction? So, we have blood and gore everywhere. All human skills are used to invent more and more powerful means of killing the followers of rival religions. The more 'kafirs' they blast out of existence, the easier it is for the 'blasters' to enter Paradise!

"What you call the 'clash of civilizations' is in essence the clash of these bizarre religions. The clash, therefore, cannot end until these religions come to an end. Since this does not seem likely, man's evolution towards a better race, much less towards a perfect race, is a near impossibility."

The second structure Darwin discussed and documented was Plutocracy. This was the only form of political structure that had ruled over men since times immemorial. All the other forms of rule were either its variants or colourful charades to camouflage its glaring inequity and indefensibility. I quote below a relevant passage from the book:

"Since human beings began to think clearly and live in groups, the rich have always ruled the poor. This went on for a long time. Long enough for humans to begin to be born programmed to be rulers and the ruled, to be tyrants-exploiters and willingly exploitable victims. For long periods of time, we had big feudal lords and their tribute-paying chieftains. Men were evolving only biologically; socially, they were being stunted in a systematic way.

"These feudal structures in good time or bad led to the so-called national states and absolute hereditary monarchies. These absolute monarchs became absolute tyrants over time, and with the help of a handful of cynical and mad henchmen reduced their subjects to literal slaves, whom they bought and sold, raped, maimed and killed at will. However, no situation, good or bad, can prevail for ever. History with its inherent dialectical inevitability heaved heavily through the inertness of total human subjugation and threw up revolutionaries and thinkers. There was a shimmer of light in the horizon, and we had a few 'enlightened' monarchies and later even some new-fangled things, called 'democracies'. Naked force, which was no longer a practical strategy, gave way to a clever orchestration of 'people's governments'. But far from being people's governments, they are the most treacherous forms of plutocracy till date. Have you ever seen a poor person or a group of poor persons ruling over people? Money and muscle are the real rulers and will remain so till another revolution heralds a still more clever, treacherous polity.

"Feudal and monarchical structures were ruthless exploiters of common people, but they seldom claimed that they were ruling over them to better their lot, much less to lead them to perfection or even a higher state of evolution. But our present-day constitutional monarchies and democracies are booby-traps. People are told day in and day out that they are being led across all hurdles to a virtual paradise, a state of equality and plenty, where enslavement and starvation will have vanished into the pages of history. But what they actually get in return for their valueless votes are broken promises, worse starvation, still worse enslavement.

"If we still delude ourselves into believing that people are progressing towards a better state of evolution and should one day end up as supermen, we are either idiots or damn fools."

Some other parts of the book, especially those that dealt with comparisons between the Neanderthal man and our 'great twentieth-century Man', made an equally depressing reading, but the part I have quoted above forms, to my mind, the book's central core and easily takes the cake.

I called Darwin to congratulate him on publishing such a well-researched, well-written book. However, the tone of my voice did not quite match my words. A palpable degree of depression in my voice did not depress him even slightly, and he thanked me for my nice words like a seasoned politician.

Sheila's comment on this was rather hard-nosed. He had a right to his point of view, she said, as we had. He had, in fact, a greater right, she added, especially because he had been working hard for years to propound a theory.

PART FOUR

ONE

Robert Darwin's image in my mind had always fluctuated between good and ungood. After his *Structures for Antievolution* had stopped raising dust in my mind and kind of stabilized, I seemed to veer to the view that his attitude to Religion was, after all, not so nihilistic as I had thought immediately after reading his book. When, later on, I was reading his graphic description of 'honour' killings, which he preferred to re-designate as Religion-induced 'sacred' killings, my constant reaction was that he was overreacting to hammer out his theory. But now I was rather inclined to believe that his angle of looking at things was not too negative, if not quite objective.

October was a month of 'sacred' killings, it seemed. The media were in full spate, writing and talking about colourful killings in nauseating detail. Initially, I thought they were exaggerating and sensationalizing beautiful girls' murders to transform them into great copy for their publications. But, no, these things were actually happening in substantial numbers in large areas in India and Pakistan. Religion had clear precedence over biology like man's all other 'great' creations have come to have over God's 'humble' creations!

Reportage varied from the exciting to the melodramatic from publication to publication. Certain reports in ghetto tabloids and sometimes even in highbrow journals bordered on the lurid. A 'respectable' broadsheet reported the gruesome murder of a beautiful Muslim girl at Moth, a village near Meerut, but could not resist the temptation of making it like a scene from a horror novel. I went there with Firoz to see for myself what had actually happened. A 16-year old

Sania Khan had her throat cut by her father, Javed Khan. She had been meeting a Christian boy from Sardana. Javed Khan became so disgusted and distressed by her 'dishonourable' conduct that he put a gag over her mouth and stabbed her 10 times. She bled to her death and was secretly buried in an unused cemetery far from the village.

'Honour' killings were being reported from some Western countries as well. Nuziat Mirza, a student from south London, was found strangled in her house. Her husband, who reportedly killed her for her 'emancipated' views and ways, was believed to have fled to Pakistan.

Reports of such killings remaining excellent copy for several newspapers, many horror stories from Pakistan enjoyed the first page status for more than a month. Most of them were disgusting to the extreme, though repetitive in terms of the violence perpetrated upon beautiful young girls and the outrage it caused among the 'liberated elite'. The notion of honour was being invoked as a justification for such horrible murders. Eighteen-year old Tasleem Shah, a Sunni Muslim near Islamabad, offended her great family honour when she fell in love with a Shia Muslim boy. Her brother, Shabir Hussain, had no option to retrieve his family reputation but to murder her in a most gruesome way. He ran her over in his new Merc, reversed over her body and sped forward, crushing her to gory pulp. To cleanse his conscience of the impure blood, he drove his bleeding car to a nearby mosque, parked it outside and went in to say his *namaz-e-janazah*.

In Islam, a woman cannot divorce her husband. Rukhsana Naz, 20, had hoped for a divorce from her beast of a husband, who was drunk most of the time. Seven months pregnant, she wanted to marry her lover. The family was so outraged that her brother strangled her with a piece of plastic flex while her sweet mother held her down.

Honour killings were certainly not a new social phenomenon. Numerous hapless young women and men had been killed over the ages to save family and community honour. The difference is that the media 'now' needed lots of grist to their mill, but 'then' the media were practically non-existent, and history was reticent in favour of the honour-saving forces.

These killings and many others I saw reported in the media made me sympathize more and more with Robert Darwin's point of view. History is witness to the fact that more than half the bloodshed in the world was caused by Religion and more than half the social evils and superstitions would not be afflicting us today if Religion had not come into existence. I am adducing history because it is the least biased of all our social constructs. Out of the numerous social evils that Darwin listed, I cite here just one example, which he discussed under the title 'Vrindavan's Widows' and traced back to the vagaries of Religion. Young and middle-aged widows rejected by their families travel from all corners of the country to Vrindavan in search of hope. In this 'paradise', they are regularly exploited physically and made to chant Krishna's name day in and day out in return for a princely sum of three rupees and 200 grams of rice per day. And you have to look at their glazed faces and soulless chants to see for yourselves how disillusioned these things are with their paradise.

Darwin's second structure made me sympathize with him even more. That every form of government is ultimately Plutocracy is beyond all rational question. Those who have the means have the muscle to rule. And this is more true of democracy than of any other form of government. Democracy, in fact, is the worst form ever, since it is the most treacherous form. It does the opposite of what it professes to be doing. Vote politics absolutely negates what it is supposed to achieve theoretically: you need money to buy votes; you need more votes to retain power and amass money; you need obscene amounts of money in your coffers to buy votes perpetually to retain power down your dynastic line; and, all the time, you discreetly call it people's rule to ward off as long as possible those 'predatory' kings and queens of yore.

Darwin's book took some time to be noticed by the media. But once it had been noticed, it got wide publicity. Generally, for the wrong reasons. It was no doubt praised by the so-called intellectual elite, who some critics called 'mavericks'. But this little praise was overwhelmed by the massive ridicule the book was subjected to. Critic after critic condemned it and called its author all kinds of sophisticated names: a cynic, a nihilist, an iconoclast, a crackpot, a psychopath.

But the more the book was denigrated, the higher it climbed the best-seller list. Darwin became a celebrity and was adjudged by a mass media agency, called *The Arbiter,* the 'most notorious celeb' of that decade.

I felt very bad, thinking that Darwin's book deserved anything but this treatment. I called him and he talked to me as if nothing had happened. All the same, I wanted him to come over. Faith was very keen to see us, and thus they were with us at the weekend.

Faith held Sheila in such a long embrace that both Darwin and I suspected an unending supernatural communication going on between them. Disengaged, they heard us talking about the view the press had taken of the book. Darwin was absolutely unfazed, and so were Faith and Sheila. For a moment, I felt so left out—among the initiated. Why did I not believe like him and the two spiritualists or clairvoyants that the works of this kind are universally condemned initially? Despite momentary chagrin, I felt greatly relieved that Darwin's perspective on antievolutionary structures had not been disturbed at all by the whole body of savage diatribes against his book.

The four of us lived like a wonderful single family. Darwin was to work on a kind of epilogue to his *Structures* in some of the Delhi ghettoes. But his work looked incidental to his desire to stay with us for a few days. We enjoyed every moment of our togetherness in a state of unbroken bliss. I did not need to take leave. It suited Darwin and me to be out in the day, attending to our duties. When we were back in the evening, we were back to our paradise, the two ladies receiving us like angels waiting in it. We were together all the time and yet tea, coffee and meals were ready to be served at the right time. For brief moments during this great togetherness, I was befuddled by an overdose of bliss. So much so that I found the whole atmosphere unreal, rather surrealistic. I could not decide during certain moments who was who: Faith became indistinguishable from Sheila; and Darwin looked a wide-eyed seer scanning my soul.

During my normal moments, I enjoyed our four-sided chat. I had a feeling I was speaking more than anybody else. Darwin spoke less and said more. Sheila spoke only when addressed, and occasionally when her intervention was unavoidable. Faith's part was most spontaneous: she spoke most naturally as if cued by her role in our play.

Suddenly, Faith stepped out of the play to tell us something important. It was about Rajneesh. He had almost succeeded in escaping from jail. She had come to know about this piece of jailbreak and prevented it! She assured us that he would not be allowed to leave his prison cell until he had reformed himself and resolved to live a normal life.

She told us about Kapila also. She had bribed her way out of the jail. The jailer came to know about it within an hour and had her re-arrested and put behind bars. When she was caught, she was on her way to Rajneesh's prison. Faith assured us she would not find it easy to escape again. She would keep an eye on her. In fact, she had already paid her a 'visit' to understand her situation and read her mind better.

We 'lived' with the Darwins for several days even after they had left. Apart from their aura permeating the flat, we had moments and words hung everywhere. We heaved them up into our mouth like cows and chewed and rechewed them till we squeezed fresh kinds of *rasa* out of them. Faith had scripted a new meaning of faith for me. Sheila could not disagree, but she had a better take on her. Love, she said, summed up Faith better: love, in her view, was inclusive of and richer than faith. And now it was my turn not to disagree.

I am now saying something which I would not believe if somebody else said it: The more we missed the Darwins, the more the two of us complemented each other. We had never needed and enjoyed each other's company so much. Love is nurtured by faith, and Faith had given wider and richer meaning to our love. Earlier on, Sheila had, perhaps, known me inside out, but I had had only occasional glimpses of her mind; but now I had clearer peeps into her, though I could not sustain them beyond a few seconds.

We agreed that the Darwins had enriched us qualitatively. Thus, the reciprocity bug began to bite us. To enrich them, we wanted to go behind them. Initially, I had thought only Faith was an unknown quantity in respect of her past. But I soon realized that I did not know quite a chunk of Darwin's life either, especially the part which antedated my first encounter with him all of 20 years before.

As we were busy resurrecting the dead part of the Darwins, we struck against an unexpected stratum of hard rock: a horror of a serendipity. Elizabeth welled up in our minds. Why had she abandoned Darwin? And why in the first place had he left or 'rejected' Faith in favour of her? And Elizabeth did not just pop up in our minds; she actually materialized outside our minds as well, in our solid physical world, in real flesh and blood!

I had just closed the door behind me on my return from office when I heard the doorbell ring. Sheila did not let me turn back. She had, perhaps, expected the unexpected guest and was at the doorstep in a minute. She let the stranger in and instantly sensed it was Elizabeth. My eyes blinked very fast to recognize a face that I thought I had seen somewhere. Without waiting too long for my blinking to slow down to its normal pace, Sheila introduced her to me. Shortish and shrunken, Elizabeth stood before me trembling and breathing rather heavily as though somebody had been chasing her. Two dried tear-streams showed up clearly on her wrinkling cheeks. Her hair bun had opened and her long black hair was still in a state of unfurling. I motioned her to a chair lying behind her. Sheila had brought a glass of water. She stood up, took it from the plate very respectfully and gulped it at one go. As Sheila left to fetch her some more water, she slumped back into the chair. When Sheila returned, she rose again. I motioned for her to sit down. We were in the little lounge between the kitchen and the drawing room. Sheila sat down on my right, facing her directly. She was reading the vibes of conflict sweeping through my mind. Since Elizabeth was Darwin's 'enemy number one', I was not too sure whether we should keep her with us even for a few minutes. Sheila set my doubts at rest, and I was very clear now as to what we would do to her.

Sheila knew now how to go 'behind the Darwins'. Suddenly, there were steaming cups of cream coffee in front of Elizabeth and me since Sheila was on a half day's fast. The very first sip of coffee orientated her to Sheila's face.

'How are you feeling now, Elizabeth?' asked Sheila in a tone of voice that would make even a dumb person speak.

'I'm better, thank you. It was very kind of you both.'

'How is it that you have come to us? To strangers' house?'

'No, Mr Verma is not a stranger. He was one of Robert's close friends.'

'What's your problem right now?' I asked. 'Is there something we can do?'

'Yes, you can, Mr Verma. Some very dangerous criminals of a powerful gang are chasing me. I've barged in here to request you to save my life. Can you . . . ?'

Of course, we'll save your life. But, first, we'd like to know a few things about you.'

'I'll tell you everything, Mr Verma.'

'This will help me to help you, but not for ever. As soon as you step out of this house, these criminals might waylay and kill you. So, unless you determine to give up their company . . .'

'That's why I'm here, Mr Verma,' she said very pleadingly. 'I want to turn over a new leaf, but these gangsters would not let me . . .'

She broke down in the middle of her sentence. A fresh glass of water helped her to get over her choked voice. She was trying to resume her explanation when I interrupted her. I was not quite convinced of her intention and, therefore, wanted to ask her a few more questions.

'You've been a criminal by choice,' I said in the tone of a judge. 'Nobody forced you into a life of crime, did they?'

'That's true, Mr Verma. I wouldn't say I'm innocent.'

'Then, why do you want to turn over a new leaf now, after so many years of association with the underworld?'

'I've failed there utterly. Crime isn't in my blood. I've suffered too long and too much. My haggard face, my anguished mind, my tatters, through which you can peep into my mind, my heart and my soul, are witness to my intention.'

'I'm not too sure there. Anyway, what'll you do when you've got rid of your mafia?'

'I'm not quite clear about that, Mr Verma. I think I can hide in some *Nari Niketan* or somewhere, and after the things have cooled, I could take up a small job and live on my own.'

'I'm told you wanted to go back to Robert and even threatened him with dire consequences if he refused to take you back.'

'I'm very sorry about that. That's history now.'

'But you still pester him with nasty phone calls, and send him threats even now.'

'No, that's not true, Mr Verma. I haven't called the Darwins for months now. I know he's happy with Faith and would not accept me back. And, to be fair to him, I don't think I have any right to reclaim my old place.'

I did not have any more questions to ask. I felt a ring of sincerity in her words, and yet my eyes were scanning her face for any sign or trace of deception hiding behind her skin. As she was waiting for my reply, I caught a look in Sheila's eyes, signalling that she would not mind our helping her to get out of her dark and dangerous world.

She was to stay with us for two days. I went to office as usual. I did not fear for Sheila, though I put her on full alert despite her disarming confidence. In the few hours of my absence during these two days, she was able to gather everything about Elizabeth in respect of her life before and after she had run out on Darwin.

She came of very poor parents. Her father was a drunk, and her mother was, therefore, obliged to do odd chores in their neighbours' homes to earn for the family. She had two sisters and one brother. Good education was out of the question when even two square meals were a serious problem. Being the eldest, she was expected to look after her siblings and help her mother with the household work. She was too sensitive for her years, and the family misery began to impinge upon her too hard, too soon. Her mother was a pitiable little creature, much too overworked and starved and ill. She just could not bear her condition as well as the plight of her brother and sisters, and one day she just burst out and held her father squarely responsible for the misery. He had already sold away the little family property to buy his daily quota of booze, and now he was planning to dispose of the little house they were living in. The head of the family could not take the little squirt shouting at him. He charged at her with a little club he always kept by his side to scare away the street dogs. She escaped, but her helpless mother bore the brunt and bled to her death in hospital. The old drunkard got seven years in prison, and our poor Elizabeth was left in charge of the family. She had to leave school, but she would not in any way let her little sisters and brother drop out.

This is how her real struggle began, which sowed the seeds of crime in her. A young handsome Christian boy tried to befriend her. Casual visits became regular. Bouquets and goodies started coming in to suit the different occasions in the house, and then the inevitable happened . . . She needed money very badly to run the household, and when it was offered, she capitulated. After that day, there was no going back. The young man was not only a philanderer but a crime-prone hoodlum. He had seen in her a potential for earning himself big profits. That is why he had invested in her. He engineered a scheme, which was a combination of blackmail, temptation, glimpses of a happy future. Only in a matter of two years, this clever spider web had become a dragnet from which only a mythological hero could escape.

So, when she married Robert Darwin, she was more than half-buried in the dark world of crime, though she still had surviving in her a desire to escape that world and serve him with dedication. The underworld rule is: 'once a criminal, always a criminal'. Thus, however hard and persistently she tried to cut herself off from the mafia, she could not succeed. The dragnet closed in on her, and she was hauled back into the abyss. She certainly had 'not run out on Darwin'. Her fatal fault was that she had not shared her past with him—for fear of being misunderstood and abandoned.

Sheila did not find any big holes in the story, though certain bits and pieces here and there, in her view, seemed to have been glossed over or slightly exaggerated.

She was 'more or less sure' now that Elizabeth's repeated attempts to get in touch with Darwin, and later on her frantic calls, which were taken as threats, were sincere, desperate attempts to escape the mafia and reform. When I raised my eyebrows at her *more or less sure,* she confirmed with her look that she was fully convinced.

Elizabeth had little hope left of Darwin or somebody else rescuing her. So, she gave up on him and gave her masters the impression that she was reconciled. In point of fact, she was biding her time, for momentary flickers of hope did occasionally throw light on her mind's secret corners. On several occasions, she could have easily escaped to freedom, but she had no safe place or person to go to. When she thought of me, she knew she was taking a risk, but a risk that was worth taking.

For the two days she was with us, she did not betray any desire to disturb Darwin. She knew very well that he had been living a life of bliss with Faith. But she wanted both me and the Darwins to help her get out of her hell. When Sheila spoke to Darwin on the phone and explained the whole thing in her own special way, he at once agreed and even suggested a practical way out. She was to be hidden away in a remote unknown *Nari Niketan* for a reasonable length of time, until it would be feasible to rehabilitate her. Sheila was after all Sheila. She even made her talk to Darwin, who said a few morale-boosting words, and Elizabeth thanked him tearfully without any rancour or bitterness in her tired voice.

TWO

"Those who say that India is a poor country are perfect idiots and can, therefore, be forgiven." This is the opening sentence of a celebrated industrialist, Padamshree Vinay Kumar's welcome speech at his son's wedding ceremony at Pune. The bridegroom, Shravan Kumar, was a very finicky and fastidious young man, who had condescended to enter into a wedlock after sampling a large number of girls. Vinay Kumar was extremely happy that the wild animal had agreed to be domesticated at long last. There were twin advantages in this: the bride would bring a dowry worth a hundred crore odd rupees, and the groom would be hopefully obliged to attend to the family business.

In fact, he was so pleased that he could not but share his pleasure with everybody present under the huge marquee. His expansive style of speech was a verbal equivalent of his wide open arms to embrace the whole country. Thus, his personal pleasure overflowed its banks and tended to inundate the whole nation: "India is a rich country, a very rich country indeed. We have made great progress since 1947. We had only half a dozen truly rich individuals then, but we have scores of them now." The response was a long hand, which continued until the industrialist raised his benedictive right hand to quieten his guests. "This poverty-line concept is nonsense, which these politicians keep on moving up and down to suit their electoral requirements. It suits them wonderfully to keep large numbers below this line. But to keep public attention off this malaise of poverty, they sometimes hold us, the rich, responsible and tighten the screws on us." The gesture of his right hand revolving clockwise to imitate the action of tightening a screw made people break into a roar of derisive laughter. "As birds of a feather flock or fly together, so riches attract riches and poverty attracts poverty." There was a loud general chorus of approval, and from a sophisticated corner of VIPs, a remark of highly discerning appreciation: 'how logical!' All that he had said constituted a number of highly quotable dicta, but the most memorable one was this: "If you let more and more people become rich and remain rich, they will attract more and more rich people. Thus, when the number of the rich increases, the number of the poor will decrease automatically. This is inevitable logic, which our politicians must appreciate if they . . ." The rest of the words were drowned in the sky-rending ovation, which started like a sudden burst but never seemed to end.

Vinay Kumar wanted more people to become rich, thinking that a strong flow of riches would sweep poverty and squalor under the carpet and take the heat off the people like him. He certainly would not like anybody to dislodge him from the top slot in the hierarchy of rich Indians. To make this point unambiguously clear to his rivals, he often made a powerful statement to this effect in everything he did or contemplated.

So, his son's wedding made a history of sorts. Never, perhaps, had any wedding been so grand and never perhaps would any wedding be so splendid. He got a replica of the Amber Fort near Jaipur built to serve as the facade of the marriage *pandal*, which cost him all of 80 crore, just a fraction of the total amount he wanted splurged on the wedding. The most lavish ceremony of all time, it cost him 500 crore, far less than he actually wanted to spend. Nothing better or more extravagant could have been done in spite of some of his brilliant financial whiz kids tapping all their inventiveness to burn money. The wedding was followed by celebrations that lasted 11 days. The festivities were based on themes, one full day having been assigned to each theme. The most memorable of these themes was a film stars' night. A hundred Bollywood and other film stars had been invited. Just the invitation cards to these gods and goddesses had cost around 25,000 rupees each. Next in order of the cost were corporate personalities' night and the fashion designers-and-models' day.

When the wedding celebrations were finally over, Vinay Kumar got some time to relax, but he was not satisfied. He thought he had not been able to make his statement loud enough. A fear lurked in his mind that his record might be broken soon after his lifetime, if not earlier. He should have spent a few hundred crore more. His fear was not quite unfounded, keeping in mind the story doing the rounds those days of a rape-and-murder-tainted minister owning a wrist watch worth over 25 hundred thousand rupees.

A highbrow national paper went gaga over the splendour of the celebrations and regretted that most of these hugely rich industrialists were such misers and did not spend even a fraction of what Vinay Kumar had spent. The celebrated editor was of the firm view that even if a dozen of these rich people loosened their purses and spent their moneys a little more liberally on such ceremonies and celebrations, the quality of life in this country would be a lot different.

This editor was lampooned by a few leftist papers and some other publications, which still kept up the charade of a 'socialist' viewpoint. But the majority of the mainstream publications heaped praise on this 'daring' editor. One article in *Our Nation* wrote a fulsome eulogy on 'the guts of this celeb of great integrity'. Another, called *The Elite*, described him as the 'Prince of Indian journalism'.

Darwin had been amused by a highly readable report of Vinay Kumar's eleven-day bash. Such 'retrograde moronic nits' had always been beneath his contempt and worried him not a whit. But this 'stinking fart of an editor' really got his goat. He was so enraged on reading the report that if he had come across this man at that moment, he would have knocked his dirty brains out. He told us on meeting us a few days later that he had never blown the lid so high even during his most rebellious youthful days.

He was on a professional visit to Delhi. We were together for two whole evenings. When I brought in the subject of Vinay Kumar's blooming bash, he only wrinkled his eyebrows in disgust and made a grimace as though he would throw up. Sheila was not clear either why I wanted to talk about such a disgusting character, though unlike Darwin her attitude was that even such people had a right to live. But I was rather keen on engaging Darwin.

'Don't you believe, Robert, that man has been 'disevolving' since the time of Charles Darwin?'

'Yes, I do, very much.'

'Then, why on earth do you negate your own view?'

'How do I . . ? I don't really understand.'

'Well, this Vinay Kumar is a good example of degeneration or your antievolution, isn't he?'

'Yes, he very much is.'

'Then, you shouldn't be so hard on him.

'Now, this is sophistry, my dear Vigyan. I only hold that human beings are degenerating; I'm not obliged to like or love the likes of Vinay Kumar; I'm not supposed to approve of decay, am I?'

'No. But if your antievolution is inevitable, why fret about it?'

'I've never said it is inevitable; I've said it's been going on contrary to the old man's evolutionism. I "fret" about it because I don't unbelieve that it can be delayed or even prevented.'

'So?'

'So, I'll do whatever I can. If I can't act by way of launching an activist movement or agitation, I can at least express myself against it loudly and clearly.'

In spite of what the likes of Robert Darwin had to say or do, Padamshree Vinay Kumar's unpoor country had to go on the way it had been going, if not at a better pace. The margins of society were expanding. We had ample space for such expansion. The more such vanity- and luxury-spenders needed or wanted to spend, the more helpless and hapless people would work for them in order to earn their survival pittance.

The poverty line was moving 'down' as more and more marginers' attrition threshold was dropping, thus obliging them to accept whatever labour for whatever wages. This is what Vinay Kumar actually meant by his most popular dictum. "If you let more and more people become rich . . ."

Till the advent of Vinay Kumar brand of 'dynamic neo-capitalism', Indian economy had long laboured under the airy-fairy notion that by a random redistribution of social, legal and employment opportunities and privileges, the poverty line could be gradually brought down to zero and a kind of socialist structure could be put into place. But, somehow, things went seriously wrong. The poverty line mounted to the half-way mark. The economy choked with the tightening noose of controls round its neck, leaving the country gasping for a breath of fresh air. Vinay Kumar's predecessors had been a prescient lot and had seized the opportune moment in a most perspicacious way. Soon the media were at their feet, and a movement towards the restructuring of the economy began. It worked like a hall of mirrors: one person imitated another, and one party mirrored another, which mirrored the other, which mirrored the other . . .

The noose was thrown into the garbage bin. Powerful currents of fresh air rushed in. The economy was now being liberalized and the means of production and distribution were being privatized. It was now a different kind of choking, like a child choking on too much milk being forced down its throat by its overloving mother. Vinay Kumar brand of neo-capitalism was taking this laissez-faire to its 'logical' conclusion.

Darwin could not decide whether he should be sad or happy. Anyway, it was not a matter of making a rational choice. Instinctively, he was sad, very sad like us, like all sensible people. Obviously, he could not rejoice that the society was living out his social philosophy to the full. He never wanted Charles Darwin's human beings to degenerate, to retrogress. His theory of antievolution, though rationally extrapolated from the social trends and practices he had dispassionately observed and pondered, was more in the nature of a stern warning to them to tread carefully so that they could stop short of the precipice.

He was so depressed that evening that he wanted to 'freeze to a weed or a clod'. He needed Faith around immediately! Faith, perhaps, sensed this at once, but she could not grow wings. Luckily, his depression did not last for more than an hour, and we were able to retrieve the evening. Sheila played Faith besides playing herself. There were eats and drinks galore. There were poetry, songs and witty anecdotes till late in the night. And before we woke up in the morning, the doorbell rang persistently and Faith appeared like an angel to re-rehabilitate our faith in things.

Although Robert seldom needed any crutches to be himself, yet Faith's presence did make him sound a little more than normal, that is, a little more than normally cheerful. I did not have to make any effort to persuade him to stay with us for another day or so. It was a rare joy for the four of us to be together again. There was a thorough give-and-take. A perfect understanding. A full communion. No problem remained a problem. Elizabeth's contorted face peeped from her Bikaner

Women's Home and soon waxed wrinkleless. Kapila's malicious scowl loomed from her cell and morphed into a simple smile in a minute. The problem was we were unbelievably without a problem, and thus we two, the pragmatists, started to have suspicions! Then the two clairvoyants looked at us, and the suspicions dissolved. And then we had no problems, no solutions; there were just us and life and the world at large.

As it happened once before, this time too when we parted, each one of us was different from what we had been, for each one of us had more of the others in us than before.

THREE

This time, surprisingly, the Indian Cultural Fair was being held in the Exhibition Maidan under the aegis of *India Yesterday and Today.* Hall No. 11 was the venue. The popular culture part had been sponsored by the Sheetal Group of Industries and the semi-classical and classical music and dance part by the West Indian Society of Culture.

A time-slot of three hours had been assigned to each segment in the line-ups of programmes proposed for the two major categories. The organizers had carefully done a kind of market survey of the consumers' prevailing tastes, and the latter were, by and large, in favour of starting the fair with the popular culture part and being through with it before taking up the classical-semi-classical part. However, two senior members, whose voice could not be ignored, were opposed to separating them. So, it was decided that each day the popular culture items would be interspersed with the classical or semi-classical items. On the second day, the structure was like this: the programme would begin with a pop culture segment, go on to the classical or semi-classical segment and end with the former segment.

The first day began with a bang. The programme started with a Panjabi *bhangra* pop. The spectators mostly comprised young people below the age of thirty. Every pair of hands was clapping and every pair of feet was tapping in sync with the rhythmic beats of the bhangra, performed by Gurjeet Singh and his troupe of nine girls and eight boys. The fast varying rhythmic tempo with the lighting and other stage effects created a psychedelic mood in the first few rows, and the boys and girls there were on their feet, dancing like mad, forgetting that they were part of the audience rather than the artistes. The gruff male voice of Gurjeet Singh had such a sensual appeal to an exclusive group of highbrow girls in the middle of the left side of the auditorium that one could almost hear the sound of fish being fried. When the dance came to an end, there was a standing ovation lasting for several minutes. And, then, suddenly the performers were mobbed by a big crowd of frenzied fans, so much so that Gurjeet Singh had to be literally rescued by the security men.

After the interval, the curtain rose on a big Indipop performance. The first words were *aao muhabbat karlo*, *gar tum chaho to*, which meant 'Come and love me, if you want to love(.)'. The chief singer was a very sexy boy in a flashy costume. Choreographed by one Urmila Khan, the video part was provided by six boys and six girls. The boys were clad in tight black jeans and blood red shirts with black bow ties. The girls, of course, had stripped to their bare basics. The girls' pelvises gyrated and the boys' groins gravitated towards them. As the rhythm of the number quickened, the pelvic movements and the legs' locomotions naturally speeded up to keep pace. The refrain recurred after every two lines, sung on a slightly higher note and a shade faster. And at every recurrence of the refrain, the girls' bikini-clad pelvises lunged forward to meet the boys' protuberances, then moved backward and then revolved like neon lights on the marquee of a cinema.

'Superb! Marvellous! Wonderful! Wow! Come here, you lustful hotties! We're coming over, you lusty guys! Wait for us! Come to us!' These were the verbal responses heard above the high-decibel voices of the singers and their reverberations in the auditorium in the form of the re-echoing of the song, clappings and foot-tappings and seat-tappings. There were moments when one could not decide which was the more exciting of the two—the stage frenzy or the off-stage madness. Before the curtain went down, the dare-bare hotties were trembling in the steel grips of a few coercive hunks from the auditorium like a calf being ceremoniously *halaled.* It took the security men a good many minutes to rescue the victims and scare away the hoodlums.

The third item for the morning was a song in literary Urdu. It was being presented in typically pop rhythms, though it looked back on account of its good memory and resisted a rape on its chastity for a few moments before it finally gave in. Hamid Quraishi had changed over from the *ghazal* to the *qawwali* and finally to the pop style. Now he was a name in the field, and his name was enough to set the stage for any kind of song he could set to Indipop. He began slowly. His video, consisting of tastefully made-up girls and boys in minimalist costumes, had the entire hall going in raptures over them. The rhythm quickened slowly as though working up measuredly to an orgastic conclusion. The refrain of the song was: *jab kabhi chhedaa janoon ne deeda-e-khoonbaar ko*. A rather serious line was being sung with a progressively quickening pop beat. Hardly anybody could have understood the tenor of the words. None possibly had even the foggiest idea of what it was all about. They were just some anthropophonic sounds strung together, which, of course, had to denote or connote something to pass for words. Nor did the singers seem to be interested in them or their cohesiveness. They only wanted hooks to fix their rhythmic beats on.

The beats became faster and faster. Hamid's lips and limbs slogged to keep pace, and the words got slurred and then blurred to indistinguishable complexes of sound. The girls had become sensualities incarnate and the boys were melting in the heat of their frenzied gyrations.

The spectators, one and all, were a vortex of amorphous flesh and blood churning dizzily. Hundreds of wild youths had gatecrashed and there was a virtual spate of flesh and blood, drowning everything and everybody in its way. The security men, suddenly splitting from their psychedelic oneness with the mass of humanity, declared the show closed abruptly. The abrupt quietness and motionlessness was something like a sudden power breakdown, instantly shutting down every sound and movement.

There was an interval of one hour after this morning show. The post-lunch period of three hours was meant for a line-up of classical items, beginning with a vocal performance by Pandit Vasant Raj. When he began his warm-up *alaap* or prelude, there were about 50 people in the auditorium. A few more people came in as he was beginning to move on to the alaap set to *taal* in slow tempo. It was a difficult *raga*, and the transition from *vilambit khayal* to *drut khayal* took more time than expected in a normal classical vocal presentation. Quite a few listeners seemed to be enjoying this part, and some faces had brightened up, expecting that something really great was going to follow. The middle part of the raga was a marvel of vocal virtuosity, and the few connoisseurs in the front rows were in a state of ecstasy. But soon the atmosphere changed. One could hear a buzz of voices from some of the back rows. Some youths were talking in whispers. Either they had come in expecting some exciting songs or rhythms, or they had come in to scoff at the expected 'antics' or 'capers' of the vocalist. The connoisseurs were perturbed that their enjoyment was being marred by the noise behind them. The buzz had now really become a loud noise. The artist found it more and more difficult to continue. He was now reaching the next stage of his superb composition when there was a sudden fracas at the main door. A hundred odd youths broke the resistance of the security men and rushed in. They had with them two bagfuls of tomatoes and rotten eggs. The 50 youths that had formed the buzz crowd earlier joined them and tomatoes and eggs rained in torrents. Pandit Vasant Raj and his accompanists had nowhere to look to. They made for one of the side doors, and the audience were all up on their feet, appealing, cajoling, protesting. When a reinforcement of the security personnel arrived, the rioters had run out of their tomatoes and eggs and were now themselves running out to escape arrests.

The remaining part of the classical-semi-classical programme for that day was 'shelved'. But the afternoon pop-culture show was to start at 3 p.m. as scheduled. Meanwhile, a quick enquiry revealed that the disruption of the classical vocal was the result of a conspiracy on the part of two youth organizations that had set their face against such 'mindless, time-wasting, uncultured' programmes. These 'modernist' organizations and their ever-increasing followers had disturbed and stopped such 'silly' things at a number of places before, but had not attracted much publicity. The Exhibition Maidan Cultural Fair was a high-profile show, which assured them that their action here would prove to be a big blitzkrieg.

Before the afternoon show began, a quick agreement was thrashed out between the organizers and the modernists, according to which the time for the *classical-semi-classical* items was cut down to just two hours every day and that day's shelved program was cancelled.

The entire three-hour programme was divided between two items. The first was an unheard-of combination of Indi-pop, jazz and a kind of 'fancy-dress' reggae. Pop, jazz and reggae are not just forms of popular music with strong rhythms and rather simple tunes. They also present a spectacle that would seduce anybody's mind. The hall was full to more than capacity. Quite a number had 'standing seats' along the side walls and the middle aisle. The composite rhythm enthralled the audience. In between, swathes of them broke into raptures. At certain climactic turns, sections of them would suddenly stand up and clap vigorously. No external force was necessary to guide or control them. The performers remote-guided their responses and evoked their cheers and leers.

The leers remind me of the way our youthful spectators eyed their icons moving and shaking on the stage. If their eyes had been their sex organs, they would have ravished each one of the guys and 'gals' on the stage.

The guys wore jeans and shirts of different shades and shoes with heels of varying heights. But the girls appeared to be dressed for rampwalking rather than for dancing. Sometimes, they would be in such a formation as to present a virtual rampside view. One of these beauties sizzled in a kind of swimwear that left very little to the imagination; one was wearing bright red undies on top of sleek leather trousers; two of them flaunted really cool hot pants in lycra and spandex with brief halter tops; still another revelled in an aquamarine bikini with gold and silver embroidered motifs. One very tall girl was clad in an eye-catching backless gown, and two rather short ones were in off-shoulder tops and real mini skirts with broad red, black and blue floral patterns. But the one who stood out among all these ravishing seductions was a porn-star-type sizzler, who extemporized a kind of striptease every minute or so, generally when she happened to be in the front and within the straight eye-range of the front rows.

The rhythm quickened and voices rose in volume and pitch. The words had no meaning. The poor things stuttered and sputtered helplessly and unintelligibly in the overwhelming din of voices, drum beats, tappings and clappings: all sound and fury taken to its extreme. I had never seen such a synergy of give and take between artistes and their audience. Their relative storms and lulls coincided. When the girls on the stage sparkled and exploded, the youths in the audience burst into their high-voltage squeals of delight; when the guys on the stage gigged or boogied, the girls in the audience imitated their gods in their psychedelically induced dream sequences. When the show trailed to its end, the audience swooned into quietness. But, no, they were not yet satisfied. They wanted more and shouted 'encore'.

The performers were too tired to continue, and the time for the next item had been fixed days before. So, the organizers tactfully expressed their inability to respond to the encore cry. The tact had no effect, and some youths, who perhaps had never taken no to anything, started vandalizing furniture and stage property. The organizers had no choice but to be very strict this time and the vandals had to be thrown out by force. But, while going, they warned that they would not let the show go on. To avoid any more damage to the auditorium, the second and last item of the afternoon programme was cancelled.

The security arrangements were tightened for the next day. The first item for the morning line-up was a piece of comic theatre: a comic play enacted by cartoon characters. The actors and actresses were made into cartoons. A commonplace theme of a rich old man marrying a young woman was being presented as a grand idea. The aim was to ridicule the idea and thus the cartoon-like characters were most suited for it. But the whole scheme got out of hand, and vulgarity got the better of the comedy. Vulgarity of the type which would make any sensible person blush with shame, which therefore resulted in ridiculing the actors themselves rather than the idea they set out to scoff at.

Ironically, the response was positive. Most hands clapped to express their appreciation. One dandyish dude with a face suffused with attitude went on to the stage to even formally thank the performers for their 'great' performance.

The next item was of a type which had never been presented to any audience in the world before. It was a disco on a stage for an audience. For a disco, you cannot be an audience; you are present in it and you dance and you change partners.

But here two dozen professional dancers were discoing for the youthful audience and expected them to watch it quietly! Oh boy, there was a peaceful pandemonium! The entire auditorium turned into a disco room, or rather disco rooms. Almost all the boys and girls were dancing wherever they found the space. The squeeze necessitated by the obstructive topography of the fixed seats was a godsend for the boys and girls, who otherwise could never have approximated to one another so amorously. Of course, in the spaces where the seats were moveable and were not so conducive to cohesion, the discoers felt rather cheated. Anyway, these satisfactions and dissatisfactions apart, the stage disco and the participative auditorium disco were in a kind of sync seldom encountered among such a large population.

When the stage boogieing trailed off, the audience were still dancing. But the cessation of the tune made the dancing rudderless, and it gradually crawled to a clumsy halt. The doors suddenly opened as though the stoppage of the noisy movements had created a depression in the air pressure inside.

The authorities were now worried about the midday programme. The first item on the list was a classical instrumental. Ustad Shaukat Ali Khan was to present a rendering of *Yaman Kalyan* on the sitar. The hall was not exactly full, but it was not empty either. Among the audience were not only a few reputed musicians and music-lovers but also some mid-level highbrow VIPs. A couple of VVIPs also shone in a protected niche along the left wall.

The warming-up was reduced under instructions from the organizers. The Khan led the accompanists in style to the mid-point, where the rhythm was beginning to quicken a second time. The sweetness of the raga was ravishing, to say the least, and the audience were shaking as if it had touched the central nodes of their nervous systems. The Khan's own ecstasy went into his composition and held everybody in thrall. And, then, suddenly there was a hell let loose. Oops! the laxity of security at the main door. The glowering dudes and frowning glamorous girls would not let that 'stupid noise' go on under any circumstances.

The show, of course, had to stop. But along with this was stopped the Indian Cultural Fair. The hall was closed and the 'dirty' dudes and their 'cultureless' girlfriends were 'arrested' and respectfully dropped at their homes.

These pop-addicted, noise-loving modernists had come to know the line-up of the classical-semi-classical programme. The items that were to follow were two *ghazals* and a *thumri*. The ghazals were to be performed a la a classical raga tempered with a light-music touch. The thumri, of course, was to be presented in the style of a Begum-Akhtar thumri. The modernists were furious that the three precious hours were so 'callously being wasted on such silly items'. They threatened serious violence if they were not replaced by some 'sensible' items.

The press was at pains to perform a balancing act. A few highbrow publications criticized these 'vandals' and 'philistines' for their lack of taste, and at least two sophisticated editors strongly condemned them for their gross vulgarity. But, by and large, the media sympathized with them. After all, the so-called vandals wanted what was fashionable. The organizers had no business to show off their culture snobbery and impose their private aesthetic upon others. "Those who go against the trend of time are like those foolish swimmers who swim against the current." Paper after paper and channel after channel went on: blah, blah, blah!

The abandonment of the Indian Cultural Fair only highlighted the change that had been taking place over the Indian cultural landscape for over ten years. High culture was all but submerged under the flood of popular culture. One could only see its tiny tips over the surface like bubbles winking over a soap solution. The classical music was all but gone. Even the hugely popular semi-classical ghazal and a number of other serious, life-sustaining melodies had almost vanished, their remnants here and there serving only to stir nostalgic memories among the aging population. The classical dance was still there, protectively cloistered and aired on certain rare occasions, perhaps to reassure ourselves that we had once been 'cultured' human beings.

Even the popular culture had been progressively diluted. Those semi-classical dances, which had once formed the backbone of Indian films and held the average cine-goer in thrall, had all but disappeared. And those extremely lovable melodies sung by a Noor Jahan and a Lata Mangeshkar were now available only on those gramophone records or at best on those old-fashioned audiocassettes. The present regimen for our entertainment and emotional (and perhaps moral) edification consists in Indipop with its strong local and imported rhythms and combining song and dance and gymnastics and slea3ze into one composite 'art' form.

And when its juggernaut moves forward, it incites everybody to 'action': it excites and shakes and stirs the 'primordial slimes' of hate and horniness rather than sending its audience to a blissful state of peace and tranquillity like those classical melodies and movements.

When this great modernist change was beginning to raise its head, some 'visionaries' saw in it the beginning of the end of social harmony. But nobody heeded them. We are now all in an overcrowded countryside bus, blaring at us, at the highest decibel possible, a girl-boy song-dance-sex sequence, drowning the external sound of the ramshackle vehicle violently shaking on the bumpy non-road, and muffling the head-splitting internal noise and the *bidi*-smoke pollution. And yet those visionaries and their ilk strike us as obsessives and crackpots.

All complications of calibrated complexity gone, life at the level of culture has reduced to two elemental strands: noise and nostalgia. Noise of everything we say and do; nostalgia for what we used to say and do.

As after my earlier encounters with sociopolitical realities, I duly returned to Robert Darwin's theory after this India-Yesterday-and-Today experience as well. As on earlier occasions, this time too, I had a self-spat, one part of me enveloping my alter ego, materializing outside me and having a bellicose face-off. Earlier on, this kind of fight lasting for hours or even days was often mediated at some stage by Sheila the Great and finally ended in a reconciliation tilted in my favour. But, later on, this kind of spat moved more and more to the central point of the scale, until it was impossible to decide the issue. After that, once or twice, my alter ego had a clear edge over me. This was the point where Darwin's theory began to impress us and earn our recognition and even respect. Respect in the sense that it was our moral duty as civilized people to be open to viable and valid points of view.

This time round, our respect had more to do with the situation on the ground than our moral duty as civilized beings. Darwin was too much with us for a whole evening. Was it just a coincidence that he called that very evening? He did not say anything about the Exhibition Maidan happenings. Perhaps, because he was now far above those younger days when he used to arrogantly hammer his 'Didn't I say this(?)'. Sheila, however, thought he was either unaware of these happenings or just uninterested because of their repetitive character.

FOUR

Summer was gradually giving way to winter. I was in a true Sunday mood after more than a month. After a heavy lunch, I was feeling really sleepy. Sheila wanted to go out with a big shopping list. Instead of helping her, I just let go of myself. I could not have slept for more than three quarters of an hour when a big explosion shook the entire apartment building. I got out of bed in panic and rushed out into the foyer between four flats on our floor. My neighbours had also come out. Nobody knew anything until some urchins suddenly emerged from the lift cabin, agog with fun. They were amused to see anxious faces and sure that we were confused like those panicky 'idiots' outside the building. It was just a cracker, not a bomb or a blockbuster, which we thought must have blown up half of the city. The urchins giggled and we were all embarrassed that we had acted silly.

The 'bomb' heralded the advent of *Diwali*, the great pan-Indian festival of lights and sounds. Such a powerful bomb had never been a forerunner of this festival in the past. And, in any case, Diwali was still five days away. At a citizens' meeting held some three months before, it had been decided by a process of consensus that noise and pyrotechnic displays were to be brought down to the minimum level possible and to be confined only to the Diwali night. So, such a powerful explosion occurring not less than five days before the festival night was more than a rude shock even after we had come out of the panic that perhaps half the city had been reduced to rubble and we were about to be exploded to smithereens.

As we moved towards the dusk, there were more explosions—first sporadically and then continuously, first small crackers and then sky-rending bombardments, first the children going crazy and then their excitement-seeking parents. Half an hour into the evening, and the towers, houses, huts had morphed into garlands, festoons, embroideries of lights.

The next morning, a CP-based paper excitedly reported a 'scoop'. 102 people, mostly slum-dwellers and a few enfant terribles in the downtown areas, had been killed, and countless huts and about 20 houses had been burnt to ashes. Some calculated voices tut-tutted and a few important people even clicked their tongues in sympathy.

But the light and sound show was to continue to flourish from night to night and then from night to day-night. Diwali comes only once a year after all. It was impossible to enforce whatever tattered local rules or fuzzy national laws existed. Partly helpless and partly indulgent, our delicate and peace-loving aging population took the ear-splitting noise and blinding lights on the chin as they had been doing from Diwali to Diwali for years. But this time, things were to turn out to be different. We had made great progress in manufacturing our explosives, and by the time the Diwali night changed into dawn, the losses in terms of life and property had already run into billions. The people and their managers had taken all this in their great stride. *Chalta hai* was a great morale-booster. And this stoic attitude made this D-night the most unforgettable of all such nights in history. All of 2000 human beings had been burnt to cinders, never mind hundreds of houses and animals. *Chalta hai* was toned down a little, and some leaders, ministers and activists of high-profile NGOs went into huddles to plan for 'non-violent' Diwalis in future. The consensus emerging from these deliberations proudly formed the first page news in several newspapers. The main point in the recommendations was that we did not need any strict law to arrest the degeneration of the festival into the ruinous chaos that it had become; we only needed to be cajoled back into its pristine serenity and sacredness. If this did not work, then alone was a strict law to be enacted to restrain and regulate its celebration. The consensus had a strange footnote appended to it. It was in the form of a question, which a 'mad maverick' had asked while walking out in a huff. It was: 'how long would we try the "cajoling back" experiment?'

My *Structures for Social Evolution* had talked about the main Indian festivals. Two of the more important among them were *Holi* and *Diwali*. I had tried to evaluate them in respect of their contribution to social evolution. The crux was that they had been degenerating progressively and thus hampering social progress, if not negating it. When the book was published, it was criticized for being much too harsh on Indian festivals despite the fact that, as a whole, it had earned international acclaim.

In the wake of this historic Diwali, my book became the focal point for some academics and other intellectuals again. In fact, it had supplied some inspiration, if not statistical information, to the huddles in their effort to frame the recommendations they had made. These intellectuals, who chose to call themselves social scientists, were now discussing the Indian festivals, belonging to different communities and observed in different regions, in relation to social harmony. Sharply opposed views were expressed, which broadly divided into two categories. One view was that their fast deteriorating celebration created tensions in communal relations and, sometimes, even in regional equations or relations. The other view was that they did not contribute to any tensions whatever, that all of us should make the celebration of all festivals more and more harmless and meaningful, that we should all help revive some of those tribal and peripheral customs and festivals which were dying out and that we should all encourage inter-communal and inter-regional participation in all of them.

The first view stated what was happening on the ground and indirectly suggested that all the festivals should be banned if we wanted some unity to survive through the chaos of our bewildering diversity. The second view had it that all of these festivals should continue to be celebrated, in a better way as far as possible, to enrich this unity to fight chaos and achieve meaningful diversity. These two views could be possibly harmonized if the first could be taken as a diagnosis and the second as a remedy.

Robert Darwin saw some of these intellectuals using my book in Hyderabad. He had read it a few months after its publication but did not remember all of its contents. He read it again to collate the views propounded by these two categories of intellectuals and the perspective I had put forth in it. He was furious that these 'disingenuous guys' were bending my book to express their one-sided views like schoolboys at an inter-school debate. They should have tried to gain a proper perspective on my book before attempting to score over one another childishly. His reaction I found to be rather impetuous in view of the level of intellectual sophistication he had attained. We were on the line for more than 20 minutes, and when I told him mischievously that he was too harsh on them in order to glorify my book, he diverted his anger to me. When I put the receiver back, Sheila pinched me on the back of my neck and we had a hearty laugh.

We had not celebrated Diwali and Holi for several years, although I had not made any principled point against them as such in my book. Among other things, I had said that most festivals across the board had been over-ritualized and reduced to hulks that served no social purpose. They could have been refilled with meaning by us, but we had not done so. Sheila had been spiritually-oriented instinctively, from the beginning, and I had started to see things in a similar way soon enough. Spirituality in our case at least was not in any way opposed to rationality. In fact, it made us more rational. We worshipped God because we were intellectually convinced that there was a Supreme Power, who not only deserved worship but whose worship gave us pleasure and peace. We believed in clairvoyance because it was a form of heightened and expanded awareness, which anybody could attain. There was no place for any kind of 'religious' mumbo-jumbo in our scheme of things, which festivals had actually come to mean to us. And, in any case, they were only social interactions (or confrontations?) on the largest scale rather than a means of individual advancement on the intellectual or spiritual path.

Was it possible to decide that Sheila and I had become more rational or spiritual over the last two years? The attraction between us now was of a different kind and quality. The strange distance-maintaining 'magnetism' that existed between our male flesh and female flesh was gone. We worked and sat together without being conscious of sex or even gender difference. Quite often, she would come and sit in my lap and kiss me unpassionately on the eyes and the nose. Sometimes, we had afternoon naps on the same bed. A few weeks before, she had climbed on to my bed at night and taken me into a tight embrace. After that, we had been sleeping together almost every night. But why did we not have sex even once? She did not ask me why. I would feel her between the legs. She did not need it, but she often became one with me. I would want her to come closer, but it was not possible to obliterate no-distance.

I had never been so fulfilled. My office life was now very different. My subordinates looked upon me as a demigod, and my colleagues looked up to me for my 'guileless guidance'. I was absolutely confused for a while: In what way was I more informed and efficient or superior to them? Why had the chemistry between them and me changed? Even my boss behaved differently. Perhaps, the revival of my book was responsible? But no. Not many people in the office were aware of this. Only the boss knew that I had been praised again on that score.

FIVE

Rajneesh was a free man now. He had bribed his way out of prison. His criminal background and his hidden money hoards had come in handy. A junior jailer belonging to his caste had been won over. Through him, he contacted a police officer, again bearing his caste label. Appeal to caste is a heady brew, and money mixed with caste is a cocktail, which works on anybody in India. This police officer, Niranjan Singh, was at his command for anything. What Rajneesh wanted was a very small thing. Niranjan Singh just said abracadabra, and the case was weakened to a joke. The judge found it an open-and-shut case and set Rajneesh free at the first hearing, but not before passing serious strictures against the 'corrupt' police officers who had been responsible for keeping an 'innocent' and 'honourable' citizen in jail for so long. His magnanimity went even a step further during an unprecedented review of the judgment just a week later. He awarded our innocent and honourable man three million rupees in damages, which covered all costs plus contingencies. One could hear muffled voices in the bar room, making amusing comments. One clearly audible quip was: 'the judge seems to be equally honourable.' Another less audible remark, which was more in the nature of a wisecrack, was: 'this judge appears to be more just than justice itself.'

The next logical step for Rajneesh was to seek out Kapila, his friend and enemy, or contact me. The latter step was an easier option. So, I was on the line within a day of his release. He wanted to see his beloved old teacher and as usual was 'dying' to see me. This time, I did not quite mind meeting him. I wanted to update myself about him, and there could not have been a better way for doing so than by letting him come to me. But I had to keep him waiting for a few days since I was not too enthusiastic about meeting a man, who every time in the past had left me either deeply disturbed or depressed or angry.

Sheila was not opposed. She just said it was no harm meeting him. But Darwin said I must meet him as soon as I could. We could defang him, or forestall his future moves in the interest of our safety, or get to know more about Kapila and their possible future relationship and explore the possibility of keeping them apart.

Rajneesh called me according to the date and time we had fixed. This time, my office and home were out of bounds for him. I wanted to meet him in camera, so to say. *Care and Comfort*, a cosy restaurant in South Delhi, was the venue for my 'sincere' student to meet his 'wise' teacher.

We met on the dot. He had never been to this restaurant before. So, it took him some time to get over his sense of surprise. The décor was the reason: it was a strange mixture of French furnishings and local flooring. Such hybrids were common in Delhi and I had never been impressed by such eerie mixtures and glitzy decors. My coldness to his surprise made him rather conscious, and this made us focus on each other.

'How are you, sir?'

'And you, Rajneesh?' I replied in a tone which meant nothing more than the words.

'I'm very fine, sir. I've come here to tell you what I've been doing all these months and . . .'

'I'm here to listen. You just go ahead.'

'For some time, I was in jail. But the case against me was false. Kapila madam had got me framed.'

'Why call her Kapila *madam*, when she got you entrapped?'

'Because she was once your wife, sir.'

I controlled my temper with great difficulty. I did not want to waste my time giving vent to my personal feelings and bringing in things extraneous to my purpose in agreeing to meet him. So, I asked in a neutral tone: 'But why are you telling me this?'

'I'm telling you this to prove that I could've avoided this jail term which I've undergone.'

'Were you innocent?'

'Not quite. I did indulge in a few irregularities, sir.'

'Then, why did you want to escape punishment?'

'Because many people have escaped after committing much more serious irregularities, sir.'

'Do you mean crimes?'

'You may call them crimes, sir. But it depends upon how you look at them.'

'You don't think they're crimes?'

'I have no quarrel with this point, sir.'

'Anyway, what you want to say is that if Kapila hadn't got . . .'

'Yes, sir.' He cut me short.

'So, now you want to get even with Kapila?'

'No, sir. I only wanted to say I'm not even half as bad as my name.'

'You realize you've earned a bad name?'

'Yes, sir, and I want to become a better man, sir.'

'I wish you all luck.'

'Thank you very much for this, sir. But I need your help too, kind sir.'

'Help? Need some money?'

'No, sir. I need some work.'

'What kind of work?'

'Some job to sustain myself. I have some property and money, but I can't lay hands on them for some time.'

'Why?'

'If I go back now, my enemies might kill me. They must be already prowling around to trap me.'

'You'd better go to your friends.'

'Sorry, I have no friends. I've just come out of jail after seven years, sir.'

'For the same reason, you may not have any enemies either.'

'I wish it were so. But, as you know, sir, it's friends, not enemies, who fall off in adversity.'

'You're right. But I have no job to offer, nor can I get you one right away. I'd advise you to look for some old acquaintances or friends around. If you don't find any, you may find some clues. Then you could cautiously feel your way back to the place or places where you have your money and property.'

'Thank you for your kind advice, sir. But if I can't go back, can I see you again?'

'Well, you may give me a ring in a week or so.'

'But before I go, can I see Madam Sheila?'

'Now, why do you want to see her?'

'I'm told she can tell a few things about one's future, sir?'

'You're mistaken. She can't tell anything?'

'Sorry, sir. Somebody misinformed me, it seems. But please tell me where Mr Darwin lives. I'm keen to meet him. I'm told he's written a wise book on some social structures. I want to consult him on an important social matter, sir.'

'When you come to see me again, I'll give you his address. At the moment, he's away to Australia.'

On this note, I took his leave. But I was getting rather suspicious now. He wanted to see 'Madam Sheila' and then 'Mr Darwin'. His interest in astrology and social problems did not quite go with his character. Even if he was genuinely trying to get closer to all of us so as to change a bad name into a good one, I could not have taken any risk with a confirmed criminal. Sheila could not have agreed with me more. The very next day, I rang up Darwin and Faith. Faith was very keen to see us at the earliest opportunity. But Darwin was finding it difficult to get out of a serious commitment even for a day. We were not in a position to go to Hyderabad because of some pressing problems in my office. An enquiry into a case of malfeasance had kept my nose to the grindstone, and there were no signs of its coming to an end in less than a fortnight. The MD was rightly very concerned about this matter and wanted me to wrap it up speedily.

As a meeting was not possible immediately, I told Darwin everything about my encounter with Rajneesh. He reacted very strongly to the very mention of the word *Rajneesh*. But soon he understood my mind. Of course, he would not like anybody not to have suspicions about Rajneesh. We agreed that the door to a second meeting with him should be kept wide open. He was keen that I should trail the man's activities from now on in a thorough way and on a permanent basis. John D'Souza was immediately available for my work. And now I was enthusiastic about meeting Rajneesh. For a change, *I* was eagerly waiting for a phone call from him.

That evening was a Sheila day. We had christened the 14th of November 'Sheila day' a few years before, when we had first celebrated her birthday. The occasion was a birthday party at a neighbour's house. It was probably 14 October. When she congratulated the birthday boy, Mohan, he asked her about the date of *her* birth. Instead of answering the question, she cast an amused glance at me. It did not take me even a fraction of a second to say that her birthday was exactly a month away. Since then, we had been celebrating this day in our own way. Sheila was strongly opposed to making it a formal public affair. Yet, every 14th day of November was a special day, celebrated without excitement or fuss: a present was there, music was there, sweets were there, hugs were there, tears of joy were there. But nobody, not even these tokens, were allowed to come between us. That evening too, all these tokens were there, but they were just tokens; what they betokened was inexpressible. We sat hand in hand. We talked heart to heart, without much speech. She became a little pensive. I looked into her eyes. She said she was trying to locate her actual birthday, lurking somewhere in the folds of her past. But was it necessary to locate it? Maybe, she thought, that would give her . . . Identity? Raison d'être?

The nine o'clock newscast reported many sad things. A huge slum in Delhi comprising about 2000 shanties and 1000 tents was on fire, and over 100 fire engines were busy dousing the flames. A bomb blast in a busy market in Aligarh had killed 'many' people and reduced two huge plazas to rubble . . . 'The situation was under control', of course.

This was enough to pull Sheila out of the folds, and we were fully together again, mulling over fire, blood and rubble. The symbols and tokens were still there, staring at us wistfully. Not to disappoint them, Sheila opened the gift-wrapped packet and could hardly stop her tears from flowing down. I wiped them gently and then I fed a piece of *barfi* into her half-open lips. Simultaneously, I found a similar piece sliding into my mouth.

Years before, I had solemnly resolved not to celebrate my birthday until a brand new nation had risen from the mounds of bones and rubble. Darwin had initially laughed it off as one of the most ridiculous resolves of the century! But later on, when he began to respect my feelings, he empathized with it. And, anyway, since he did not have any faith in these birthdays and other celebrations, the subject never came up again, even when we were present together on such occasions.

A few days after Sheila's birthday, a very interesting thing happened. I had just come home and Sheila was making coffee. She called out, asking me to open the door. I had not heard the sound of the doorbell. I opened the door to a stranger, a middle-aged woman with grizzled hair and a face rich with wrinkles. She said she had come to meet Sheila. She claimed she was the latter's mother. Sheila's presence there did not show any sign of surprised recognition or delight on her face. It was clear she was an impostor. But we let her in and gave her some coffee and biscuits. As she was busy with her coffee, I scanned her thoroughly. I did not find anything in her which could reflect any kind of genetic connection between her and her claim. Sheila was all the time inspecting her mind to determine why she was trying to pass herself off as her mother. Yes, she had been sent here as a kind of spy. But who could have sent her? Suddenly, Sheila's face lit up as though she had seen something she had been scouting for. She took me aside and just uttered the word *Kapila*. Everything fell into place. Her 'mother' was still sipping her coffee and needed some more. She darted towards her and ripped off her disguise. Her hair and face had been meticulously made up. We completed our own investigation before sending her to the police station near my office. Just a little threat was enough to pump her.

Kapila had come out of jail before Rajneesh. Whereas Rajneesh was in close pursuit of her to avenge his arrest and possibly to get her killed, she was chasing him to befriend him. She was a typical criminal. Since Sheila and I were her high-priority enemies, everybody else including Rajneesh was her friend for the time being. This impostor could not tell us much beyond admitting that she had been hired to pose as Sheila's mother and snoop on us. This pose would have clicked if Sheila had not possessed the ability to see through all exteriors, however solid or opaque.

After this incident, we raised our guard to the optimal level. As we were prepared for Kapila's next move, we waited for it with interest. Good things, and even bad things, do not happen when you expect them. Your interest is none of their concern. We did not have to worry because we never lowered our guard even for a minute. Our phone had a caller ID device fixed on it. Thus, we kept a tab on any blind calls. For one month, there was only one blind call. But it was from a harmless number. The caller apologized for disturbing us.

About two months later, there was a nervous call. A rather whispery voice told us in a lower register that somebody was plotting to hurl a grenade upon our apartment building. The call was traced to a privately owned phone kiosk and from there to a shanty in a sprawling slum in east Delhi. A pale-looking, emaciated man lying supine on a dirty mat stood up in panic as two policemen entered this shanty. Before he was asked any question, he panicked and told them he had been paid to pass the message. He was arrested for further investigation. Kapila had hired him through one of her associates and she was out of bounds for such lazy arrests and enquiries as one could expect of such policemen.

The arrest of Kapila's hireling must have alerted her, and she must have decided to do something solid rather than making hoax telephone calls. For the next few weeks, we got no news about her. Then D'Souza suddenly came alive and had something interesting to report. Kapila had finally joined Rajneesh and they had mended their fences. She was now working on his old love for her, and he was melting gradually.

Rajneesh probably did not know that we knew more about his moves than he about ours. One evening, he called me and wanted to start from the note we had parted on. He told me in his characteristic theatrical tone that he had been working hard to improve himself since our last meeting. And I told him rather cryptically that nobody could 'improve' and 'deteriorate' at the same time. Half a minute's silence on his part meant to me that he had understood my remark.

'Sorry, sir, I don't understand you.'

'Isn't Kapila sitting by your side just now?'

'No, sir. Not at all, sir. I'm . . .' At this point, I rang off. Sheila said I should not have cut him off. She was right, but nothing could be done now except waiting for his next call.

There was no call from him for more than a week. And then one morning, Firoz told me that my 'old student' wanted to see me as soon as possible. We met an hour later.

'Good morning, sir. How are you, sir?'

'And you?'

'I've come to tell you that Kapila was not with me that evening, sir.'

'But you've been meeting since you were set free?'

'We've met only twice, sir. I swear, sir.'

'But you're friends again. You must've been hatching conspiracies.'

'No, sir, not at all.'

'Why did you meet, then?'

'She came to meet me. She said she wanted to apologize.'

'So, you forgave her?'

'No, I didn't. I just kept mum. She called me a few days later and insisted on meeting me.'

'And you melted, thinking that you could use her to . . . ?'

'No, sir. I let her meet me so as to know her mind. I was determined to finish her before she could get me trapped again or eliminated.'

'Do you still stick to this plan?'

'Yes, sir. Very much, sir. Trust me, sir.'

Well, nobody in their full senses could have trusted him. Nevertheless, this meeting was a pretty good input into our strategy to ward off any danger from him, Kapila or their evil associates. I was reasonably sure it would considerably delay their banding together to conspire against us. I also had a contingency plan in place in case they happened to put their scheming heads and dirty hands together later.

Sheila was satisfied that I had done all I could to pre-empt any possible attacks. The evening after this meeting with Rajneesh was a very peace-giving time. We toasted it in a glass of red wine each. We played our choicest music and also danced a bit as an expression of our joy. Strangely enough, we wished, contrary to our general practice on such occasions, we had invited some of our friends and neighbours. But it was just a passing mood.

The fortnight after this toast evening was not only very peaceful but also unusually eventless. The office routine and the daily cycle at home were not exactly dull, but they could hardly be called exciting events. But did we desire excitement? No, we did not, and yet it looked rather strange, the way things were going.

And then exactly on the sixteenth day after the toast evening, Darwin dispelled the quiet that we were mistaking as eventlessness. He broke the news that Kapila had been seriously wounded in a 'gang war'. He did not know for sure who had shot at her. But my immediate suspicion was that Rajneesh had struck the blow. D'Souza this time was much too tardy for our curiosity. Sheila asked me not to bother about this. And why did we need to care who had killed whom and why?

The very next morning, Sheila said she had 'found out' who had attacked Kapila. 'Found out?' I blurted and then realized she knew everything. Rajneesh had not yet made up his mind. A member of the mafia, Ghazi, she had earlier worked with had been after her life. She had two-timed him with a slightly more powerful mafioso in the same gang. This brute, notorious for his utter disregard for human life, would have killed her when she was found two-timing him. But her arrest and imprisonment in a secret jail had saved her life. She was lucky this time again. The first bullet missed her heart just by a millimetre and the second bypassed her left arm. She was now recovering at the Shekhawat Hospital near Jaipur under heavy police protection. Luck seemed to be favouring her at every step. When Ghazi came to know that Kapila was still alive, he went to this hospital with some of his top shooters and tried to force his way into it. In a fierce encounter that followed, he was killed along with three of his supporters. One fellow was arrested, who the police was milking out now, and two escaped as they usually do in such encounters.

SIX

We generally get lots of excitement out of springing surprises upon our close friends. Robert Darwin's rather subdued contact with us over the last few months did make me a bit curious at times, though I did not quite suspect that he was going to drop a real bombshell. We had not spoken to each other on the phone for over a fortnight, and I was more than curious to speak to him. As soon as I entered my office one morning, Firoz, who had been eagerly waiting for me, rushed in with a newspaper in his hand. He just placed it on my desk and left. It was open on page 16. A news item had been marked for me. The title was 'All Ads Are Lies'. I did not find it too exciting. But why had this fellow marked it for me? I started reading it carefully. Half way down, I found Robert Darwin glaring at me with his book, *The Seedy Indian Society*. My surprise bordered on a shock! Why had he not told me anything about it during all the months the book must have been in gestation? It was like a woman hiding her bulging pregnancy until she delivered a baby. Anyway, I rushed straight to the page which carried a review of the book. It was a mean-minded write-up by a trainee journalist, who seemed to be trying to primarily show off the use of some new words and fashionable phrases, which she had recently learnt from her sophisticated senior colleagues, and incidentally training her arrogant malevolence at the book a la book reviews in some Delhi newspapers. Anyway, it did give me some idea of the theme. I wanted to read it right away. But it had not yet arrived at the book stores.

When I went home in the evening, I was feeling more intrigued than before by that highly intriguing question: why had this fellow kept me in the dark? 'Because he wanted to give us a surprise,' Sheila said in answer to the unspoken question. The suddenness of this answer did not intrigue me any the less. Yet, she wanted me to first freshen up, take some coffee which was waiting and then ring up Darwin. But she did not quite succeed in her purpose. As soon as Darwin picked up the receiver, I started shouting at him.

'But why're you shouting, dear?'

'Because of your *Seedy*, Robert.'

'You can't have read it, Vigyan?'

'That's why I'm annoyed. Why don't I know anything about it?'

'You know my nature, don't you? I enjoy springing surprises upon my dear friends.'

'But I'm more than a friend to you. I can't take any sudden surprises or shocks from you at your bally convenience.'

'Do you prefer gradual surprises, dear?' he said impishly and laughed.

'Yes, friends should grow into their friends gradually rather than storm into them.'

'I should've thought my method fertilizes the soil in which friendships flourish. I'm sorry if . . .'

'Now, don't embarrass me,' I cut him short. 'I need the book here immediately. Can you have a copy sent?'

The line went dead suddenly. Perhaps, this point was the best note to end on.

The next morning had a couple of highly depressing things in store. Sheila had brought in Firoz, who was standing before me with something ominous oozing from his face. 'Anything serious, Firoz?' I asked with a degree of put-on poise. 'Yes, sir, very serious!' He immediately left on his scooter. I followed him in my car. My aunt Lakshmi, who lived at Guwahati, was waiting at his house, absolutely dishevelled and distraught. She had come to Delhi in the morning on the Guwahati-Dadar Express. She had been accompanied by her friends, an Assamese family of a sixteen-year old girl, Usha, her mother and her father. The train was detained at two stations for several hours before Jamalpur, where two other trains had been looted and damaged by marauding gangsters and political hoodlums.

'Why was it detained and what happened?' I asked very anxiously. 'Aunty, please tell me everything. I'm very worried.'

'The reason given out was that the railway authorities were waiting for the security men to arrive at Jamalpur in sufficient numbers. Everybody in my compartment was in panic. One middle-aged woman, who was being brought to Delhi for a serious heart problem, had a sudden cardiac arrest. Her husband and mother could do nothing beyond crying disconsolately.

'Then the train started suddenly and crossed two stations at more than its usual speed. About this time, a person in civvies, possibly a railway man, entered the compartment and asked the passengers to bolt the doors and shut all the windows and warned them not to open them at Jamalpur.

'The train stopped as suddenly as it had started. Just before a tunnel between Jamalpur and Ratanpur, a place which, some people later said, was most suited for marauders' favourite operations. First, the train was treated to a barrage of heavy stones, which softened up the defence provided by the windows and doors. For full one hour, it was these hoodlums' *raj*. "Catch the Assamese, kill them all!" was the loudest war cry. They grabbed all the Northeast-looking passengers and beat them most brutally. I tried to shelter my friends like a hen spreading her wings over its helpless chicks. But three heavy moustachioed fellows kicked me away, and as I was smarting with pain in the solar plexus, one of them dragged Usha away by the hair and the others beat up her mother and father. In spite of my pain, I ran out like mad and shouted for help. Usha was being stripped as also some of the 16 other girls from Arunchal Pradesh and Nagaland, who had been hauled out of S-6. I saw at least six cops moving about on the platform. I called out to them loudly and frantically, but they moved away unconcerned! I tore through the circle of hoodlums and covered the now fully naked Usha with my shawl. Somebody hit me with a club and threw me off her. The circle then opened, and in full sight of the train, the hoodlums raped her turn by turn and shouted the filthiest of abuse at her and everybody around! And then one of them thrust a bamboo stick into her genitals! I couldn't see what was happening to the other girls. I'm sorry. My only concern was this heavily bleeding girl.'

'Where's she now, aunty?'

'She's at the Ram Manohar Lohia hospital, struggling for her life, and her battered old parents are waiting for their nephew to arrive from Cuttack.'

We immediately left for the hospital. We were not allowed into the ICU ward but were told that a panel of doctors were trying their best to save her life. She had been brought there from the operation theatre half on hour before. All the wounds inside and outside the vagina had been 'successfully' sutured, but she was not out of danger yet. Her parents were sitting on a bench outside the ICU. The mother was almost on the verge of collapse and the father was desperately trying to keep up her spirits. Our presence helped them a little bit. I assured them I would do my utmost to get them their Usha back alive and healthy.

Leaving Aunt Lakshmi with them, I went to see the Chief Medical Officer. He listened to the tragic story and was all sympathy. His assurance of help verged on the sentimental.

Said he would bring her back from the very clutches of death. He allotted her a private room out of his special discretionary quota and moved the old people there. We were by their side, attending to their emotional and physical needs till their nephew, Vibhu Mahapatra, arrived late in the evening.

Aunty was on her way to Chandigarh. I took her home and informed her Chandigarh hosts, who were anxiously awaiting word from her. They agreed that she could change her programme to suit our convenience. She was with us for two days. She liked our attention and fell in love with Sheila. Aunts and uncles generally turn you into question marks when they meet you after a lapse of time and, especially, when they find something unusual about you. But Aunt Lakshmi's uneven life had already predicted for her answers to all such questions about us. And Sheila's presence had imperceptibly answered all the questions that might have remained still lurking here and there in her mind rather than raising them.

On the second evening, when I returned home, the door opened automatically. In the lobby, I found Aunt Lakshmi caressing Sheila so tenderly that I became quite emotional. Was she Sheila's real mother. Sheila got up with a start, but her eyes were wet with the love she had received. When she had gone to the kitchen to get us snacks and coffee, aunty almost choked with emotion. 'Sheila is a miracle of a woman!' she effused. 'I've never seen a person of this kind all my life. When you meet people like her, all questions about their origin, their caste, creed and class evaporate!'

The coffee was very delicious. Aunty wanted more. Sheila had brought it in the biggest coffee pot we had at home. Aunty poured herself the fourth cup and yet she wanted to go on. Sheila knew it would harm her and, so, she stopped her craving after the fourth!

Then, suddenly, Sheila started crying. She wanted aunty to stay with us for ever. The latter felt very sorry that she could not do that. She, however, wiped her tears and consoled her very tenderly. She also assured her she would be in touch with her regularly till her last day. Sheila's tearfui eyes looked into hers, and she said she would stay with us for another two days.

Vibhu Mahapatra arrived as expected, and aunty felt as though a heavy boulder had been suddenly taken off her head. Anyway, Usha was my duty from now on, not hers. So, she had two wonderful days with Sheila and me and confessed she had never been so free of questions and doubts before.

SEVEN

Darwin's *Seedy Indian Society* arrived within two days of my telephonic spat with him. It came trailing clouds of Darwinism II. He had worked out some more of the remaining problems in his theory. It was now thicker on quantity, but longer on quality. He had made the most judicious selection from his facts, which he called 'data', and subjected it to the most rigorous interpretation possible. Though, as usual, I had predecided not to be over-influenced, yet he seemed to be subtly breaking my defences. I found myself believing what I did not wish to believe. He had marshalled his data like an infantry line with their fingers on the trigger. He had only to utter the word *fire*.

His scope was global; his focus was the Indian society in that most of his data had been drawn from its highways and byways. Society had moved well from barbarism towards a civilized state. Half-way down the line, it lost its way. It missed the right milestone and ran on very fast towards decay. Even decay has seeds of regeneration. But, no, it did not stop there; it suddenly and impetuously turned back to the state from which it had started.

"Its hallmark is falsehood, bloodshed, destruction. Everything is a lie, a pretension, a dissembling: from friendship to love, from ritualism to devotion, from advertising to branding. Look at its professions and practices. Are there any other correlated things so opposed to each other? Just take the case of advertising. It is universally taken as a respectable and charming way of conning the consumer. But is it always faithful to the product it cons them for? No. It double-crosses the product it is intended to boost. A hen fed on *fevicol* lays an egg, which is more unbreakable than a bronze pitcher! Is this ad hyping up fevicol or ridiculing it? When a powerful Tide of a detergent zips past a soiled shirt and blazes a trail of dazzling whiteness on it, does the ad expect even a worst imbecile to buy the detergent? Or look at this most astounding way of advertising the price (reduction) of a new cola bottle. Because the Pandus were five and the protagonist's hand also has five fingers, the price of the bottle must be five rupees despite the fact that the hapless interlocutor of this man has only one father, not five! This 'jokad' is a lethal combination of vulgarity and illogicality, and yet intended to help the product? Or look at this Time-defying miracle, called our great Colgate. A 60-million-year-old skeleton of a dinosaur has its teeth intact! When a little lisping girl wants to know whether her teeth will also survive as long, a triumphant tiny tot breaks into a grin and bets that *his* teeth will because he uses 'my Colgate'. And the Jockey brief may last for ever because it transcends our 'stupid' social morality and is premised on the avant-garde social assumption that nakedness is the best thing, or at least the most approved thing! It is the 'next best thing to nakedness'.

"Or take this poor thing, called love. The Indian cinema, the father of a brand-new species of love, advertises its pampered progeny in the most 'convincing' way known to history. Two over-made-up characters, quickly exchange their ritualized *I-love-you* and *I-love-you-too*, after the woman has spurned or slapped the man enough, rush on to the nearest garden or grove or field, start cavorting like colts and fillies or going through some of the most grotesque choreographed gymnastic motions to loud tunes and rollicking rhythms and soon rally round them scores of weird capering gymnasts to keep them company in their enactment of this charade. No wonder, love has all but disappeared from the hearts of the

GenNow. Parody survives and might flourish *till death do us part*.

"One of the most precious gems of our heritage-treasure was dance in some of its most revered genres. Seers saw them and agreed that dancing reflects the rhythm of the cosmos. What do the ringside 'seers' see and say now? They *see* rhythms that turn them inside out, movements with meanings beyond their mortal grasp, words with resonances only in their nerve-endings. And look at our tiny tots, teeny-boppers, adolescents, post-teens reacting to them. And look at them behaving and growing in their post-ringside career.

"Secularism? It is a great ideal simply because it is unreachable. Everybody, eyeing a shimmering political chair at a distance, swears they are secular. You may have seen many secular *bodies*. But have you ever seen one secular *mind*? Everybody's motivated private exceptions only prove the rule. All our comrades and their beardless and *tilakless* fellow-travellers hide their 'opium' in their bloodstream more effectively by hiding behind their simulated transparency."

When I was reading this part of the book, I was very upset. There surely were and are some secular minds in this country as elsewhere. Did he forget that there was a man by the name of Mohandas Karamchand Gandhi, who had equal respect for all faiths? Was he himself not, very much like the conmen he was criticizing, tailoring reality to fit his theory? Sheila was looking across my right shoulder, and then into my left cortex.

'He has a right to his way of thinking, sir,' she said with a calm poise.

I was rather startled. 'But he's telling blatant lies!'

'Is he? Is he telling bigger lies than some of these "fellow travellers", sir?' she said with the intonation of a muffled question. My mind suddenly calmed down. I started reading the book again. Certain points and passages disturbed me, but

I wanted to go through the entire thing dispassionately before reacting to it sensibly. Back with me with her steaming cups of coffee, she wanted to listen to some passages in the book. She was getting more and more involved as I read through strings of ironies and innuendoes. Direct hits, however, did not affect her even as they did not impress me.

Education in *The Seedy Indian Society* was a real cutting edge. He presented some home truths, which not even the best of our educationists could have refuted.

"Democracy is still our goal, though we have discovered to our great chagrin during these fifty odd years that we have neither ever worked for it nor therefore deserve it. However, what we have to our credit is that we cherish it as an ideal and hold it aloft as a big banner. But are we doing anything even as a token to realize it? The only long-term means towards its realization could have been and still is education. But look at your education, your system of education, I mean, and see for yourselves what it does to your ideal of democracy and an egalitarian society. Does it not do just the opposite of what you want it to do? Your five-star schools and technical institutions spawn elitism, surely not egalitarianism! It is creating a new caste system in place of the old caste system, which you all are vying with one another to demolish to garner votes, to win polls. And not too far from these five-star centres of exploitative excellence, you have your stinking slums, which ghettoize millions of midday-meals beggars, thereby contributing substantially to the consolidation of your new caste system."

I stopped here for a moment and stole a glance at Sheila. Her eyebrows had contracted and risen rather high. I felt free to say what I honestly felt about the last few paragraphs. 'Isn't he laying it on a bit thick, Sheila?'

'Perhaps, yes. But he may have better things to say later.'

'But this is such a bad picture, Sheila. This would send a wrong message to the world, wouldn't it?'

'Yes, you are right there,' she agreed, with her forehead still creased in concentration.

To some other comments I made on the book, she did not respond. When I goaded her to speak up, she said she was finding it difficult to persuade herself to believe that Darwin could be so negative in his approach. I left it at that and deferred the reading of the remaining chapters to the following weekend.

Darwin rang up just to say hello. He did not betray any curiosity to find out my reaction to his book. This was nothing new. Earlier too, he would never talk about his writing unless I mentioned it. He was about to ring off when I told him casually that I was still reading his book.

The rest of the book also was a little too bleak. All social systems and structures were bad, restrictive, constrictive, convoluted, antievolutionary. Some positive links between them were snapping, crumbling. Any way out? None to his mind. He did not rule out miracles, though he did not believe in them! One important point, which impelled our engagement at an intellectual, logical level, related to the traditional debate over the relationship between individual and society. But as against the tradition of general consensus that the two were mutually supportive, his view was that they were mutually destructive.

"It was sensible to expect that as humans evolved further biologically, they would develop socially too. But something went wrong somewhere downstream. Somebody pressed the wrong button, and the orientation reversed mysteriously, without our knowing about it. We have been reverting since at a terrific speed towards our natural condition of barbarism. The only hope now lies in another mysterious hand rising and accidentally pressing the right button."

I wanted to see the reviews. Firoz was very helpful. He took the help of an assistant and collected a number of reviews from as many as 15 publications. Normally, book reviews of one book do not appear in so many newspapers and other publications. Obviously, this book was being looked upon as above normal. But almost all the reviews were negative. Three of them condemned the book downright: 'It is not worth the paper on which it is printed.' One said: 'It is a blasphemy against human society.' And one even said unprintable things about it, which I rejected out of hand.

Now that the book was many reviews old and I had had more time to think over it, I had a 'right' perspective on it. Most of the points made in it were partly true: our society and its constituents have regressed too fast and too far; and in spite of our much-flaunted increasing control over nature, some individuals are not much better, in certain aspects, than the earliest Homo erectus. Nevertheless, I felt that a person of Darwin's calibre and perspective should not have missed the wood for the trees. I even suspected that he was possibly slashing off his victim's limbs to adjust them to his Procrustean bed.

My chief gain from reading this book was that I got to see the facet of Sheila's personality which had been hidden from me! Or was it a new division of the cells to form a brand-new tissue? I do not know this till this day. Her looking at things 'objectively' even when she had to painfully contradict me was nothing new. But the insight into things which she so casually and unobtrusively showed during one of our exchanges over *The Seedy Indian Society* was something I had not anticipated. I felt very bitter over the way Darwin was rubbishing everything. 'So negative, my!' I fumed, with my eyebrows squeezed to their limit and my hands pressed against my tingling temples. And Sheila, who had all along reacted very cautiously to my point-to-point responses to the book, did not take a second to utter something, which seemed to have been waiting ready-made in her mind: 'It is the negative that complements the positive.' And when she saw only surprise where my face had been a fraction of a second before, she added so innocently: 'It is such views that power societies to move forward . . . I was able to understand parts of that simplified book on dialectic, sir, which you had brought home the other day.'

I knew she had been growing steadily, but I never expected that she had taken such a big leap forward. I was sure this thought had not been just auto-cued by her clairvoyance but had welled up from her logically developed mind. I was delighted to the point of euphoria. And when I started gushing with praise, she gently covered my mouth with her right palm.

EIGHT

We had a mind to invite the Darwins. Sheila was really missing them very much. But Faith had not been well for some time. It was, therefore, inconvenient for them either to come over or to ask us over. But something much more exiting, though infinitely less desirable, was ours for the asking! Rajneesh wanted to come over. Why? The same set of reasons: was dying to see me; had so many things to discuss with me; needed my 'most valuable' advice on a 'very important' matter. I also gave him the same old reasons for my inability to meet him immediately. But I kept his hope alive, saying I would give him a ring as soon as I was relatively free. Since he could not give me his contact number, he asked to call me in a week or so. His phone call or his asking to call was no more a threat to me. He had been defanged since his last visit. This time round, I did not have to ask him what his hidden agenda was. I wanted him to expose to us all that he still had hidden or submerged inside him.

We were convinced beyond all doubt that this fellow was a leopard who would never change his spots. We, therefore, thought it prudent to hedge our bets very well. A thought suddenly fell from the sky: why not catch hold of Kapila and work on her? When I broached this to Sheila, she smiled the way she had never smiled before and then said 'Yes, of course (.), as though she had transferred her own idea to me without my knowledge.

The next weekend was the earliest we could implement this idea. On the Saturday afternoon, we were on our way to Jaipur. When we reached the Shekhawat Hospital, the visiting time had just begun. We had full two hours to work on our plan. Kapila was in a private room. When she saw two 'unknown' visitors entering with a bouquet and a basket of fruit, she squeezed her eyes hard to read our faces. She did not recognize me until I reached her bed. Then, suddenly, she sat up and said *namaste* with her hands folded and raised respectfully. I said 'How are you(?)' and offered the bouquet, which she accepted with a grateful face. She did not betray any ill feeling towards Sheila either. Sheila was sitting on her bed and looking into her eyes all the time. I was wide-eyed witness to Kapila's face quickly changing from grateful to gloomy to cheerful to kind. Accordingly, her words went on morphing from formal to neutral to personal to warm. The right time to talk things over had come. But we wanted to give her some time between this first encounter and our real business. When we were taking her leave, she wanted us to stay for some more time. We promised to call again at the same time the next day.

In a room in a suburban hotel, we got down to preparing our strategy to deal with Kapila. I dialled the number of D'Souza. Fortunately, he was on a visit to Jaipur. In less than half an hour, he was with us, giving us his latest information on Kapila and Rajneesh. He told us that Rajneesh had not come to know till just two days before where Kapila had vanished suddenly but was in hot pursuit of her. It was also true that she had tried to befriend him when she had come out of jail.

Armed with this dope, we were in Kapila's room at the appointed time punctually. She had had her room specially cleaned and even perfumed to receive us. When we entered, she quickly got off her bed and walked towards us. The moment I realized that she was trying to bend down to touch my feet, I caught her mid-air and stood her straight. She stood there motionless for a few suspenseful seconds, her eyes slightly misting over. I had a strange feeling coursing through me. I cannot say to this day whether it was sympathy or tenderness or pity, or a mix of all these. But I clearly remember being touched quite a bit. I walked her back to her bed and motioned her to it. As she was shuffling to sit comfortably, I stole a glance at Sheila and found in her eyes a go-ahead signal.

I told Kapila clearly but very sympathetically that I was ready to help her as much as possible if she had already decided or could decide to change the course of her life. In this mellowed mood, she said a prompt and grateful yes and confessed at the same time that she had no doubt been trying to conspire with Rajneesh to hatch an evil design against us. The help I offered was twofold: she would be protected against all the enemies she had accumulated in all her days of lawlessness; and she would be placed in a secure and comfortable Women's Home and all her essential needs would be looked after.

For a minute or so, her face became a shade pensive and then gradually cheered up as she saw Sheila looking at her. I waited for her to say something, but she only smiled with tears in her eyes. Assuming that she needed some more time to think over my offer, I said we would not mind calling on her again.

'No, I wouldn't like to keep you waiting,' she said promptly in a palpably anxious tone. I accept your offer and am ready to move to the place you've so kindly suggested.'

'I'm glad you've agreed to turn over a new leaf. I hope this means you understand things as they stand between us.'

'Yes, I have no illusions now, and no expectation beyond what you're doing. And more than that, I feel very obliged. But I wonder if I can call you Vigyan once again.'

'Yes, you may. We are friends as of now.'

'Yes, and thank you very much.'

As soon as we came out of the hospital, we rang up Robert. He liked the idea of Kapila being sent to the same Women's Home at Bikaner where Elizabeth was. He had kept track of Elizabeth on a regular basis and told us that she was not only reconciled to her new life in a new habitat but considerably changed and happy. He chuckled a little when he said in a lower register that the two *very bad* wives would hopefully make a *very good* couple together. When I joked that his phrasing smacked of a double entendre, he just laughed and turned the phone over to Faith. She was ecstatic when she heard our voices turn by turn. She surprised me when she said that she had already visualized these two women staying together not only at one place but also in one room!

One advantage in despatching Kapila to Elizabeth's embrace was that she would be safely away from the reach of her enemy-friend, Rajneesh. When he called to ask to see me at my 'kind convenience', I gave him an appointment for the Friday afternoon as the Darwins were expected on Saturday.

As soon as he entered my office, he wished me in his usual theatrical way and then quickly walked towards me and made a gesture as though he was going to touch my feet. I stopped him doing that and motioned him to the chair in front of me. As he was lowering himself into the chair, he put on an embarrassed smile to say:

'Sorry, sir. When I met you last time, I concealed one little thing from you, sir.'

'What was that?' I was a bit curious.

'I did try to approach Madam Kapila, though I told you that she was all the time looking to see me. But I assure you, sir, I had no intention of patching up with her.'

'What exactly was your intention, then?' I was all the time looking at his face intently to read his mind.

'Believe me, sir, I only wanted to find out what she was up to.'

'Why?'

'Because I was keen to stop her from conspiring with some of her old criminal friends to harm you, and of course me.'

'Anyway, do you still intend to see her.'

'Yes, sir, I'd very much like to.'

'Do you know where she is?'

'No, sir. I'm still chasing her.'

'That's good. But please inform me as soon as your chase is over.'

'Yes, sir, I will.'

'And bring that woman to me, will you?'

'Yes, sir, without delay!'

'I want to teach her a lesson. But, unfortunately, my information at the moment is that she's either been killed or is in the possession of one of her old gangs.'

'Have you got this news from some reliable source, sir?' he asked, in a tone which made me a little alert.

'No, not exactly. But if I get to know something new, I'll let you know. Meanwhile, you must continue your pursuit with the same perseverance until you catch this dirty criminal.'

'Yes, sir, I will.'

Sheila was happy when I gave her a lowdown on this meeting in my office. We agreed that if he succeeded in tracing the whereabouts of Kapila, it would give us a lever to know his intentions better and thus control his movements and actions.

About a fortnight later, a boxed news item in a Delhi newspaper gave us some relief as well as worrisome suspense: "A Hardened Criminal Killed in a Gang War." The name of this criminal was Rajneesh. A few other points about his native place and case history confirmed that it was no other than 'our' Rajneesh. But I knew him too much to give credence to this news item. It could have been planted by him to keep us as well as some other 'friends' of his off our guard.

So, the relief we felt was already over, and complacency had not been our strong weakness for quite some time.

I was thinking of informing Robert about this new Trojan Horse when he called to check with me about it. He was also of the view that this news could be a plant. His worry was not that he or I might become careless or complacent soon enough; his concern was how these reporters could be so naïve as to publish such items without adequate verification. He was not too unglad when I said that naiveté or gullibility was not their fault as much as their vulnerability to bribes or blandishments.

Within a month of this Trojan Horse exchange between Darwin and me, D'Souza called to say that he had got a breakthrough. His excited tone clearly indicated that he had something very serious to tell me.

'Something important, John?' I asked coolly.

'Yes, sir, something very important and urgent!'

'What's that?'

'That man Rajneesh has been spotted!'

'What do you mean by *spotted*? Do you mean to say you haven't seen him yourself?'

'Yes, sir. But my assistant, Salman, has seen him. I'll check on this information myself and get back to you by tomorrow.'

He kept his promise. He saw Rajneesh with his own eyes before calling me. The latter had been seen coming out of a hotel on the MI road at Jaipur. He was living incognito either to scour the area for his victim or to escape those for whom he was a possible victim.

I had nothing much to worry about. I only had to be vigilant. I relayed this news to Darwin and waited for Rajneesh to resurrect himself. I was prepared for what he would say when he finally chose to surface. Meanwhile, I wanted D'Souza to keep track of him on a day-to-day basis.

NINE

Darwin was much too busy rounding off 'The Post-script' to the last book of what he called his 'trilogy'. To pre-empt my 'friends-should-not-storm-into-their-friends' complaint, he had prepared me for it. His earlier books had both shocked me and shaken me. So, I was extremely curious to know what he was going to say now. I called him one evening and asked him what kind of 'mischief' he was now up to. He chuckled a little and said cryptically that he was writing something on what he had written in the two 'prequels' to this sequel. His coinage amused me more than it intrigued me. Perhaps, that is what he wanted. To make him open up, I just said I did not like the title. But he was careful to avoid the trap.

This time, the first copy came to me. I did not have to wait for a review to tell me about its publication. The title had changed to 'The Epilogue'. Why? Well, I did not bother much about 'why'. I just 'stormed' into the book, thinking I would retitle it or even 'detitle' it, if necessary, after I had gone through it. When Sheila asked me what I meant by 'detitle', I said I meant 'erase'.

The Epilogue was a well written book. Darwin had taken a fresh look at what he had said in the prequels and attempted a revised, coherent perspective on his theory. The most intriguing part, or the gravamen, of the book was the new data he had worked into it to broaden his perspective.

The new data consisted in what was happening in the society now. And the point was that whatever was happening was the consequence of the existing 'structures for antievolution', as described in the first book, and of the 'seedy' depths to which the society had fallen, as discussed in the second. If we did not want what was taking place to happen, we would have to roll back those structures and thus stop their consequential social degeneration or decay, which, according to *The Epilogue*, was almost impossible because "the time once gone cannot be recalled".

I wanted to take a critical look at the data, or what he called 'The Consequence', in the book in order to decide for myself whether or not the data were authentic and if they were a natural social consequence of what the antievolutionary social structures as postulated by him had done to the society.

First of all, I examined his elaborate description of a plethora of scams, warping the very fabric of the country's economy. He zoomed in on a very short period of four years and had a sizable list of scams and scamsters. "A lowly clerk in a bank, Sobhraj Mehta, shook the very foundations of the Main Stock Exchange single-handed by manipulating share prices. He was a 5000 crore man overnight. The law went about pussy-footing, and he went around free and fine, cocking a snook long enough to kill off any social values still surviving. This spawned a culture which encouraged and by default 'trained' many of our ambitious bounders in the art of pulling off much more colourful economic coups. Among them was a stamp paper scam, under which stamp papers and stamps worth 30 thousand crore had been sold off to unsuspecting customers in 10 states. This staggering amount being quite a chunk of our total national economy, what damage it must have caused to it boggles the mind. Worse still: when the lid was taken off this scandal-box, we saw exalted personalities and powers jumping out for cover. Obviously, such a huge scam could not have gone on for so long without support and sustenance from these sources."

As I thumbed through some of the remaining pages in this chapter cursorily, I could see scandal after scandal staring at me. All these scandals or scams had one thing in common with pornography: they were irresistibly seductive. Thus, although I found them satiating, if not sickening, I could not help being drawn towards them, not the least for the way they had been presented.

"Taking a cue from the genius of this man and the impotence of our criminal law and law-enforcing agencies, a bright young trader innovated brand-new products for export to Asian, African and Arab countries. He had acquired printing devices, paper and all accessories for printing fake currencies and stamps (for different purposes) for most of these countries. He had been keeping these stocks at several places in the country for years, and not a soul among many of our vigilance and police departments had come to know of them! Not only that. He had been printing fake currency for this great country too, and it might take our smart vigilance agencies quite some time to gauge the percentage of fake currency notes circulating in our burgeoning economy."

The topmost of such scandals in terms of their destructive power, however, was the system of the Exam Scam, which had permeated almost all examinations in the country and reduced them into a total farce. This system, in Darwin's view, had been devised to strike at the last bastion of our society. It was supposed to destroy whatever of its core entity might have survived the attacks on its economy.

"The Exam Scam had been invented and perfected by a young man, called Ranveer Don. He devised a number of clever ways of helping students to cheat in any kind or level of examination. His tentacles having spread to the green rooms of almost all examinations, he had in his super-grade office the question papers of any examination ready 48 hours before it was due to start.

"By far the best way of cheating in an examination was our Ranveer Don's 'Engine and Bogie' system. His clients could apply for and pass any examination under the sun: for a professional degree, for a decorative degree, for a job. The only problem was that the fee for each of them was a bit too steep: ranging from two lakh to 20 lakh rupees. But he had provision in his system of concessional rates for depressed castes and classes. Whatever the fees, there were thousands waiting to take their exams the Ranveer-Don way. He would make groups wanting to take different exams apply en masse so that they could get consecutive roll numbers and were able to sit in one examination room. Depending upon the subject of the examination a particular group were taking, he would hire a 'scholar', who would be made to write that examination along with them. He was the 'engine' of the train. He would quickly solve all the problems and pass on the answers to all the students in the room, called the 'bogies', using a specially devised code.

"The CAT was finally out of the bag, certainly not because our tactile Vigilance got to feel a mobile bulge in the bag but because of the CAT's own goof-up or carelessness. The combined entrance test spilled its own beans: our celebrated Don had become much too carelessly overconfident even for our conscientious, privacy-respecting Vigilance gentlemen. Of course, the entire examination was cancelled, after hundreds of all the earlier scam-tainted bogus exams had done their irreparable damage to the system of education and competitions."

There were many other scams peering at you from the next 30 pages or so. My interest was flagging fast because the similarity between them was gradually getting the better of their differences. In fact, I would not have gone through them the way I did but for the way they had been presented.

The last chapter, however, was a 'true' epilogue. The dark glasses were gone. The coloured glasses, which he had worn at times during his checkered journey, had been put off. He had seen everything, subjectively or objectively, and was now trying to distance himself from those pictures in order to place them in perspective. And he was succeeding?

"Humans made fast, though unsteady, progress to what we might call a civilized state, where they were able to live together without excessive bloodshed and, sometimes, even with love for one another. At a jinxed milestone into their journey, they lost their sense of orientation and turned back weirdly instead of moving forward, and have since been hurtling to a state of barbarism. This second barbarism is infinitely worse than the first because they cannot regain their primeval simplicity. Armed with their mind-boggling inventions and colossal engines of destruction, they delude themselves into the belief that they have progressed to the limit of their natural leash and can create and destroy, as they wish, like God Himself.

"There is still hope, though very dim, of an about-turn. Another milestone on their regression path might awaken them to the fact that they are moving in the reverse direction. It would be very difficult indeed to turn back, but should this realization dawn on them, new social structures might emerge and start a new paradigm of syncretic, co-operative social life."

I was not too impressed by this epilogue, for it did not flow quite logically from the prequels. Besides, it was much too bleak for the hopes he deliberately tried to raise in the concluding lines.

Sheila's comment on the epilogue was rather direct, perhaps, for the first time. She just did not like it. When I asked her the reason, she said that despite the scenario he had pictured for the world to come, she hoped for the best.

Darwin was with us a few days after the publication of the *Epilogue*. A few 'wise' reviews had taken him lightly, a number of 'unwise' ones had shot at him from the hip and some had condemned him in intemperate, vituperative words. He was unfazed. I called a spade a spade, and Sheila listened patiently to him as well as me. When Darwin urged her to speak up, she subtly suggested that he write a post-epilogue to develop a new perspective on the basis of the prequels and the sequel. For the first time, perhaps, he did not take her seriously. He said with a touch of tartness in his voice that he had done what he had wanted to do.

He wanted to go back immediately. Sheila said a big NO, and he had no choice. She knew he had been missing Faith intensely every moment since he had arrived here. The same thing was happening to Faith in Hyderabad with eerie synchronicity. Sheila had only to click on the right number in her communication system before Faith was on board the first morning flight of Sahara Float.

Darwin had to wait for five long minutes for her to disengage from Sheila's arms. The longer embrace that followed gave Sheila enough time to serve tea and some spicy and crunchy snacks. Over the table, Sheila and Darwin eyed Faith at the same time.

'I love Robert too much to distance myself from him,' she said very slowly.

Her intonation showed she had not finished. And yet Sheila uttered 'oh', to prompt her to continue.

'Even being part of him, I'm his alter ego. So, I've told him what you two have told him.'

'Told him?' I blurted, and then immediately realized that she must have had 'access' to us all the time.

'So?' Sheila was curious.

'So, we should leave it to him now.'

This clinched the issue without any hard feelings or angst in anybody's mind. The human society had the potential to sort itself out in the context of the globe as well as in the larger context of the cosmos. Did we all think this way? Darwin's face was a bit Sphinx-like again?

Faith wanted to stay on, but not without Darwin. He too was inclined to stay for a day or two, but his 'duty' was much more demanding apparently.

Duty? Even Sheila did not know anything. A corporator, Rama Reddy, wanted to extort some money from Darwin. Because Darwin did not oblige him, he had him put on notice: "Two hundred square yard area in the front part of your bungalow is public property. You are hereby notified that you must remove this encroachment within 15 days. Failing which, the Municipal Corporation of Secunderabad will forcibly demolish the illegal construction, recover from you the expenses for its demolition and slap a heavy fine on you."

The bungalow was 150 years old. Darwin had bought it as such from a Parsi trader. Not an inch of it had been added to the original construction. Obviously, the idea of 'encroachment' had been suggested to this Reddy man for the purpose of extortion. He was very close to the core of the Andhra Pradesh government. Anybody would have paid the extortion amount or bribes to get rid of this problem. But Darwin was not anybody.

This time, I was determined to be one up on him. I did not give him time to spring a surprise upon me. A senior secretary in the AP government, Mr Rakesh Sinha, was a very close friend. I just gave him a tinkle to explore if he could do something. Perhaps, the mention of Ram Reddy was enough to ignite a light in him. In a provoked tone, he uttered 'Wait a moment, please (.)' and rang off. I could not guess the meaning of his 'moment', nor did I need to. In less than an hour, he called to say a cryptic 'Don't worry, Vigyan (.)' and went off the line.

The next day, when I called Darwin to ask him whether he had been able to attend to his 'duty', he said an upbeat yes. I think we did not sound too tongue-in-cheek when Sheila joined me to congratulate him.

This was only part of Darwin's 'duty'. Why had he not told us about it? Well, it was against the grain for him to burden friends with his 'piddling' problems. The other part of his duty, which he did want to share with us but could not, was to do with Elizabeth and Kapila. These two women had established contact with Faith some days before and urged her to intercede with Darwin and me on their behalf. Instead of 'rotting' in that sexist prison, called *Nari Niketan*, they wanted to live life on their own terms. Perhaps, they had their boyfriends waiting somewhere around, or they just wanted to go out and try their luck. In their reckoning, enough time had passed since they had entered this 'bleak' house, and their enemies must have gone off their trail by now.

Darwin told us all this when we congratulated him on his relief from the Reddy entrapment. His perception was exactly the same as ours. Those mafia gangs were very much there, and these women would be killed or enslaved within hours of their exit from their secure nest. He agreed to warn them in clear terms that they would venture out at their own risk.

A few days later, they had a glimpse of Rajneesh making enquiries at the reception counter, and within days of this incident, Elizabeth spotted a suspicious character prowling around the Home. She could not recognize his face because of the distance. But the moustachioed man she saw whispering into the receptionist's ear two days later was definitely one of her underworld chief's men. They put their heads and fears together and gave Darwin's stern warning serious thought. They had a clear choice before them now. They could break into their 'freedom' and risk their improving way of life and even their life, or continue reforming in the security of this Home. They were free, yes, quite free.

Kapila called Sheila after about a month of Darwin's warning to them and told her that they had decided to act on his advice.

TEN

Darwin's trilogy had latterly caught the attention of the avant-garde readership in Western Europe. Several reviews had appeared in widely different publications and they were generally negative. However, one end of the sociopolitical spectrum, which had long lost faith in democratic or liberal capitalism, found its new bible in the trilogy. Just about this time, several bizarre things were happening in some Semitic, Western and South Asian societies, which had found a clear 'prescient' expression in the trilogy's antievolutionism. A detective investigating a Germany's infamous cannibal case reported a flourishing cannibal scene in Germany and two neigbouring countries. Three young men were blinded in the Middle East for 'lasciviously' looking into the eyes of a Muslim woman, which they said were visibly blinking through her *burqa* eye-slits. Two men's ears were slashed off for drinking during Ramzan in Jammu and Kashmir. A middle-aged woman was burnt alive at a police station in Bangladesh for burning a copy of the Holy Quran in a state of depression.

I was rather baffled. I could not quite see the connection between these isolated freaks and Darwin's 'prescience' in his books. To my mind, these readers, like most of us at any given time, were dissatisfied with the working of the existing sociopolitical structures and suddenly lighted upon their eureka moment in these books. Anyway, Darwin had only demolished these structures without proposing any alternative ones to surrogate for them. It has always been easier to deconstruct—about every philosopher's great pastime, at any time. Has any system ever ensured, or will any system ever ensure, the supply of bread, clothing and shelter to the last man? Okay, let us leave these stupid necessities out. Let us deliver or promise to deliver justice to one and all and leave it at that, shall we?

These thoughts crossed my mind after I had cleared a column of files on my desk. I was quite pensive. The MD peeped into my room. I stood up to welcome him. He found an unusual expression on my face. Firoz had some coffee sent in, and over it I told the boss what had stirred my mind in the last half an hour or so. His eyes blinked quickly, and he proposed a conference to deliberate on these and related thoughts under the aegis of our Company.

We had an elaborate infrastructure for hosting conferences, seminars and cultural performances. We had just a mini conference in mind tightly focussed on the subject, arising from the thoughts that had crossed my mind. We invited intellectuals who had done a good amount of thinking and research in the areas of democracy, capitalism, socialism and (social) evolution. Robert Darwin was prominent among them. Our company was to be represented by the MD and me. The audience was to consist of individuals representing different sections of the people in Delhi and around.

The conference started according to plan. Many more people were present than we had expected. Faith and Sheila were attending the first formal conference in their life. Faith's graceful poise among the sophisticated audience and luminous intellectuals did not surprise me as much as Sheila's balanced nonchalance.

I was supposed to give the keynote speech. But because my instrumental thoughts had been inspired by Darwin, I managed to get him to be the keynoter.

The MD introduced Darwin as the keynote speaker and father of antievolutionism. Even though several articles on Darwin and many reviews of his books had been published in

English and several Indian languages, none among our elite audience had heard of this weird-sounding 'ism'.

So, when the 'father' of this eerie creature started to speak, there was quite a stir in the audience: "We've been evolving biologically but disevolving socially since animals' first transition into humans." Before his pitch fell to the bottom of his range to coincide with the period, the storm among the 'listeners' rose to a crescendo. This was possibly the biggest shock of their lives. 'We are the best turned-out, sophisticated swish set,' one gab-gifted speaker was heard saying above the noise. 'Does he mean to say we've disevolved socially to our present state of picture-perfect human beings?'

The MD rose to appeal to the audience to listen to the speaker quietly. The noise subsided to a buzz, but continued. Darwin waited at the lectern. A leaderly-looking man stood up and requested his fellow listeners in a pompous tone to let the speaker first say what he has to say: 'Let's demonstrate to his face that we have socially evolved to this level of tolerance and discipline despite his great theory of antievolutionism.'

To Darwin as to me, this 'discipline' was a complete sham. But this did not bother him. He just wanted to expound his theory and he seemed to believe in every syllable of what he was now saying. I had never seen such eloquence in an intellectual presentation all my life. The audience were spellbound. Their jaws had dropped by several millimetres. But did they really appreciate what he was saying? He was deconstructing everything. Every social structure was now a heap of debris. One could visualize a real Apocalypse or *Pralaya* with its Noah's Arc and all its paraphernalia. And when this image had played itself out, nothing appeared to signal a new Beginning.

The second speaker was a social scientist from Varanasi. He pitched in with his turgid defence of the working of the democratic institutions in India and the consequent steady progress to social justice. After he had done that in his jaunty professorial manner, he changed his tone and style to demolish Darwin's 'original' social philosophy. His harsh language undid the effect of his attack to a large extent. When he sat down without evoking any applause from any section of the audience, he was visibly disappointed. There was some more disappointment in store for him. An extremely well dressed man with an arrogant air about him trashed the professor's speech in equally strong terms. 'At least, Robert Darwin had something fresh to say,' was his last sentence.

Two more speakers' addresses revolved round Darwin's theory, which they dismissed out of hand. The first speaker, a socialist-economist, rejected Darwin's theory as a piece of 'crazed eccentricity'. The second, an academic from Bhagalpur University, was extremely hard on Darwin. He did not say a word about the latter's views. He just wanted to know how a person of Darwin's credentials could have been invited to present his 'mad' theory. A number of people among the audience raised a serious objection to his use of the word *mad.* When I reminded the speaker in a firm tone that, in the realm of ideas, the line between validity and invalidity was extremely thin, he sat down in a huff.

The MD did not want to speak. He motioned for me to move to the lectern. When I opened my file and surveyed the audience, I found myself being auto-cued to read out the text in front of me! At least, this is how I felt at that time. From the time I uttered the words *Ladies and Gentlemen*, the audience went into a trance, as it were:

"The theme of this conference is Robert Darwin's thesis that humans have been socially disevolving even as they have been biologically evolving. My main objection to the thesis is that the twin evolutions cannot move in the mutually opposed directions. If this thesis was accepted as a valid postulate, then we should be prepared to accept the conclusion that when the biological evolution finally reaches its culmination, we will have become total brutes in social terms. So, I would say that Mr Darwin's thesis is a sensitive man's over-reaction to our rapidly degenerating social values at the present time. But, at the same time, I must add that his views have a great social value and might prove a significant contribution to human civilization in the long run. In this context, I would like to quote a young colleague (who wishes to remain anonymous): 'It is the negative views like this that power social revolutions and advance human civilization.' "

Some ears pricked up, especially among my Company colleagues, who started looking around at their colleagues seated here and there to identify the 'culprit'.

The remaining speakers thought that I had put Darwin's thesis on a pedestal whereas I had only put it into perspective. As a result, there was very little interest left in the conference. The speakers went though the motions and tried to make things interesting at Darwin's cost. One even tried to drag poor Darwin on coals, but ended up blackening his own hands and face. Apart from these few attention-drawing moments, all these speeches ended on a tame note.

A few days later, in an official meeting with my senior colleagues in the MD's chamber, when I gave the credit for my speech to Sheila, she became a celebrity. 'Must be a highly educated person,' the MD remarked. 'Never been to school even for a day,' I said in reply. Though nobody had normally questioned my statements before, this one did raise a few eyebrows. In their place, I would also have reacted in the same way. Anyway, I had never seen the MD so pleased. He said he would call at my house shortly to congratulate her in person.

That evening, when I gave the credit squarely to Sheila, she started crying and would not stop. I was absolutely baffled. No amount of caressing and cajoling helped for over ten minutes! When she finally calmed down, her head was on my lap. She spluttered something. I listened for it but could not understand what she was saying. Gradually, she became a little articulate:

'I owe my language, my knowledge, even my existence to you, and you give me credit for those few words which had just escaped my lips. I was only the medium. And how can you deny that you had inspired them and even powered them into expression!'

The Darwins had not come home. They had left for Hyderabad from the conference venue. We missed them very much for days. There was no response to our phone calls. Were they preparing to spring another surprise upon us?

Rajneesh called several times after the conference. He complained that he had not been invited to attend it. When I told him that, to our knowledge, he had been dead for some time, he feigned great surprise. He said he was sorry he had not been in touch with me for a while. He also tried to assure me that he had been trying to improve himself as an individual, as a 'social animal'. When I asked him why he was taking such trouble, he said in his usual glib way: 'Sir, I want to make myself worthy of you and Madam Sheila. I want to be an intellectual, a thinker, a writer.' I wished him all luck, but refused to give him an appointment for a meeting. The world was a vast place, and there were many better places and many better people in these places that could trigger his reformation better than me and my place. This is how I tried to rationalize to myself my unwillingness to meet him.